BIG DOGS

BOOK ONE IN THE **BIG DOGS** SERIES

S.L. DITMARS

WILDBLUE
PRESS

WildBluePress.com

BIG DOGS published by:
WILDBLUE PRESS
P.O. Box 102440
Denver, Colorado 80250

WILDBLUE PRESS is registered at the U.S. Patent and Trademark Offices.

ISBN 978-1-957288-90-1 Hardcover
ISBN 978-1-957288-91-8 Trade Paperback
ISBN 978-1-957288-89-5 eBook

BIG DOGS

This book is dedicated to the men and women who wear the uniform and work with dogs. No matter their task, they spend endless hours seeking perfection in something that cannot be perfect. They do this because they know other people's lives, as well as their own, may depend on their actions. Assignment as a working dog handler is one of the most rewarding jobs there is.

There are few things more beautiful than watching handler and dog together, in perfect synchronization, and there is nothing more devastating than to have a K9 partner injured or killed in the line of duty. A K9 is not only a part of the law enforcement or military family, but also part of the officer's family at home.

We owe them all a prayer of thanks and safekeeping.

S.L. Ditmars
Prescott, AZ

*"We serial killers are your sons, we are
your husbands, we are everywhere.
And there will be more of your children dead tomorrow."*
—Ted Bundy

*"There is no hunting like the hunting of man, and
those who have hunted armed men long enough and
liked it, never care for anything else thereafter."*
—Ernest Hemingway

PROLOGUE

January 2019 – Long Beach, California

Lieutenant JW North of the Long Beach Police Department sat quietly in his car, listening to a police radio that was almost silent. The engine of his police car idled quietly; he needed to keep it running as it was cold and damp tonight. He was waiting for a radio call that he hoped would not come. A few more hours and the sun would be up, and he'd have survived another night.

He glanced at the clock—0300 hours. *Oh boy, the witching hour.* JW had the heater on high, and it could still barely keep the chill out of the car. The radio squawked and he hung on the words of the dispatcher over the air, but all he got was a unit heading to jail with a drunk driver. It was dead quiet this morning; it had been that way for several weeks now. *Who in the hell would want to be out on a night like this?*

Christina Anderson drove out of the parking lot of Bellow's Coffee Shop, on her way home after working a full shift there. The streets were mostly deserted due to the early hour. Although the job didn't pay much, she enjoyed the people she worked with and her customers, especially toward the end of her shift when her regulars came in. Everyone at work called her Chrissy; they loved her infectious smile and easy laughter.

One of her regulars was a police officer who had offered to follow her home to make sure she was safe. She knew about the rapist—the "Shadow." Everyone did. She knew four women had fallen victim to him already, but she felt safe driving in her car. Although she liked the officer and wouldn't mind a date after she got to know him better, she had told him, "No, thanks. I'll be fine."

Chrissy's uneasiness returned as she turned into the alley that led to her unattached garage. *Maybe I should have taken that officer up on his offer.* She knew she would feel safe once she was inside the garage. It had an electric door opener, so she wouldn't have to get out of her car until she was inside. She let out a small sigh of relief as she heard the click-clack of the door closing behind her car.

Exiting through the garage's side door, Chrissy stepped into her backyard and paused. *Odd*, she thought, *the motion detector light on the garage did not come on as I opened the door.* It was especially dark tonight since there was no moon to provide any light. The darkness made her feel even more uneasy.

Calm down, she thought as she started toward the back door of her unit. She knew there was another light there and she would soon be safely inside. Chrissy gasped as she heard movement to her left. *All right Chrissy, stop being a little girl, afraid of the dark. Probably just the cat,* she thought, and started to turn back to her right. The yard seemed too dark to her, matching the darkest corners of her mind where her fears lived.

The blow to the back of her head came suddenly. It stunned her and she dropped to her knees, her head swimming with pain and confusion. A second blow rendered her unconscious and she fell to the ground.

A voice came from the darkness. "If you thought you were safe, you were wrong. No one is safe from me."

The Shadow reached under her arms and pulled her back into the garage. He flipped on a small light on a workbench and began to go to work. He rolled her onto her stomach and reached into his backpack and pulled out a roll of duct tape and a pair of shears like the EMTs carried to remove clothing.

He bound Christina's ankles and wrists behind her back and taped over her eyes and mouth. Confident his prey was secure, the Shadow began to cut off her clothing.

Christina awakened to cold. She realized she was naked, and she couldn't move or see. She tried to speak, but there was tape over her mouth. She panicked and almost threw up in her mouth. She began to struggle against her bonds, but soon realized it was futile.

She heard a voice from behind her. It was quiet yet demanding.

"Oh, I see you're back with us. Good. It's not nearly as much fun for me if you don't wake up. Now, Chrissy, this is how it is going to be. You will submit to me, or you will die. Personally, I don't care. I am going to have you alive or dead. It's your choice."

He picked up the shears and used the pointed tip to trace a heart on her right butt cheek. She winced and pulled away from the pressure. He knew this wouldn't leave a mark; he wanted her fear. This wasn't about sex for him; it was about control and domination.

"Chrissy, I have a knife here. It is very sharp. I sharpened it especially with you in mind. Now, as I said, you can submit, or I can cut you up while you are still alive. Certainly not an attractive alternative for you. So, will you submit?"

She was panicked. She did not want to give in to this animal, but with her only other choice being a painful death, she gave in. She nodded her head.

"Good, Chrissy."

She felt like he was praising a dog. She heard him undo his pants and then felt him kneel behind her. He pulled her hips up and entered her roughly from behind. She started to pull away from the pain and he slapped her hard across her back and said, "Submit."

She squeezed her eyes shut tight, but the tears still found a way to leak out. Quietly, she prayed for rescue, for salvation, for survival.

After he was finished, she could hear him fastening his clothes.

"Chrissy, you were a good girl. You just stay there, and your roommate will be home in a few hours."

She heard him go out the side door and it closed quietly. Christina lay there for a while, thankful she was alive, but humiliated beyond reason. She was angry and ashamed and so many other things. She thought about what she should do next and whether she would call the police when she got free. *Wait a minute, he knew my name. He knew about my roommate and when she comes home. How did he know so much about me?*

When her roommate came home and discovered Christina, she quickly cut her free and called the police.

Lieutenant North snapped back to reality as the dispatcher came on the air. "Unit 2 Adam 14, a 261 occurred two hours ago…" He used his computer in the car to put himself on the dispatch. As he scanned the call and read the narrative, he became angry. "You sonofabitch," he screamed as he began striking the steering wheel with his hands. *One of these days your luck will run out and I will be there.* He put his car in gear and started driving to the call.

Christina didn't know the officers who arrived and, thankfully, the officer she knew from the coffee shop was not there. She did not want him to see her like this and was grateful for his absence. She was seated in her living room. Police officers seemed to be everywhere, making notes, taking photographs, and occasionally asking her questions. She noticed an older officer standing off to the side. He wore silver bars on his collar. *Most likely he is the watch commander.* She knew this from her work at the diner. He said nothing to those around him, just watched. There was a quiet calm about him, strength, confidence. But there was something else, something boiling to the surface. He was angry—pissed was probably a better word. He looked toward her and their eyes met. His eyes appeared to soften a little. *Sympathy?*

They took her to a hospital where she was treated and then examined by a forensic nurse. The detectives talked to her and tried to calm her fears, but she was scared. The Shadow had come into her life and violated her. From now on, she would never truly feel safe.

The rape changed Chrissy on several levels. She no longer felt safe either inside or outside her home. The fact that the Shadow knew so much about her made her think he could come back at any time. She didn't even want to go the grocery store and had to ask her friends to pick things up for her. As she withdrew more and more into herself, the number of her friends slowly diminished. Her fear grew to such a level she was even afraid to return to work. When she realized she had to work in order to survive, she did go back, but there was no longer any joy in her eyes and her co-workers never saw her smile anymore. The Shadow had changed her, and she would never be the same.

1

MARCH 2019

Field Training Officer Donald Harrison cruised eastbound on Pacific Coast Highway from Santa Fe Avenue. He and his trainee were working unit 1A2 and had just finished their squad meeting at the West Division Police substation. The Long Beach Police Department divided the city into four areas: North, East, South and West. Each had its own assigned officers and, when it was busy, each had its own radio dispatch channel. Harrison had been a police officer in Long Beach, California for over twenty years and was still working patrol. It was his choice: he liked patrol and he liked the responsibility of being a Field Training Officer (FTO). It gave him a sense of value to take new officers who had just completed the Police Academy and train them in the ways of the street. After all, there is only so much a rookie can learn in the classroom. His rookie, Officer Leandra Gonzalez, had shown good potential so far. She was sharp and confident, and she wrote good reports, which in the opinion of Officer Harrison was one of the more important aspects of the job, along with officer safety and about a thousand other things.

Don was a demanding FTO, known as the "Axe-Man" because he usually got the trainees who were having the most problems. Don was good at what he did: he would either fix them or start the mound of paperwork that would eventually lead to their resignation. Don didn't like that part of the job, but not everyone was cut out for this line of work. Some got in it for the wrong reasons, believing the badge gave them a lot of power. What those people failed to realize was the badge only brought responsibility—to the community, to your fellow officers and the profession, and most importantly, to yourself. Being a police officer was different from many professions in that you rarely had a supervisor with you. As Don had learned in a leadership class, integrity was doing the right thing when no one was looking. He had forgotten who said it, but he tried to imbue that philosophy into his trainees. Police work was not easy and certainly not for everyone. It was time to find out if Leandra had what it takes. Officer Harrison felt lucky this rotation. The FTO Coordinator had assigned a sharp trainee to him. He was happy to have a break this time, as his last rookie had nearly gotten him killed.

Don spotted a dark green Toyota pickup truck pull to the south curb just west of Long Beach Boulevard, stopping near one of the local streetwalkers. Prostitution was a problem in many cities; Long Beach was no exception and it led to a variety of other problems, including illegal drugs and street robberies. *I wonder what this is gonna lead to,* Don thought as he reached down to the center console of his Ford Explorer black-and-white police car and activated the overhead red and blue LED light bar and pulled in behind the Toyota. Without taking his eyes from the vehicle and its driver, he told Leandra, "It's all yours, rook."

Lieutenant JW North had just concluded his squad meeting at the East Division substation and finished his pre-shift inspection of his black-and-white Ford Explorer. He left the station parking lot and turned east on Willow Street and then south on Lakewood Boulevard. He was heading down to Pacific Coast Highway to a local coffee shop to meet up with his friend, Don Harrison, for a quick cup of coffee to help get the night going. It was still early in the shift and there was a four-hour overlap with the afternoon shift to help cover the busiest time of the night. It was March and the weather was a bit cooler than normal. There were patches of fog around the city, especially in the lower areas.

JW had worked Watch One or "Graveyard" for most of his career. He liked it because there was no command staff around and he and the other area lieutenants could run the show. Of course, someone had to oversee the city. Tonight, he and North Division Lieutenant Brynne Heathrow would split the watch commander duties. The watch commander acted as the chief of police while everyone else was at home. It was a Thursday night, and he wasn't expecting a busy shift. He called Brynne and volunteered to take the first half of the shift as watch commander.

It was JW's last night as a police officer. After thirty-two years, he was going to retire and focus more on his golf game. He had tried the game earlier in life and found it too frustrating. The job was hard enough, he didn't need the frustrations of golf too. His blood pressure could only take so much. But now that he was about to retire, all bets were off. He had visited a local golf shop and been custom fitted for a new set of clubs and had started going to the driving range. He still had no idea what he was doing. He had put his trust in the young salesman and silently prayed the clubs would work a miracle and help him improve his game, so he wouldn't continue to be embarrassed in front of his friends.

Before that, at the end of his shift, he would go to breakfast with his fellow officers one last time. JW found that even though he had promoted to the rank of lieutenant, he related better to the officers that worked the streets. He had asked Chief of Police Michael Estrada for permission to have several police units at one location. The citizens of

Long Beach sometimes became upset if too many officers ate at one place at the same time.

Police Dispatcher Cynthia Hewitt had been with the Long Beach Police Department only six months. She loved her career choice and was looking forward to growing with it. She had breezed through the classroom training as well as her call-taker training. There were a lot of things you had to know as a dispatcher, and you had to be good at the job in order to survive the pressure. Her trainer, Wendy Sanchez, had told her she was doing great and, because of her success, she was working the dispatch console for Area II tonight. Area II, which consisted of the East Division, was usually a little quieter and had less violent crime than the other three areas. So far, it had been a relatively quiet night and she had only dispatched a few "hot" calls. Her trainer was sitting behind her listening to the radio and watching her every move. This might make some people nervous, but Wendy had been incredibly supportive and treated Cynthia like a future colleague and not some rookie to be harassed. She felt very confident that she could handle anything that came their way and, if she panicked, Wendy could step in and take over.

Cynthia quickly scanned her dispatch screens and saw that all her units were either on calls or self-initiated activities like traffic stops. There were a couple of calls holding, but they were low priority report calls and the units assigned to those beats would be back in service soon. Also, she knew that the Watch One units were coming out of their squad meeting and would be available soon. She glanced to her right and looked at the mapping software that showed where all the police units and calls for service were located.

All in all, she felt pretty good about this. Unfortunately, that good feeling was about to end.

A priority-one 921 call flashed on her screen. She quickly translated the radio code of 921 to prowler. She was confused at first because she knew prowler calls were priority two. The call taker had upgraded the call to priority one for some reason, but why? The answer occurred to her even before she read the text of the dispatch: "Shadow?" The calling party had seen a shadow in his neighbor's backyard that moved quickly across the yard and then disappeared. The call taker believed the suspect could be the Shadow and had bumped the priority to one rather than have it possibly wait to be dispatched. "The Shadow" was the name the media had started calling a serial rapist who had already claimed five victims in Long Beach.

His M.O., or modus operandi, was to break into homes in nicer neighborhoods and attack the female victims. The really scary part was that it appeared the Shadow did some surveillance of his victims, because they were always alone when he attacked. The Shadow had always been a step ahead of the officers responding to the previous dispatches; many officers believed the Shadow was using a scanner to listen in on the police radio channels. Because of that belief, the area lieutenants had a meeting with the communications supervisors and together they arranged that any potential Shadow dispatches would be made only by sending a typed message on the computer inside each police vehicle—no audio over the radio.

This call was at 824 Santiago Avenue. Cynthia had been on a ride-along with East Division but did not know this neighborhood. The mapping software showed it was right next to Recreation Park Golf Course. She knew the car assigned to the beat of the call was out on a report and could see that all the other area police units were unavailable. Rather than wait, she keyed the alert tone on the radio channel for East Division and said, "All East units.

Code One your computers." She knew the officers would understand the Code One call as a priority request to read her message.

JW North had just turned south on Lakewood Boulevard from Willow Street when he heard the dispatcher, a new one whose name he couldn't recall, put out the Code One. He had met her once during a visit to the Police Communications Center and knew she was still training. He could tell by the tone of her voice that this call was potentially something big. He turned to the center console and quickly scanned the message. A prowler call at 824 Santiago. The calling party had seen a shadow in his neighbor's backyard. The call taker had noted the address of the residence next door—828— and seemed to believe this was possibly the Shadow. JW agreed. Shadow. He hated that name. *Damn media always trying to come up with a snappy nickname for criminals.* The problem was it glorified the scumbag to a portion of the populace, and that did not help at all.

JW used his computer to put himself on the call and accelerated his Explorer. He knew the location of the call in the 800 block of Santiago Avenue. It was on the east boundary to Recreation Park Golf Course, where he had a tee time the next morning. Ironic, he thought. He knew if he continued southbound, he would arrive at the Traffic Circle in less than thirty seconds. The Traffic Circle was the largest of several roundabouts in Long Beach. Three major arteries fed into it, and so many accidents occurred there that it had its own pre-drawn sketch for officer accident reports. From there, he would go around and exit eastbound on Pacific Coast Highway. He started to turn on his overhead red and blue lights, but then changed his mind. The Traffic Circle was hard enough to navigate normally, and people tended to do stupid things when they saw a police car with its emergency lights on.

As JW cleared the Circle, he turned on his emergency lights to enable him to easily drive through the next two intersections. He would not use the siren as he did not want to announce his arrival. Traffic was light and he knew he could be there in another minute. There was a problem, though. The houses on the 800 block of Santiago Avenue faced west onto the golf course. The Shadow would have good lines of observation west, north, and south. Smart move. He reached down and turned off the overhead lights before he reached the north side of the golf course. He then decided he would drive one block past Santiago, to Terraine Avenue. He quickly glanced at the unit status screen on his computer and noted that several East Division units, including some of his Watch One units, were on the call. He smiled to himself when he saw Unit 2S9, his old friend, Sergeant Eric Fletcher, was also responding. Looking at the map, he saw that he was closest and would arrive first.

As he turned south on Terraine, JW pushed the 10-97 button on his computer to notify the dispatcher he had arrived. He drove until he reached Eighth Street and turned right toward Santiago. He stopped mid-block between Terraine and Santiago and turned off his Explorer. He got out quietly and pushed the door closed, just latching it. He looked up the alley that ran between Terraine and Santiago and silently cursed. *Damn it, I forgot about the alley.* Nothing like giving the bad guy easy, direct access to the back of people's houses. JW hated alleys. They were dark, full of trash, and had a thousand places to hide.

JW started to walk toward Santiago, pulling his service weapon from his holster. Long Beach PD was different than many police agencies. With certain limitations, you could carry almost any reliable handgun available. The downside was, in a firefight, different officers could be carrying different types of magazines and/or ammunition. JW favored the Springfield Armory Operator Long Beach Special in .45 caliber. Although the Operator was a top-notch handgun right out of the box, Sergeant Mark Powers, his friend and former rangemaster, had insisted on replacing certain parts with upgrades. Springfield Armory had been more than accommodating and their pistol was one of the more popular ones carried in the department. JW's Operator was even more distinct than others—he had replaced the factory grips with a custom set he had made with an engraved image of his badge on the right side and the Marine Corps eagle, globe, and anchor on the left. JW had always loved woodworking and had seen a laser engraving machine at a woodworking exposition. His purchase of the expensive machine had confirmed to his wife, Bonnie, that he was indeed crazy. He used the engraver to make custom grips as rewards for his officers. You couldn't buy a set of grips from JW, you had to earn them.

JW approached Santiago slowly. The light here wasn't great and there were patches of fog drifting in from the golf course. He didn't want to bypass the suspect if he was not at 828 Santiago. He was walking past a parked vehicle when he heard a very low-volume ticking. He looked at the car and noticed it did not have a heavy coat of dew like the car parked across from it. As he listened, he continued to hear the car tick. It was the sound of the engine block cooling off.

He took a couple steps back and looked at the license plate. He reached up with his left hand and keyed the microphone to his portable radio. "Unit Edward 21 to run a plate on an unoccupied vehicle at Eighth and Terraine."

The dispatcher responded with, "Go ahead."

"Edward 21, the plate is 2 George, Adam, Tom 1-2-3, California."

The dispatcher quickly responded, "Edward 21, that vehicle is 10-29 Victor. Are you Code Four?"

Her response indicated that the vehicle was stolen, and she was asking if he was OK.

"Edward 21, I am Code Four for now. Vehicle is unoccupied."

"10-4, copy, you are Code Four, the vehicle is reported stolen from Arcadia two days ago."

JW knew that if this call was the Shadow and if he did have a handheld scanner, he had just told him the police were there. He decided to raise the response of this call.

"Edward 21, how many units do I have en route?"

"I show four units and a field supervisor are also en route." JW again keyed his microphone. "I copy that, please find me some more units. I want three units here with me and let's start setting up a perimeter. Also, see if the helicopter is in service."

Before the dispatcher could respond, the police helicopter cut in. "Unit Fox 2, we have been monitoring. We are currently in North Long Beach and en route with an ETA of five minutes."

JW decided it was time to get to 828 Santiago. He started walking in that direction, northbound, when he heard something behind him. Thinking it might be one of his assisting units, he turned and looked over his left shoulder. As he did, he caught a flash of movement to his left. Before he could face whatever it was, he felt a hard impact on the left side of his chest, followed by the loud report of a firearm. JW rotated and raised his Operator, but as he tried to raise his left hand for a two-hand hold, he found his left arm was not working. *What the hell? Have I been shot?*

He saw movement between two houses and placed the front sight on the silhouette as he fired instinctively, two times in quick succession. JW saw what appeared to be someone falling to the ground. As he started to sight in for a follow-up shot if needed, he began to feel lightheaded. His vision blurred and he felt dizzy. He dropped to his knees because it felt like if he didn't, he would fall down.

As he continued to lose consciousness, JW realized he was seriously injured. He reached for his handheld radio, but everything was going dim. Adding insult to injury, he fell forward onto his face, breaking his nose. As he started to black out, he could hear the dispatcher coordinating responding units and something else—the sound of someone climbing over a fence.

2

Sergeant Eric Fletcher, Unit 2 Sam 9, had quickly left the station after the Watch One squad meeting. He needed to run by the restaurant where they were having JW's going-away breakfast to make final arrangements before they closed for the evening. He heard the Code One dispatch for the prowler call and thought he'd better roll to that. It might just be their boy. Lieutenant North was tired of that asshole wreaking havoc in town and had placed a bounty for the arrest of the Shadow. Of course, that was not what JW called him. He remembered the LT saying, "Hey, you guys catch this idiot, and I will buy breakfast for whoever does. Hell, I will come back from retirement to celebrate with you." JW and Eric had been friends for a long time, and it was not the first time JW had placed a bounty on a suspect. With the "heavy" bounty, Eric thought this call might attract a lot of interest from the officers and perhaps he should respond to make sure there was adult supervision. Eric then thought, *Adult supervision. Who am I kidding? I'll be there.*

Sergeant Fletcher used his computer to place himself on the call and then scanned the contents of the call on his screen. He saw Edward 21 en route to the call and thought, *LT is always lucky on these calls. He'll probably get himself into the middle of it. I better pick up the pace.* As he accelerated toward the call, he heard the dispatcher come on the air. "Units responding to the 921, we have a report of shots fired in the area. Unit Edward 21 can you confirm?"

He listened for a few moments and did not hear anything from Edward 21. Eric didn't like that and reached for his microphone, telling the dispatcher, "Unit 2 Sam 9, continue to try and raise Edward 21. I am responding Code Three!" indicating that he was turning on his overhead red and blue lights and siren.

As he sped toward the scene, he could hear the dispatcher trying to raise JW. "Unit Edward 21, Code One channel two."

There was no response, and Eric's feeling of unease grew rapidly.

Dispatcher Hewitt updated 2-Sam-9's status on the call to Code Three. Her anxiety level increased as she worried that the "shots fired" call she had broadcast just moments ago was actually Lieutenant North being shot. She had never been on duty when an officer was injured, let alone shot, and she was not certain she could deal with it. She took in a deep breath and let it out slowly, hoping it would relax her a bit. She felt a hand on her shoulder, turned her head and looked into the eyes of the communications supervisor, Wendy Sanchez. She looked concerned, but confident. "Relax, you have this. Handle one issue at a time and everything will come together." Cynthia turned back to her dispatch station and said a silent prayer. *Please don't die...please do not die on my watch.*

Sergeant Fletcher decided to take a direct route to the scene. With Lieutenant North's status uncertain, he did not want to waste time with a more tactical approach. He drove north on Santiago from Seventh Street. As he approached Eighth Street, he could see a body lying in the road just ahead. He slammed on his brakes to avoid hitting whoever it was and threw his car door open. *Oh no!! That's gotta be JW! Damn it!*

Eric approached his friend and then slowly rolled him over and felt his neck for a carotid pulse. He knew what he was doing went against all the rules of officer safety; he should be ensuring the area was clear. *To hell with that, JW North is down!* Eric felt a weak pulse and saw the bloody, broken nose, but could not see any other injuries. JW was unresponsive, but Eric wasn't sure what the hell was wrong with him.

Eric took a deep breath; it was time to get this party started. He keyed his microphone and said, "Unit 2 Sam 9, I am on-scene. I have an officer down, Edward 21 is down. I need paramedics ASAP, 999," using the radio code for Officer Needs Help—Emergency. Eric looked JW over more closely and noticed blood on his left front chest. He reached down to his pocket and unclipped his Spyderco pocketknife and flicked it open. He cut through JW's shirt near a little hole that appeared to be from a small caliber bullet. His police car's headlights were lighting the area and he could see a small penetration into JW's chest. *Bad luck, JW, just missed your vest.*

Dispatcher Hewitt nearly jumped out of her chair when she heard the radio code for Officer Needs Help—Emergency. Her system flooded with adrenaline and she remembered what her trainer had told her about these types of emergencies. *You must slow it down. Your adrenaline will speed it up for you, so if you slow down, it will sound normal.* As she prepared her broadcast, she could hear the dispatchers on the other channels. Dispatchers routinely listened to their assigned channel and monitored others at low volume in case of an emergency. It was almost as if they were one voice.

Cynthia heard, "All units stand by for emergency traffic." They all turned to her as if to say, *It's yours now, run with it.* After switching over to a city-wide broadcast, she sounded the alert tone over the air, then keyed her microphone and said, "All units, per 2 Sam 9, officer down, 999 at 828 Santiago. Units assisting switch to channel 2 for further. Units assisting, use your vehicle computer to put yourself on the call." She turned her head slightly and looked at the mapping screen. She watched in amazement as every unit in the city stopped for a moment and then began moving toward E21 and 2S9.

Officers Harrison and Gonzalez had completed their business on their traffic and subject stop. Nothing illegal had happened yet, so the two subjects were sent on their way. Don turned to Leandra and said, "You know what, I want you to drive for the next couple of hours."

The words had no sooner left his mouth than he heard the dispatcher simulcast the Officer Needs Help—Emergency call. He had not heard the beginning of the dispatch, so did not know his friend JW was there or that he might be seriously injured. It didn't matter, when an Officer Needs Help call goes out, everyone rolls.

He turned to Leandra and said, "Change of plans, rook. I'll drive."

Harrison and Gonzalez both hurried to the car to get moving. Don told her, "Use the computer to put us on the call and get me some details."

Officer Harrison activated the red and blue lights and siren and, after checking that the intersection was clear, he accelerated through it. He had the green light at Atlantic Avenue and traffic was light, so he was able to build up speed quickly.

As Leandra scanned the call information from the vehicle computer, she said, "It looks like it was a prowler call and Lieutenant North was the first on-scene. Then there was a shots call in the neighborhood. Then 2 Sam 9 got there and found the LT down and put out the 999."

JW North and Don had been good friends for many years and were roommates at the National Police Shooting Championships competition every year. The speed of the Ford Explorer crept even higher.

They continued eastbound, slowing a bit as they approached intersections, Leandra looking for cross traffic and shouting "Clear" to be heard over the siren. As they passed into East Division at Cherry Avenue, Don asked her to change the radio to channel two in order to monitor the situation. The radio was a mess, officers were talking over one another on the air and no one could be understood. Finally, the dispatcher activated the alert tone with a loud beep and told the units to keep the air clear unless they had emergency radio traffic.

Don was not the only one amped up. He needed to watch for citizen vehicles and other police cars now that he was getting close. After they passed Redondo Avenue, they began a slow drop toward the traffic circle. Don started to slow the vehicle, but he was going fast and the downhill road added to his momentum. As he entered the Traffic Circle, he had to swerve to avoid a white PT Cruiser that was surprised by his sudden appearance. The sudden change in direction caused the rear end of the police vehicle to break free and Don corrected into the skid, but then he was struck from the rear by the PT Cruiser. He lost control of the vehicle but was somehow able to avoid the other traffic on the Circle. He went over the curb and flattened both front tires as the rims bent. The underside of the police car also hit the curb, puncturing the oil pan and leaking oil all over the grass on the inside of the Traffic Circle. The car slowly rolled to a stop near the center of the fifty-yard-wide grass center area. *Oh shit! Well, at least I didn't hit one of the palm trees.*

Officers Harrison and Gonzalez would remain there for the next several hours. Other officers would have to come to their aid and take an accident report. Don looked around the Circle; the PT Cruiser was gone, having fled the scene. After waiting a few minutes, Don switched the radio to another area's channel and advised of his location and the accident. He was told there were no units available, they were all on the 999. Don looked at Leandra, a deep pain in his eyes she did not completely understand, as he said, "Well, what did you learn tonight, Gonzalez?" She was uncertain what to say. Officer Harrison seemed to be in pain, but neither of them had been hurt.

She shook her head. "I don't know, sir."

Don motioned toward their ruined police car and said, "You don't do anyone any good if you don't get there. JW North is a good friend and I let him down tonight. I screwed up. I should have let you drive." Leandra nodded. She wished she could say something, but she was certain that nothing she could say would make Officer Harrison feel better.

Sergeant Fletcher did not like the idea of an armed suspect somewhere in the area and he wanted his officers to have an advantage. He keyed his microphone and transmitted, "2 Sam 9, Code Adam Robert. I am authorizing the deployment of patrol rifles for any units on this call that have them." He wasn't sure how many officers would have AR-15s with them, but now they could break them out and perhaps shift the odds in their favor if the Shadow decided to start shooting again.

Sergeant Fletcher knew the injury to JW was potentially life threatening. However, Long Beach Fire Department Station 14 was nearby with both an engine and paramedic unit. He hoped they were at home and not out on another call. He could hear the sirens of approaching police units and knew help would be there soon. It was all just a question of whether they could get JW to a trauma center soon enough. He was tempted to grab JW, throw him in a black and white, and take him there himself. Unfortunately, Eric knew his duty was to stay on-scene, take charge and get things organized. It was going to be a long night.

He could hear car doors slamming behind him and the sound of boots slapping the ground toward him. Eric didn't need to look up to know the cavalry had arrived. He smiled when he saw the first officer was John Walker, a very experienced officer assigned to his shift.

"Walker, take as many officers as you need and set up an Emergency Action Team. I need you to check 828 and see if anyone needs help. If necessary, make an entry and clear the residence. Be quick about it but be safe. We need to get a handle on this call now!"

Officer Walker turned to several officers and began giving them instructions. The group then moved quickly up the street toward the house at 828 Santiago.

Eric turned his attention back to JW. As another pair of officers came up to him, he realized it was Mary Castillo, one of his field training officers, and her rookie. With everything happening around him, he couldn't recall the kid's name. Jones? They were assigned to unit 2 Adam 12 tonight.

He told her, "Mary, you and your rookie take care of the LT, monitor his vitals, and see if you can find something in your first aid kit to apply pressure to his chest wound. Take a look and see if you can find anything else wrong with him. I think the bloody nose is superficial, but I really haven't had time to check him over. I need to take charge of this cluster and see if we can catch our shooter."

Mary turned to her rookie, Officer Jones, and told him, "Run back to the first black and white. They all have a first aid kit in the trunk. Bring it here and we can start first aid until Fire responds."

Mary then began quietly talking to JW. Eric couldn't hear what she was saying, he just hoped it would help keep JW in the land of the living for a while longer.

3

Within moments, John Walker, unit 2A11, and three other officers arrived at the front of 828 Santiago. The structure was a light blue, two-story home. It was dark and quiet. He turned to two of the officers and told them to go around back and see if they could find a point of entry. He keyed his handheld microphone and advised dispatch that he was in charge of the Emergency Action Team (EAT) and the residence appeared quiet for now. He knew there were other officers moving in on the house and wanted to avoid a friendly-fire situation. He told dispatch he had two officers moving into position in the rear. As soon as he finished his transmission, the police helicopter, unit Fox2, arrived and lit up the area with its searchlight. *Well, if the Shadow didn't know we were here before, he certainly does now.* A few moments later, Walker heard one of the officers in the rear advise dispatch, "We have an open door in the rear."

Walker keyed his microphone and said, "2 Adam 11, I copy that. Advise those officers to stand by. As soon as I get some more officers to cover the front, we will come back and make entry."

He had no sooner finished his transmission than two more officers ran up behind him. *Ask and you shall receive.* The area was being flooded with police officers. *Could they get them in the right places in time?*

Walker quickly briefed the two new officers on his plan and what he wanted them to do—specifically, contain the front and stop anyone coming out. He then took his backup officer and went to the rear. He could hear officers in the alley behind 828 and knew the containment of the house was complete. He could hear the helicopter on the radio, coordinating with dispatch and the responding units to expand the perimeter and, hopefully, contain the suspect if he wasn't still inside the residence. He faced his Emergency Action Team, now all together again, and quickly briefed them on the upcoming search and their roles on the search team. Officer Walker keyed his microphone and said, "Unit 2 Adam 9, I am with the EAT at the rear of the residence. We are going to make an announcement inside and make entry. Please advise units at 828 and 2 Sam 9."

Walker made his announcement, stating, "This is the Long Beach Police Department. Come out now and surrender to the nearest officer." In the background he could hear dispatch on the radio telling the other units that he was making entry.

Searching an unknown residence for a dangerous felony suspect is one of the most nerve-wracking parts of being a police officer. As Walker and his team moved inside, they worked together as a team to clear the residence room by room, covering each other's movements. All officers are taught basic search techniques in the Police Academy and during Advanced Officer Training. The training is rudimentary and based on the need for a group of officers that have not worked together before to be able to perform a search safely. No one was going to mistake them for a SWAT team or Navy SEALS, but they were getting the job done.

As they moved through the home, four flashlights moving back and forth, being careful to not backlight one another, Walker noted that the house seemed undisturbed except for the back door, where they believed the suspect had made his entry. He wished he had a K9 unit to do this search, but he knew, by policy, K9s were prohibited from searching residences unless the owner was there with them to confirm that no one was supposed to be inside. The EAT finished the downstairs search, pausing at the stairway leading to the second floor. Walker was already drenched with sweat and, taking a quick glance at his teammates, it appeared they were, too. He looked at the stairs and silently cursed them. *I hate stairs. Frigging fatal funnel if ever there was one,* referring to the nature of stairs and how they forced them into a narrow tight space, making them easy targets for anyone looking to shoot them.

Walker and another officer worked slowly up the stairs, one facing forward, the other to the rear, looking up. The other two officers remained at the bottom trying to provide as much cover for them as possible. As they reached the second-floor landing and found it clear, he signaled to the other officers to move up to join the rest of the team. They began clearing the upstairs rooms, one by one. As they reached the last, Walker paused outside the door of what appeared to be the master bedroom. He swept the room with his thirty-thousand-candlepower Streamlight flashlight. He saw what looked like a body on the bed. He signaled the others and the team entered and quickly cleared the room. Walker directed the others to clear what looked like a bathroom and walk-in closet while he turned his attention to the bed. What he saw turned his stomach. A woman was lying face up on the bed. Her face was beaten savagely, to the point where he could not make out her features, but she did appear to be breathing. He had no idea how old she was. She was naked, her clothing torn from her and cast onto the floor. There was a pool of blood around her head and cast-off spatter on the headboard and the wall behind it.

Walker looked at the blood on the wall and saw what appeared to be letters in the mess. He looked more closely and held his flashlight at an angle to avoid over-lighting the letters. He could just make out a message—"Fuck the Police." As Walker looked at the letters, he wondered what kind of sick bastard would beat a woman almost to death and then take the time to leave the police a message. The more he thought about it, the closer Walker came to the realization that he did not want to understand this guy. He looked at the bloody message and thought, *Yeah, well fuck you too, buddy.*

The other members of the EAT rejoined him, telling him the rest of the upstairs was clear. Officer Walker keyed his microphone and said, "Unit 2 Adam 11, the residence is clear. Code Four for now," signaling no further assistance was needed at this time. "We are going to need another paramedic unit for the victim. Advise Fire our victim is female, indeterminate age, unconscious but breathing." As these words passed from his lips, the victim gasped deeply like a drowning person coming up for air and then lay still, no longer breathing. "Unit 2 Adam 11, correction. Our victim just went into full arrest. We are beginning CPR. Expedite Fire!"

He signaled his team and shouted, "Help me get her off the bed, we can't do chest compressions there. Try not to screw up the crime scene too much."

The team carefully lifted the victim off the bed and onto the floor, doing their best to support her head and neck. Walker slid his hand along her rib cage, found the xiphoid process and then moved his hands up and into position for compressions.

Sergeant Fletcher slowly walked away from Lieutenant North and back to his vehicle, a Chevrolet Tahoe. He kept looking back at his friend, feeling the tug of loyalty pulling him one way, while duty took him the opposite direction. *JW is in good hands. I need to get my head back in the game and start taking care of business.* As he reached his Tahoe, he opened the rear hatch, accessed the command post unit in the back and started to organize things. He had heard 2 Adam 11 request paramedics and then that they were doing CPR. He knew Fire was en route but was not sure how long it would take.

The dispatcher then called to Sergeant Fletcher, "2 Sam 9, Fire advises they have two units on-scene, however, they are staging a block out until the scene is Code Four."

This was standard procedure for Fire—they would not normally come into the scene if it was not safe—but Eric needed them here now or he might as well call for the coroner. "Unit 2 Sam 9, I copy. Advise Fire the scene is not completely Code Four, however, we have control of the locations where the two victims are. Tell them both victims are critical, one receiving CPR, and if they will come in and just do a quick scoop and run, I will assign officers to each Fire unit to provide security for them."

Within moments of completing his transmission, the dispatcher responded, "2 Sam 9, Fire advises they are coming in." Eric breathed a heavy sigh of relief, hoping the effort by Fire would be enough for both JW and the other victim.

He looked south toward Seventh Street and saw help had arrived, with three black and whites escorting two fire engines and two paramedic units. The first two continued past him to 828, where he could see an officer signaling them with his flashlight. The others stopped and the paramedics quickly jumped from their unit and opened the back to retrieve a gurney and other equipment. The station captain got out of the fire engine, turned back to the driver, and said, "We're only gonna be here one minute, be ready to roll out." The captain turned to watch his men work on the police lieutenant when he noticed Sergeant Fletcher.

Eric said to him, "I appreciate the chance you guys are taking coming in like this."

"I'm not losing an officer tonight because a bad guy might be around. It's just not happening."

"What hospital are you going to?"

"Memorial."

Eric knew there were several good hospitals in Long Beach they could choose from and hoped they were ready for the storm that would soon be coming their way. "Copy, I will assign the units that came in with you as escorts and see if we can get the major intersections between here and there cleared for you."

The captain looked back, saw his paramedics were raising the gurney, and said, "OK, we're outta here. Good hunting."

Before Eric could say thanks, they were driving off, sirens blasting into the night. Eric Fletcher breathed a short sigh of relief. His friend was on the way to the hospital, as was the victim. Now he could concentrate on catching the suspect. He glanced down at his watch. It had only been twelve minutes since he first received the prowler radio call.

After the Fire Department vehicles and their police escorts left to drive to Memorial Hospital, Mary Castillo glanced down for a moment to clear her head. Seeing her lieutenant injured like that had shaken her—she thought he was indestructible. Seeing him lying there showed her she was wrong. *No one is indestructible.* She took one deep breath after another to regain control and opened her eyes. As she did, she looked at the ground and saw two brass casings on the road. They were a few feet away from where LT's pistol lay. She looked at the brass, and then the pistol.

Had the LT fired his weapon? *All the cops and firemen and vehicles that have been through here and the evidence had not been touched...what are the odds?* She called for Sergeant Fletcher and pointed out first the pistol and then the brass. Fletcher looked carefully at the brass and noted it was from a .45. Looking at the brass in relation to the lieutenant's pistol, Eric determined the most likely direction for the shots. He was looking at a space between two houses immediately in front of where JW had been on the ground. He turned to Mary and her partner, Officer Jones, and told them to go check the area between the houses. He also reminded them to be careful, the suspect might still be in the immediate area.

Sergeant Fletcher used his radio to contact the officers in Fox, the police helicopter, and asked them to illuminate the area in question. As Castillo and Jones approached the area, weapons drawn and hyper alert to the threat, they spotted what looked like blood on a white fence that ran between the two houses. Mary looked closely at the fence and then at the ground, where she saw small drops of blood on some leaves. *Alright, LT, you hit the bastard!* She left her partner there to preserve any evidence and contain the backyard in case the suspect tried to double back.

Officer Castillo shined her light into the night sky and radioed, "Fox, this is 2 Adam 12. Be advised we have a blood trail here, going over the fence."

Sergeant Fletcher keyed his microphone as Mary finished. "2 Sam 9, advise all units to stay out of the yards and hold their positions on the perimeter. Fox, can you check in yards here with your FLIR?" Their Forward-Looking Infra-Red night vision camera would help them to locate anyone attempting to hide from them. The FLIR was a remarkable tool for law enforcement. Because it located subjects by detecting their body heat, it was difficult to hide from. He had seen suspects hiding in outdoor sheds be found easily due to the glow the building gave off from the bad guy hiding within.

He knew he was going to need more help, so Eric took a moment to call Lieutenant Heathrow and advise her of the situation. He would route his SWAT activation request through her and other resources. She told him she was on the way and would take over as incident commander when she arrived.

SWAT came and searched. It took over five hours as they had to search several city blocks and then the entirety of Recreation Park Golf Course. They used police K9s and found a few homeless people in the thick brush between the fairways on the course. They searched until the sun was cresting the eastern horizon and the dew began evaporating, driving the humidity and temperature higher. They searched until it was beyond reason to continue. They searched and they found nothing, except a few drops of blood in some backyards and then some more leading across Santiago to the golf course. They followed some footprints in the grass across the seventh fairway until they disappeared on the damp cart path. However, they all searched in vain because the Shadow was gone.

4

The Shadow was happy tonight. His months of work, scouting for his next victim and then his follow-up intelligence gathering, had all paid off. Tonight was the night all the buildup would come to its culmination. He knew he was getting a lot of media attention from the local newspaper. They had dubbed him "the Shadow" after two of his previous victims said there was no way they could describe the suspect; they had seen nothing but a shadow and then they were knocked senseless. The name had stuck, and now even the national media had begun referring to him that way. He liked the name, THE SHADOW. It had a sinister ring to it. It was a lot of responsibility trying to maintain that image, but he knew he was the man to do it.

At first, he didn't like the fact that "the Shadow" historically was associated with being a "good guy." He certainly knew the public did not view him as a good guy. So what? They didn't matter and neither did their opinions. The dichotomy appealed to him. When it came down to it, he really didn't like people. So, the more they feared him, the more his actions shocked their pathetic consciousness, the happier he would be. Right now, he was a happy man. The media, especially the local newspaper, had taken special interest in condemning law enforcement. They kept hammering home their point that after five rapes, the police did not have one solid lead or a single suspect. Well, that was the police's problem; they were stupid and were not going to catch him anyway.

His "date" for tonight, Susan Anne Patterson, was forty-two years old. A bit overweight, but still within his standards. Susan had dark hair and eyes and a smile that said, "I want you to come into my bedroom and violate me." She worked in a law office in downtown Long Beach and was very successful. He could tell that from her nice house in a very nice neighborhood. He had first seen her in a bar on Second Street in the Belmont Shore business district. She was with a group, yet she wasn't really a part of them. She would chat and drink, but no one asked her to dance or would talk to her for more than a moment. The rest of the group failed to see what he saw in her.

He was out that night trawling for victims. His previous attack had gone off without a hitch. His success emboldened him, but also placed more pressure on him. He had to be perfect, not because he feared the police, but because anything less than perfect would shatter his illusion. His Susan deserved his best effort, not that she would enjoy any of it, but he was going to enjoy her pain. That would have to be good enough for her. He had followed her home from the bar that night and then to her work the following morning. His drive for perfection made him have to know everything there was to know about her.

The reality was, John Joseph Flannery was a loser. He was five foot six and weighed 140 pounds. He went to the gym regularly and, apart from what he saw when he looked in the mirror, there was nothing much there to see. He was the kind of guy that most people didn't even notice as they passed each other on the street. He had never been successful at anything in his life until his current job working the 8:00 p.m. to 4:00 a.m. shift as a security guard at one of the Port of Long Beach's many container terminals. The job was perfect for him. Everyone, except the truck drivers, went home by 6:00 p.m. and no one came back to work until 7:00

or 8:00 a.m. The drivers were not interested in him. They only wanted to get into the terminal and get an assignment from the dispatcher for their next job. When John was at work, he was alone in a sea of activity. He was alone with his thoughts, his thoughts of what he would do when he got his Susan alone. Beyond this job, which he had held for only five months, the only other thing he had ever done right was the crime of rape. Of course, he didn't think of it as a crime. It was merely what he wanted, what he would take.

Tonight, he cruised around the major streets surrounding Susan's neighborhood. It was nice because he could see her house from both the north and south major streets. Excellent; seeing her house only served to heighten his senses and his desire. He watched the traffic, looking for police vehicles, both unmarked and black and white. Unmarked police cars were not hard to spot, if you paid attention. They looked like police cars, without the light bars, and were not painted black and white. Most important, the occupants of an unmarked car paid more attention to what was around them, than where they were going. When success was paramount, one couldn't be too careful. Seeing no activity, he turned onto one of the side streets and then onto Eighth Street and pulled to the north curb in his stolen 1997 Toyota Corolla.

He turned off the lights and sat back in the car for a few moments. Watching and listening, looking for a parting of curtains or a light coming on to indicate his arrival had aroused someone's suspicion. He saw the same thing he had seen from several other stolen vehicles over the past few weeks—nothing. One of the many things that confirmed his interest in Susan was the nature of her neighbors. They were all elderly, so they didn't seem to interact with her at all, and they all went to bed early. Also, none of them seemed to have dogs.

John hated dogs as much as he hated everything else in the world. Their incessant barking made his fun that much more difficult. Instead of seeing this as an additional challenge, he saw it as an annoyance. He would never admit he was afraid of dogs, but he was. He once tried to lure his neighbor's mutt into his yard so he could kill it but had to abort his plans when the dog bit his hand. The absence of dogs in this neighborhood was a sign to him. This was the place.

He knew if anyone was watching him, he was screwed. He didn't want to make it obvious that he was up to something, so he walked into the alley as if he didn't have a care in the world. He had a small backpack with him. He hoped it made it look like he was coming home from a late-night visit to the gym but actually it was his rape kit. The backpack held the things he would need to subdue his victim and have his fun.

In reality, his heart was racing. He was exhilarated tonight. The press had noted that each rape he committed was getting progressively more violent. He didn't think so, but he didn't spend too much time thinking about it. He knew that eventually he was going to kill one of his victims. He was OK with that; she wouldn't really matter anyway. She was just a bit player in the drama of his life.

The Shadow paused at Patterson's unlocked back gate and pulled on a pair of surgical gloves. He watched all the CSI and serial killer shows and he learned. He knew his fingerprints were on file for all the minor offenses he had committed years ago. He was glad they had never collected a DNA sample. If he left DNA evidence at a scene, no worries, he wasn't in that system. He opened the gate, went through, and quietly re-latched it. *Are people stupid or just lazy? Unlocked gates...might as well hang a sign on the front door inviting me to come in.* He moved to the back door and tried it. It was locked, but with only a simple push button lock that was probably installed fifty years ago when the house was first built. The Shadow took out a pocketknife, slipped it into the door frame and pushed the latch bolt back and pulled the door open. He didn't believe the house had an alarm, but he waited and listened for a moment anyway. The Shadow was incredulous—this was too easy! Whatever happened tonight was her own fault. She brought this on herself.

The Shadow moved quickly through the house. He knew the basic floor plan from his previous observations. It wasn't hard to figure out how a house was laid out if you bothered to take the time to look. Of course, things that were obvious to him were not to others. He went up the stairs, stepping carefully to avoid making any noise. At the top, he looked toward Susan's bedroom. He knew where it was. He had stood in the bushes of the golf course across the street and watched. He knew from watching the lights go out that this was where her bedroom was. He stopped at the door and listened to her breathing. It had a steady rhythm to it that he knew meant she was asleep.

He reached into his backpack and pulled out an eighteen-inch piece of steel pipe. He raised it over his head and struck Susan on the side of hers. He hit her hard, but not too hard. He didn't want to kill her. He just needed her out of it for a few minutes while he prepared her. The blow had its intended effect; her head shifted from the right to the left. He ripped her nightgown from her unconscious form, his anticipation growing. He could still hear her breathing, more ragged now. *Good, don't you die on me...yet.* He decided. Tonight would be his first kill and Susan Patterson's last night on earth.

The police were correct in their belief that the Shadow was using a police scanner to monitor their radio transmissions. A wired earpiece led from the scanner to his right ear. He listened with interest as he heard the dispatcher send a message to all the police cars in the area. The Shadow didn't believe in coincidences, and his paranoia was confirmed when he heard the police had found his stolen car parked just down the street. The anger in the Shadow peaked. His ultra-high anticipation was now matched by rage, a rage he unleashed on Susan Patterson. He began striking her face with his gloved fists. He hit her face over and over, using every ounce of energy in his body. Numerous cuts split open and blood began to flow over her face. As he hit her again and again, the blood began to spatter on the bed, on the walls, and on him. Her eyes quickly swelled shut, but if the Shadow had his way, she would never need them again. Finally, spent, the Shadow climbed off Susan. She had never made a sound during his assault, which frustrated him even more.

The Shadow knew he needed to get out of there. He rushed down the stairs. *Can't go out front, the police will see me.* He went out the back door. He thought for a moment; the alley wouldn't be safe, so he turned and vaulted over the neighbor's fence and then continued south through two more backyards. As he reached the house on the corner of Eighth and Santiago, he peered over the fence and saw the police car stopped there. He turned and went to the wall between the houses facing the golf course and quietly climbed over. He was standing there in the shadows when he saw the police officer moving up the street, looking toward Susan's house. The Shadow reached into his pack and pulled out a Walther PPK pistol. He had purchased the gun from a homeless thief who had stolen it during a burglary. He had researched the gun after his purchase and knew the .380 caliber handgun wasn't very powerful. He hoped he would never need it, but he believed in having options. If one of his victims were to fight back, he wanted to be able to regain the advantage. Now, faced with the possibility of being confronted by a police officer, the gun felt good in his hand.

The Shadow stood behind some bushes and watched the officer. The man was big, certainly not someone he wanted to tangle with. The officer was still moving cautiously toward Susan's house when he heard something. The officer paused and then looked over his shoulder. Something told the Shadow he was about to be discovered. He panicked and pulled the trigger. The pistol jerked in his hand and the loud gunshot startled him. He saw the officer turn and point his pistol at him. The Shadow turned to run when he heard first one shot, then another. The first shot struck him on his left shoulder, cutting one half inch deep into the meat of his deltoid. The pain was overwhelming, and he nearly fell to the ground. He knew if he went down, it was over, and he would be caught. He managed to keep his head for a moment and climb over the fence back into the backyard he had just been in. *Where to go?*

He considered going back into and across the alley eastbound. He knew there was nothing there but more houses for quite some distance. He did not want to get trapped in a neighborhood. In a few minutes the police would be everywhere, and people would wake up. It was only a matter of time before people saw him and called in about it. He needed to get out of here now! He went back north, the way he had come before, but stopped one house before Susan's. He didn't need to climb a fence this time as the gate was unlocked. He went between the houses and looked down the street toward where he had last seen the officer he had just shot. The officer was lying in the street. For a moment, he considered running down and finishing him off, but the sound of sirens in the distance changed his mind. He looked the opposite direction, up Santiago toward Pacific Coast Highway, and saw there were no cars up there. He made a snap decision and ran across the street toward the golf course.

When the Shadow reached the golf course, he ran at the low fence and jumped over it into the bushes. He was tired, but he knew he needed to keep moving. To stop was to get caught. To get caught was to go to prison and there he knew he would die. He ran. He ran across two fairways and he could see his footprints in the grass. He didn't want to leave a trail, so he ran on the cart path. He knew where he was going now, as he had walked through the golf course on several occasions. This was his backup plan. He was glad he was meticulous in his planning. As he reached the clubhouse parking lot, he began to walk. He knew there was a chance of encountering homeless around here and he did not need any undue attention.

The Shadow calmed himself. He slowed his breathing and told himself he did not have a care in the world. He strolled down Deukmejian Drive past the tennis courts and turned north onto Park Avenue. He walked past a long block of parked cars outside an apartment building until he was almost at the end, where he got into his car that he had parked there earlier in the day. He reached into the driver's-side rear wheel well and took out a single key. He unlocked the driver's door and, as he got in, he heard the police helicopter roar past overhead and then its searchlight lit up the night sky almost a mile away. He breathed a sigh of relief and started the car. He drove out into the night and began to ponder his future. He needed to look at his shoulder. It was on fire and the pain was unbearable, but he couldn't go to a doctor. It might be a good time to relocate and get out of Long Beach. Yes, it was time to find a new hunting ground.

5

JW North woke slowly, as if in a dream. It felt like a dream to him, but it also felt real. He looked around and saw nothing but beautiful blue skies, with the occasional fluffy white cloud slowly floating by on a mild breeze. The temperature felt perfect and the calm winds only served to heighten his sense of peace. He could hear a small stream nearby. He looked to his left and there it was, about three feet wide with water rushing against smooth river rock and drifting off into eddies that were teeming with small fish. A larger pond fed into the stream off in the distance. JW thought there was probably pretty good fishing down there. He sat up and discovered he was sitting in soft green grass. It was perfect, whoever took care of the landscaping around here was doing a great job. There were a variety of plants with blooming flowers all around him. He felt like he had woken up in a photo shoot for *Better Homes and Gardens*. He glanced behind him and spotted a bench. JW stood and slowly walked to the bench. It was made of some kind of hardwood and beautifully carved. He could not see a single joint in the construction. His legs didn't feel quite right, so he decided to take a seat and just watch all the beauty around him. It was then that he noticed the dogs; they were everywhere, running and playing with one another. JW thought, *OK, this is getting weird*. As he sat there, a large German Shepherd trotted up to him and dropped a green tennis ball in his lap. The dog bore a striking resemblance to his old Police K9, Asko. That couldn't be, he had been gone over fifteen years now. The dog looked at him with an unmatched intensity in his eyes. JW picked up the ball and the dog tracked every movement. As he reached back and then let the ball fly, it sailed over fifty yards in the air and bounced through a group of other dogs playing. *Uh oh, this is going to lead to a fight.* The dog turned and ran full tilt after the ball. He sped through the other dogs, who ignored the ball passing through, and now ignored the dog as it sped by. The dog picked up the ball and trotted back to JW. Again, the dog dropped the ball in his lap and the intense stare returned. *Asko?*

As JW threw the ball a second time, he noticed a pair of hands resting on the back of the bench, next to him. He spun in his seat; his eyes locked on the stranger there. As JW watched, the stranger took a step back and raised his hands in front of his chest in a "no offense" gesture. "Easy, JW," he said. "I'm not here to hurt you. No one is, you can relax for a while."

JW looked at the man, a large black man with a broad smile, and said, "This is a very relaxing place. Where the hell am I?"

The man laughed at JW in a friendly way, and said, "Well, I can assure you, you are not in hell."

"Yeah, I figured that much. No fire, no brimstone, no devils running around with pitchforks poking people in the ass."

The man took on a more solemn expression and said, "This is a nice place to sit and relax." He extended his right hand to JW to shake. "My name is Mike."

JW took the man's hand and looked into his eyes. *Nice firm handshake, good eye contact, no malice in the eyes, seems OK.*

The dog had come and gone, chasing after the ball each time JW had thrown it for him. Mike nodded at the dog, and said, "He doesn't ever seem to get tired of that, does he?"

JW looked at the dog and, as if speaking of his old K9 partner, said, "No, he never tires of it. He has a play drive that is through the roof," and then tossed the ball again. "So, Mike, this is an incredible place. I love it here. Am I dead? Is this heaven? Because if this is heaven, you can sign me right up. I'm good."

Mike looked at JW with a sad expression, turned his head a little, and it looked like there was something he wanted to say. "Some, like you, would call this heaven. But, no, you won't be staying here. There is something you need to do, to finish."

JW felt his anxiety rising; he knew he wasn't the best person. Sure, he was a cop and a Marine before that. Sure, he had done a lot of good, but like most people, he had his darker moments too. He didn't go to church nearly as often as his wife wanted, but then again, he had never felt that was necessary to stay in God's good grace. Besides, he had to work too many Sundays. God understood, he hoped.

Mike saw the growing concern on JW's face and smiled that giant smile of his. "Relax, JW, you're not coming home today… you're going home."

JW looked to the ground and thought about the man's words. Going home, going home to what? He knew that when he looked up, Mike would be gone. He didn't want to look up because he knew that would make this "dream" begin to seem more real. He looked out to the fields and watched the dogs frolicking. He felt a longing inside, but then he felt an inner tranquility. *To what indeed?* he thought as the view began to fade. His last remembrance of the visit was Mike's voice saying, "Oh, and we threw a little something in for your golf game: you kind of suck at golf," followed by his deep laugh.

JW reopened his eyes. The beautiful fields had been replaced by a sterile hospital intensive care room. OK, that was the strangest dream ever. He looked around the room and saw a lot of medical machines—intravenous drips giving him medicine and fluids, another monitoring his pulse and blood pressure. There was a tube in his throat to assist with his breathing. His mouth was dry, so very dry. He would love to have a drink of water. In the shadows across the room, he could see his wife, Bonnie. The light cast from her iPad illuminated her face. She was reading. They both loved to read and enjoyed many of the same authors. That was a good thing, as JW read voraciously. He read everything and spent most of his free hours with his head in a book. *That's what was missing.* He thought of the meadow, the brook, and the dogs playing. *That was what was missing—a good book and his wife to share it all with.* With those thoughts running through his head, he drifted back out. Bonnie never knew he was there with her, but seeing her put his mind at ease.

The next time JW woke was six days later. The tube was out of his throat, but he was still hooked up to a bunch of medical machines. Looking around, he wondered, *Am I in a hospital or a medical device showroom?* Across the room, Bonnie was still here, sitting in the shadows, reading. He wondered how long he had been there, and what had happened to him and the person who lived in 828 Santiago. Then he remembered being shot and the Shadow and he felt his blood pressure start to rise. Apparently, his heightened state set off an alarm at the ICU workstation, as a nurse rushed into the room and began to fiddle with the machinery. Bonnie looked up from her book and their eyes met. He looked at her and croaked out, "Hi, Honey."

Bonnie smiled, then jokingly scolded him, "Well, it's about time you woke up! You've been out for two weeks!"

JW thought about that. *Two weeks. What the hell?* The nurse turned to him and said, "Hi Mr. North, my name is Holly. I'm your ICU day nurse. You're getting yourself a little too excited, so I'm going to up your medicine a bit. This will help you relax. I'm also going to message Dr. Malouf and let him know you are awake." Before JW could object, he felt the medicine begin to take hold. He looked back at Bonnie; she was still smiling at him.

"Don't worry, JW. I'll be here when you wake up."

JW woke up again later that afternoon. As his eyes began to come into focus, a tall, thin man with dark skin peered down at him. "Ah, good. John, how are you feeling?"

JW looked at the man, confused, and said, "I'm fine, but who the hell is John?"

Bonnie could see that JW was starting to get agitated and said, "JW, calm down or the nice nurse will come back and reintroduce you to Dr. Feelgood," referring to the Valium they had been giving him to help keep him calm.

The man looked a bit flustered and said, "I'm sorry, sir, I am not sure what to call you. Your wife told me your name was John. I'm Dr. Peter Malouf, your attending physician."

JW looked at Bonnie for an explanation, and she laughed, "It's OK, Dr. Malouf." Then speaking to both of them, she said, "The doctor asked me what JW stood for. I told him your father had named you after John Wayne, but I forgot to tell him that he only gave you the initials."

"I'm sorry, Dr. Malouf, my wife can have a rather strange sense of humor at times. Please call me 'JW.'"

Dr. Malouf replied, "I have heard that police have rather odd senses of humor—a coping mechanism—but I didn't realize it extended to their families."

JW looked at his wife and said, "Trust me, Doctor, she had a weird sense of humor long before she met me."

Both men looked at Bonnie, who said, "Dr. Malouf, a thousand apologies. I wasn't thinking when you asked the question. JW can be rather sensitive about his name at times."

Dr. Malouf laughed it off and asked JW, "Well, how are you feeling?"

"OK, but I wonder how much dope you are pushing into my system."

"Not as much as you would think. You were seriously injured and it required a lengthy surgery to put you back together again."

"Can you fill me in on what exactly happened? I don't have much recollection of anything after I showed up on the call."

"Well, you are either the luckiest man alive or the unluckiest," said Dr. Malouf. JW nodded in encouragement and Malouf continued. "You were shot, and somehow the bullet missed your bulletproof vest and entered your chest from the side." JW mentally noted the vests were not bulletproof at all, but would resist penetration from most handgun ammunition. He decided in his current tired state not to bother trying to correct the doctor and just let it go. "I examined your vest after the surgery hoping for an answer, and I can only guess that the shooter was sideways to you and missed the vest, unfortunately for you."

"Story of my life, Doc."

"Anyway, the bullet missed your ribs and entered the chest." Pointing and drawing a line across his chest from left to right, the doctor said, "The bullet continued across the front of your chest, penetrated your left lung, and then exited it two inches later. The bullet continued left to right, fortunately passing in front of your heart and stopping on the right side, where it stuck in your ribs. Luckily, the bullet was a .380 caliber hollow point; I am told it is not very powerful and did not expand or do excessive damage.

"Even with that, you suffered significant blood loss. I believe we may have lost you for a few minutes. I had a great surgical team and we were able to bring you back. Then, we managed to repair the damage to your lung and removed the bullet. Of course, we gave the bullet to the police department for evidence. You were incredibly lucky when you passed out and collapsed. You ended up on your left side, in almost a recovery position, so you didn't drown in your own blood."

JW had enough first aid training to know that the recovery position was how you placed unconscious people on their side, using the arms and legs to hold them in position to help prevent them from choking, should they vomit.

Bonnie could not let the doctor get away with the perfect set-up he had unwittingly given her. "Dr. Malouf, the bullet didn't miss his heart. It went in there and looked around, but couldn't find his heart because it's so small."

JW looked at Bonnie and said, "Why thank you, Dear. Your concern is overwhelming. A severely injured man lying here and you are making fun of him."

Bonnie quickly retorted, "Quit your whining, JW, you're gonna be fine."

Dr. Malouf was uncertain exactly how to deal with all of this until he realized the two were just playing with one another. He had seen Mrs. North there every day since the night JW had been shot. He realized her words did not match her actions and said, "Well, I can see that couples therapy will not be needed for you two."

JW then turned to Dr. Malouf and said, "OK, that's done. Let's move on to some important stuff. I'm starved. When do they serve dinner and when can I get out of here?"

Dr. Malouf informed JW he would be in the hospital for a couple more weeks and they would begin transitioning him to a normal diet in a few days. JW was not very happy about either of those situations, but no one was asking his opinion.

"You have progressed very well. We will be transferring you to a private room tomorrow. You and your friends will find that much more comfortable."

JW looked at the doctor quizzically. "Friends?"

Bonnie answered this question on her own. "The chief of police assigned an officer to be here with you 24/7. He's sitting outside. I told him, 'Thank you very much,' even though I knew you would hate it. It did make it easier for me to go home and sleep, knowing you would be watched over. Actually, the hospital has done a great job of taking care of me while you were napping. I'm starting to take a liking to hospital food."

Dr. Malouf started to leave but then turned back to JW. "There has been a rather lengthy list of people here to see you. You must be very important. After we move you tomorrow, I am going to allow you to have one or two visitors per day, excluding your wife, of course. She can continue to come and go as she pleases. You are still very weak and I worry about you developing an infection."

JW nodded and Dr. Malouf quietly walked out, and Holly, his ICU nurse, entered the room. "Please, Holly, no more drugs. I hate the things, so please no more than you have to give me."

"OK, but if you are feeling any pain or having trouble going to sleep, you let me know immediately." Holly checked a few things on his monitors and, as she left the room said, "Bonnie, fifteen more minutes, OK?"

"Wow, she tells me how it is, but asks you if it is OK for you to leave in fifteen minutes. I see who is running this place."

"That's right. You would not believe how many administrators tried to get me out of here. Finally, the chief of police called down and asked them if I could stay. JW, I was so worried about you. What the hell is wrong with you getting yourself shot up like that?"

JW didn't have an answer to that. He knew that, sometimes in life, stuff happens, and your only choice is to hang on and not get thrown off the ride. He wasn't happy he had put his wife through hell, but then again, it wasn't like he had asked that Adam-Henry to shoot him.

JW and Bonnie talked for another fifteen minutes. She filled JW in on all the happenings over the past two weeks. Bonnie was happy to see JW engaged with the conversation, but she felt like he was holding things back. She could tell he was angry about something but couldn't make her way through the walls he had put up. Was he trying to keep her out, or was he just not ready to deal with it yet? As she stood to leave, JW said to her, "Hey, tomorrow remind me to tell you about this dream I had. Weird stuff, not scary, just maybe the strangest dream I've ever had."

Bonnie nodded as she left. It would be a long time before they talked about the dream.

6

As promised, JW was moved out of the ICU of Long Beach Memorial and was transferred to a private room. There weren't many private rooms at Memorial and JW didn't think he was all that special; more likely the administrators believed that if he were placed in a semi-private room, his roommate would never get any rest due to the constant flow of visitors. He had to laugh when he saw the procession escorting him from the ICU to his new room. The department had assigned another officer to assist with the move, and hospital security had assigned a supervisor and two of their officers to protect him. JW was old friends with the director of security at Memorial and he couldn't fault his friend for the extra diligence. Not that it was likely that anything was going to happen, but if something did happen, no one wanted to feel like they had not done enough to protect him.

Personally, JW could do without all this attention. If they weren't going to send him home, then just stick him in an elevator and drop him off at his new place. Memorial was a great hospital and they had extended him every courtesy, but he would rather be at home in his own bed. When they wheeled him into his room, he saw more flowers and balloons than any florist shop he had ever been in. As they transferred him to his new bed, JW eyed Bonnie in her spot in the corner, iPad in hand, ready to begin her watch. Opposite her was a second chair, occupied by another police officer. He glanced at JW and gave him a little wave and greeting. "Hey, LT." JW recognized him as Evan Weeks, assigned to Watch II, day shift, East Division. Weeks turned his attention to a flat-screen television mounted high on the wall. It was currently showing Fox News, The Five. The panelists were arguing with one another over some innocuous point that JW was certain was leading to the downfall of western society.

JW tuned out the show and turned back to Bonnie, who greeted him with, "Well, the ringmaster has arrived." JW was confused at first, was Bonnie making some obscure movie reference? Then it clicked; she was referring to the current three ring circus around him. As the transfer concluded and everyone began to leave, JW thanked them all for their kindness and professionalism, all the while trying to keep his annoyance from showing on his face.

After thirty minutes of checking his vitals, hooking him up to a new series of monitors and meeting his new caregivers, the room was finally clear. JW turned to Bonnie, but she gestured toward the door. Perplexed as to who was coming to see him now, JW was pleasantly surprised to see Officer Don Harrison walk into the room with a bit of a sheepish grin on his face. JW was truly glad to see him and greeted him with an enthusiastic, "Hey Donnie!"

Don replied, "Hey, LT, how you doin'?" Before JW could answer, Harrison continued, "The chief has assigned me as family liaison while you recover. He told me he wanted me to do it because he thought you were least likely to kill me."

A slow "OK" was all JW could muster.

Don said the chief would come by later to see how things were going. He turned to Officer Weeks and said, "Evan, I've got the security officer who is assigned to the floor on the lookout for any brass. He'll give you a heads up when the chief is on the way. You might want to not be watching the TV when he shows up."

"Oh come on, Donnie, if I stand around here like a guard you know he"—Weeks gestured at JW—"is just going to yell at me."

"I know, but you have to make it look good when the brass is around," replied Harrison.

JW lay in bed, watching the back and forth between the two officers, and interrupted, "You two do realize that I am the brass, too?"

Weeks laughed and Don smirked, "The hell you say."

JW turned to Weeks and said, "Isn't there a report call holding in your beat?"

Weeks look confused for a moment and then realized JW was trying to get rid of him. "No way, LT. This is my job for the next half a shift."

JW reflected on that and understood what this meant. He had stood many turns guarding prisoners or VIPs at the hospital. It was boring duty and he knew that Weeks, a good, hard-working street cop, would rather be doing his real job. JW said, "Thank you," and looked at Donnie. "So, what's up?"

Don's face took on a serious expression as he removed a steno pad from his back waistband. "As I said, the chief has assigned me to you. I am to coordinate all communications between the department and you. Check."

"Lucky you," was all JW could think to say.

"Don't worry, LT, I got a system."

"Oh, lucky me."

"I am also to provide any assistance, as needed, to your wife."

Bonnie looked up from her book and said, "I guess that's me, the wife. No, thank you, Donnie. I'm good. I don't need to get lucky."

Everyone silently looked to Bonnie.

"What? Oh, I guess that didn't come out right." Bonnie slowly turned a deep red.

Don replied, "Yes, ma'am," and checked off another line on the pad. "Moving on, Sergeant Powers wants to know if you are going to the Nationals this year." The Nationals was the short name for the National Police Shooting Championships. This year the Nationals were being held in Jackson, Mississippi. JW had been on the police pistol team for years and was looking forward to going. He had made many friends there, including members of the German National Police Shooting Team. He enjoyed the competition and camaraderie, and found the shooting courses of fire, which lasted three days, to be challenging and excellent training.

"Mark says you have three months to get it together or he is going to find some other poor SOB to take your spot," Don reported. Mark Powers was another friend and JW knew the harsh language was just his way of wishing him well. He was obviously hopeful that JW would make a miraculous recovery.

JW thought of the heat and humidity of Mississippi and the thirty-five matches and over two thousand rounds that he would have to fire—and that was if he skipped the practice matches. JW was not feeling optimistic. "Tell Mark I don't know. I will try my best to be there, but he should start working on plan B."

Don frowned, but all he said was, "Check."

"Moving on," Don said. "The public information officer wants to know if you can speak to the media."

"Easy answer. My doctor says I can have only limited visitors and am not to get excited."

"You know Sergeant Kingman, LT. He isn't likely to take 'no' for an answer."

"Last time I checked, a lieutenant outranked a sergeant. No, thank you."

For the next hour, JW and Donnie went over what seemed to JW to be a never-ending list. "I have a few 'Get

Well' cards here for you," Don said as he handed JW a large stack of cards.

Bonnie interrupted him, saying, "I'll take those," and, looking at JW, said, "You have a lot more at home. I'll start organizing them and get you an extra-large pack of thank you notes for when you are feeling better."

Finally, Don came to the end of the list. "Last item, LT. The guys on your shift want to know when you are coming back to work." JW thought about this question for a long moment, and Bonnie looked up from her book inconspicuously, wondering what his answer would be. He knew the city would not let him retire until he had rehabilitated. But there was something else going on here and he did not feel comfortable at this point saying he was not going to return to work.

JW thought about his plans for retirement. He thought of the traveling he and Bonnie wanted to do. They were both SCUBA divers and enjoyed diving in the warm waters of the Caribbean. He knew Bonnie wanted to go to Italy and other places. He knew all these things and he knew he was about to be in deep trouble when he said, "Soon."

Bonnie sighed as she watched all her plans slowly circling the drain. *Well, I knew the job was dangerous when I took it.*

"Check," replied Don, and then, "See you later," as he walked out of the room.

JW told the remaining officer, "Evan, you look like a man who needs a cup of coffee."

Weeks was confused; after all, he had a cup of coffee on the armrest of his chair. Then the light in his head went on, and he realized JW wanted to speak with his wife in private. "Ten-four," he said as he got up and made for the cafeteria in the basement.

JW knew Bonnie was going to be pissed. He couldn't think of anything to say, so he went with the old standard,

"I'm sorry, can I get you some flowers to help make this better?" gesturing to the room full of flowers.

Tight lipped, Bonnie replied, "No thanks, there are more than this at the house."

"Look, you have to admit, he kind of dropped that on me. And, well, to be honest, I'm a bit confused right now. This thing has kind of shaken me and now I feel like I have unfinished business. I don't know what that is, but I do know I can't do it without you there with me." JW gave her a sheepish look, something like John Belushi to Carrie Fisher in *The Blues Brothers*.

"Does that mean you're going back to work?"

"I'm not sure. Maybe for a few months while I go through physical therapy and sort through all this. I don't know what the hell is going on, Bonnie, or what is going to happen. But I think it has something to do with dogs."

Bonnie knew that JW had been a police dog handler before he met her, when he was married to his first wife. She knew that his dog/partner then, "Asko," was a great working dog and had been shot while on a SWAT call-out. She also knew that after he had been promoted to sergeant, he had been placed in charge of the K9 unit. She knew he loved his time as a handler as he had told her, "Probably the best job I ever had. You are always at the center of the action."

She knew center of the action meant excitement to JW. After all, most cops were adrenaline junkies, but to her it was just another opportunity to be shot at. She had read somewhere that K9 officers were more likely to be in officer-involved shootings than other police officers. Now JW was talking about working with dogs? "How would this work? You're a lieutenant, not a dog handler. As much as the guys might want you back working with them, that's not your job."

"I know. I haven't figured any of it out yet. It's not a plan, not even ten percent of a plan...more like an idea. I just don't know."

Bonnie could see JW was starting to get upset. Uncertainty for a man in JW's current condition was not a good thing.

She decided to back off for now, thinking that this was neither the time nor the place. Before she could change the subject, JW said, "To be honest, I've had a great career and everything was perfect, and then this jackass went and shot me and screwed it all up. Now I feel like a failure."

JW suddenly realized the one thing he had not thought about since he had awakened. "Hey, who was in the house I was going to? What happened to them? Did they get the bastard that shot me?"

"I don't know the details. Eric is coming by later; he can fill you in." She was concerned about his anxiety. "JW, do not get yourself all wound up. I don't want to have to go find a nurse and have her shoot you full of Valium."

Later that day, Sergeant Eric Fletcher came by. "JW, how are you feeling?"

"I'm OK, Eric. How are things?"

"Well, things have been hopping since you got hurt. The paperwork on that incident is monumental."

"Alright, can you fill me in on some of the things I missed? I really don't remember anything after running the plate on the stolen car."

"I'd better sit down; this may take a while. I know how detail oriented you are."

Eric took a deep breath, as if he were preparing to give a speech. "OK, here goes. Like everyone else, I was rolling to the call, thinking this was the Shadow. I heard you on the radio with the stolen car, and then right after that a 'shots call' went out. You didn't acknowledge, so I kicked on the red and blues and put it into overdrive. When I got there, you were down in the road and I had no idea how bad it was. I put out the '999' and the next thing I know, I have every cop in the city on the way."

"How many crashes from the 999?"

"Surprisingly, only one—Don Harrison. No one was injured, although you may want to have a chat with Donnie. He feels really bad that he didn't make it there."

"Well, shit happens. I'm just glad no one was hurt."

Eric continued the story. "Walker showed up and I had him put together an Emergency Action Team and go to the residence. I had Mary Castillo and her rookie take care of you until Fire arrived and brought you here."

"Good call on Walker; he used to be on SWAT, you know." Eric then provided a complete recap of the morning's events. "Walker and his guys did a great job. I'm putting them in for an award for their efforts with the victim. Did anyone give you an update on the victim?"

"No."

"Well, her name is Susan Patterson, forty-two. As far as the detectives can tell, no ties between her and the other Shadow victims. The M.O. has enough consistencies with the previous crimes that it seems like the same guy. We haven't been able to talk to her; she is still unconscious from the assault and the doctors have no timeline for when she might come out of it.

"We located a lot of evidence, I'm not sure any of it will help though. We had SWAT, every K9 in the department, and just about every resource I can think of. Nothing. The guy went through the golf course and just disappeared. We searched well into the next day and didn't find anything. We talked to a bunch of homeless guys that stay in the golf course and the park—nothing. We interviewed every resident in those apartments on Park Avenue. Not a damn thing. Guy's a ghost, JW. It's only been a couple of weeks, but we haven't had a peep out of the guy. Of course, Los Angeles is a big county, there is a chance he could hit somewhere else and they might not make the connection, but that's not likely.

"Oh, and there was a Federal Bureau of Investigation Task Force that came through here, too. They looked around and couldn't see anything we missed."

JW frowned. "Feds, huh? That's odd."

"Yeah, apparently they are part of a serial killer task force."

"Serial killers? This guy is a serial rapist, but he hasn't killed anyone, has he?"

"Not that I know of. What I heard was the director of the FBI asked them to come and look at this case because of the attempted murder of a police officer. He seemed to think because the suspect is serial, maybe they could help." JW nodded again but said nothing.

They talked for another half an hour, discussing the case and other happenings around the department. As Eric was finishing, Chief of Police Michael Estrada walked into the room. Eric said, "Good afternoon, Chief," then looked at JW and said, "Looks like this is my cue to hit the road. Take care, LT. I'll be back in a few days."

JW thanked Eric as he left and then turned to the chief and said, "I'm sorry, sir, but my doctor has left orders that I am to have only two visitors a day, and you are number three." JW had to bite his inner cheek to keep from laughing, and Bonnie looked down to her iPad as if she were concentrating on her reading.

The chief paused for a moment until he realized JW was teasing him. "I certainly wouldn't want to take up too much of your valuable time." The chief and JW had been friends for years. They enjoyed poking fun at one another as both had a dry sense of humor, but due to the gravity of JW's situation, the chief missed it at first. Bonnie burst out laughing, joined by JW and the chief. JW laughed until he coughed and then everyone stopped. The chief looked JW over and said, "You look like you've lost some weight."

JW had been in the hospital for over two weeks, and on a liquid diet until just recently. He had lost over twenty pounds. He couldn't let the chief's jab go without a retort, and said, "Yeah, it's the fabulous 'I got shot' diet. You get shot and you lose a bunch of weight. I highly recommend it, except it hurts like a son of a bitch. That part sucks."

They all smiled and the chief said, "OK, I'll keep this short." He looked at Bonnie and asked, "Is there anything you need? The Department is here for both of you and we will take care of you. You need something, I don't care how small, you let Officer Harrison know. He is assigned to you until further notice."

JW said, "Thank you, Chief. I appreciate it more than you can know. But can we do something about the guard? These guys are cops and should be on the street. No one is coming here looking for me, and Don Harrison is not a social worker. They all need to be on the streets."

The chief's face turned serious as he said, "Not negotiable. Sorry, but for now they all stay."

7

John Joseph Flannery was on the road. He had decided it was time to get out of town. He told his boss at the container terminal that his father had been diagnosed with cancer and he needed to go home to South Dakota. This back story had been built into his "life" in Long Beach long before the Shadow made his first appearance. Flannery was a planner for certain, but the surprising part was he was able to keep all the details straight; he wasn't really that intelligent. He closed his modest bank account (security guards were not well paid) and gave most of his belongings to Goodwill. He packed some clothes and moved on, leaving a false trail should the police ever start investigating him. He was confident that wouldn't happen, but you could never be too careful.

He drove east out of Long Beach and through Orange County. On a last-minute impulse, he decided to take Interstate 15 and drive to Las Vegas. He thought Vegas might be a good place to drive through, maybe stay a day or two and then continue east. He wasn't particularly attracted to Las Vegas, but he knew that a lot of people came and went there. There was a lot of criminal activity there, too. He had a fake California driver's license he could use. It had taken some work and some research, but he had managed to get a birth certificate for a man close to his age who had died. Once he had the birth certificate, it wasn't too hard to get other things. He had not yet decided where he was going to relocate, so he wanted to try to keep that ID clean so he could start over. Once reestablished, he could work on a new backup ID. He thought maybe reading all those spy novels had paid off. He had always wanted to be a spy and thought maybe he could be good at it too, but the asshole bosses just wouldn't hire him.

Flannery drove his Toyota and left it and the keys on the edge of a poor part of Las Vegas. He figured it would be driven around for weeks before it was abandoned. By the time it showed up on the police radar—if it did—he would be long gone. He took an Uber rideshare to the other side of town. There he paid two thousand dollars cash for a Honda Accord at a small used car dealer on the outskirts of town. It looked like the kind of dump that a gambler would go to if he lost all his money and needed to get some cash to make it back home. He didn't care about that, the salesman didn't ask too many questions, and soon Flannery was on his way east with his trail fading. The Honda seemed like a good car to have. It had a reputation as being reliable and this one was in fairly good condition. And best of all, it was inconspicuous.

He turned northeast out of Las Vegas and drove until he passed through Mesquite and into Arizona. He had considered working his way south from Las Vegas and down into Arizona, but he couldn't get the old west image of Arizona out of his mind. *No, not Arizona, too many cowboys with guns.* He needed someplace with fewer guns. He didn't like guns, even though he had one for emergencies. His decision made, Flannery continued northeast into Utah. He considered stopping at St. George, but he didn't think he would fit in there. The last thing he wanted was to just show up somewhere and have people start asking questions about who he was and where he came from.

Flannery continued north on I-15 until he reached Salt Lake City. He didn't feel as if he would fit in here, either.

He stopped on the outskirts of town at a truck stop to get some gas and food. He also wanted a map of the area. He sat in his car, parked off to the side of the truck stop and ate his sandwich and sipped on his soda while he perused the map. He was not certain where he wanted to go yet, but he did not think he wanted to go any further north. He decided to turn east on Interstate 80 out of Salt Lake City. Once he got into the large open states, he would take some time to find the right place. He knew he did not want to be in a large city; something more mid-sized like Long Beach was what he was looking for. He absolutely did not want to be in a small town. They were too claustrophobic for him. It was too likely he would be noticed, and a man in his line of work never wanted to be noticed.

He stopped in a rest stop just east of Rawlings, Wyoming. He was exhausted from over ten hours of driving. Because he had not taken a break in Las Vegas as he originally planned, he had been on the road for almost two days. He knew he needed some rest. He had important decisions to make and that was best done when you were properly rested. He decided this would be a good place to grab a few hours of sleep. There was a lot of truck activity here and plenty of passenger vehicles. He pulled into a space away from the others, got out and started to walk around. He visited a large building in the center of the rest stop. This structure had restrooms, a vending machine area, and information boards describing the area. On the opposite side was a large map showing the way east. He looked at the map for a while and decided there was nothing of value on it. He needed to get further east.

It was as he was walking back to his car that he spotted her. She was young, maybe twenty-three, with long brown hair. She was thin, but not overly so. She was perfect, absolutely an ideal match to what he was looking for. He watched her as she walked across the parking lot to her car. She must have known he was there—she sashayed her hips back and forth as he watched. He was immediately aroused, he wanted her. But, as she got in her car and sat in the driver's seat, another girl got out on the passenger side. Although this new girl looked a bit like the other—sisters, perhaps?—the Shadow immediately discounted her, spotting every minor flaw, even where there were none. The Shadow was parked on the other side of the lot, but when he got in his car and sat down, he discovered that he had a perfect view of her car in his rear-view mirror. If this wasn't destiny, he didn't know what was. He sat and watched and waited.

Stephanie Lynn Peters was tired. She and her friend, Marie Hastings, were on their way back home to Springfield, Missouri. They had driven cross country to go to Portland, Oregon, because they had heard through the Internet that Antifa and other groups were going to rally in Portland. They really weren't that radical themselves, they were just bored. They were going back to college soon and they wanted some life experience and fun before the daily drudgery of classes overwhelmed them again. They thought going to Portland would be an adventure, but it was more of a bust. Unless you wanted to get out in the street and get tear-gassed or in a fight, it was a lot of standing around and chanting. Neither she, nor Marie, wanted to get in a fight or arrested, so they stayed on the outskirts of it all. She would have had more fun at home, hanging out with her friends. Oh well, live and learn. They did not have much money left, just barely enough for gas and food, so they ended up spending the night in a rest stop. In the middle of the night, Stephanie woke, craving a cigarette. She got out of the car quietly, but still managed to wake Marie, who was a light sleeper. She told Marie, "Hey, I'm going to have a smoke and stretch my legs."

Marie nodded to her friend and said, "Be careful, smoking kills, you know."

The Shadow had watched and waited through the late evening and into the early morning hours. He watched the girl as she got out of her car and began to walk east. He knew from his earlier foray and looking at the map that the North Platte River was on the east side of the rest stop. There was a fence between the rest stop and the river, but he had seen several holes in it. Apparently, strolls by the river were a common thing. He was not sure how big the river was, but he could hear it from his car. It sounded large. One of the first things he had done when he stopped was to turn off the overhead light that came on when the car doors were opened. He got out, reached into the back seat for his backpack and stood by his car as the girl began walking down to the river. He took the long way around and was able to move in the darkness unnoticed. The girl stopped by the river and lit a cigarette. The Shadow saw the match light up her face and his excitement grew. He moved quietly toward her. He had always had that skill; it seemed as if he had been sneaking up on girls his whole life.

The Shadow watched from a clump of bushes, about ten yards away from the girl. He reached into his backpack and removed his pipe, then he slipped his knife into his back waistband. He set the bag down and slipped quietly behind her. He raised the pipe and brought it down sharply on the back of her head. She dropped to the ground like a rock and her cigarette fell from her grasp. He pulled her away from the bank and back into the privacy of the bushes where his backpack was. He quickly bound her wrists and feet and gagged her with duct tape. *This stuff really does have a million uses!* He cut away her pants and underwear and waited for her to revive.

Within a few minutes she began to come to. Her eyes opened and immediately all she could see was the Shadow's knife. It was a ten-inch chrome-bladed Bowie knife. The Shadow loved the knife because it was big and intimidating. Also, the chrome metal served as a perfect mirror, allowing him to use the small amount of light from the moon to see the fear in her eyes. "Do you hear me, bitch? Do you see the knife? If you don't give me what I want, I will cut you." As he said this, he moved the blade closer to her eyes and she tried to push herself away. "Don't you move! Are you going to cooperate and live, or shall I cut your throat? Live?" She was terrified. She wasn't certain what she should do, but she knew she wanted to live. She tried to speak, but discovered her mouth was taped shut, so she nodded. "Good, now get to your knees." She did as he asked and she heard the sound of him dropping his pants. She had not been to church in years, but now she prayed with all her heart that this would be over soon. It was.

She was aware he was getting dressed behind her and thought he would soon be gone. He knelt beside her and said, rather politely, "I would like to thank you for your cooperation." Then his voice changed—"You slut! You think you can buy your life with sex?" He grasped her hair and pulled her head back. As he did so, he slid the knife to his left and along her neck and then pulled it into her rapidly. The knife, though cheap, was very sharp and ripped into her throat and then into the carotid artery on the right side of her neck. He pushed her and tried to hold her down. Even tied as she was, she began thrashing about. She effectively bucked him off her, but by then the rapid blood loss began to take its toll. She began to slow down, but then her muscles began convulsing, making one last attempt to keep oxygenated blood flowing to her brain. Finally, she stilled. The blood flow slowed and then stopped. *Christ,* he thought, *that was way more blood than I expected.* The river provided a convenient method to get rid of the body and perhaps slow any law enforcement investigation. Plus, he thought the water would help wash away any trace evidence. He kicked the girl's body into the river and watched her slowly float downstream.

Before zipping his pants, he reached in and removed the condom from his penis. There was too much blood to try to clean up the scene. He needed to get moving before someone noticed him here or her friend noticed she had not returned. He walked away from the river and casually returned to his car. He paused at a trash can and dropped the used condom inside. He then got into his car and drove away slowly, like nothing had happened. In reality, to the Shadow, nothing had happened.

As the sun broke over the horizon, Marie Hastings woke up in the passenger seat. She noticed Stephanie was not there and remembered her saying earlier she was going for a smoke. *That had to be hours ago, didn't it?* She got out of the car and looked around. Others were also beginning to wake and get out of their cars. *Maybe she's in the restroom.* Marie walked to the restrooms and checked inside. She walked up to a woman who was looking at the map on the display and showed her a picture of Stephanie on her cell phone. The woman told her she had not seen her. Marie started to get more anxious. She looked to the east and saw a bridge. There's a river over there. *Maybe Steph is down there having another cigarette.* Marie walked down the same path her friend had and, once she was beside the river, she saw some footprints in the soft earth along the shore. *Those could be Steph's.* Then she noticed a partially smoked cigarette and some drag marks in the mud leading to some bushes. As she walked to the bushes, she saw an opening to a little area where no one could see. She looked inside and saw blood everywhere.

Up in the truck stop area a pair of long-haul truckers were chatting, talking about the road and their plans for the day. First on their list of things to do was get some diesel and coffee. They needed caffeine before they went too far. They were sipping cold coffee from a thermos, but that just didn't cut it for either of them. Suddenly, their conversation was interrupted by a scream. It sounded like it was coming from down by the river. The scream was followed by another, even more distressed than the first. The two truckers began to jog toward the sounds. They picked up the pace as the screams became more and more insistent. When they found the source, they looked at the blood. One of the drivers reached into his pocket and pulled out his cell phone to call 911.

The first Wyoming Highway Patrol officer, Trooper Dennis Storm, arrived at the rest stop in under ten minutes. He knew he had at least one backup officer not too far behind as he had left his friend, Joe Morris, at the cafe in Rawlings, to pay the bill for their breakfast. Storm had heard the call and it immediately got his attention. He had a wife and two daughters. He knew how he would feel if he woke up and one of them were missing. As he drove into the rest stop, he was waved down by some people. They pointed toward the river at the other end. He drove and parked as close as he could and then another person directed him down to the water. When he got there, he saw two men and a woman who was hysterical. One of the men was trying to comfort the woman but didn't seem to be doing much good. The other man just pointed at some brush. What Trooper Storm saw almost made him regret having breakfast. It looked like a slaughterhouse in there.

Trooper Storm reached for his handheld radio and broadcast, "This is Storm. I am on-scene at the rest stop. I have a possible crime scene here with a lot of blood, but no body. The body may have been disposed of in the North Platte River. Advise Trooper Morris, I need him to block the exit to the rest stop. No one leaves. Put in a call to the Wyoming Department of Criminal Investigations in Rawlings and let them know what I have. Also, let the County know and have them respond. This looks like it is going to be ours, but I am going to need some help. I am going to need a lot of help."

8

JW North sat in his car trying to catch his breath. He had just left Monica's House of Pain after another brutal physical therapy session. The doctors had told him that the injury, although life threatening, was not that bad in terms of his long-term recovery. Having finished another two-hour physical therapy, or PT, session with Monica, he began to wonder what exactly they meant. He recalled the first day he came to her and explained his injury and what he wanted to get out of physical therapy. She listened patiently and told him they had a deal; she would be with him every step of the way. All he had to do was everything she told him, and he would be as good as new.

JW knew PT would be challenging; he had basically sat in a bed at the hospital for a month and then spent two more at home recovering. Before the shooting, he had been in excellent condition for a man his age. Now, he realized he had lost most of his muscle mass and his overall conditioning was terrible. He was literally starting from scratch and Monica was going to rebuild him. She failed to mention that it might kill him to achieve his goals. On the first day, Monica gave him a list of exercises to complete. She supervised each individual routine and demanded perfection in how he completed each one. "You are not going to accomplish anything worthwhile doing these halfway," she told him. After thirty minutes he was exhausted. Sweat stained his shirt and he was ready to call it a day. She told him, "That was a nice warm up, now let's really get to work." He moved through a series of more complex exercises and finally she put him on the treadmill for forty-five minutes. The machine worked its way up and down, speeding up and occasionally slowing down. When he stepped off it, Monica told him, "Good first day, see you the day after tomorrow," and that was it, he was dismissed.

That had been three weeks ago, and it did not seem to be getting any easier. Each time JW reached the desired level, Monica would bump up his goal. JW was beginning to feel as if he was in Navy SEAL training. He knew that wasn't true, a SEAL could run circles around him. He also knew that if he survived, he would be in the best shape he had been in since he was much younger, when he ran marathons. He thought for a moment about where he was going to take all this and decided that might not be such a bad thing. He decided it was time to have a conversation with Bonnie.

When he arrived home, Bonnie was there waiting for him. After a quick hug and kiss, he told her he had something important to discuss. Before he could start, she said, "OK, but first I have something I need to say. I know something is bothering you, JW. It is readily apparent to me and everyone around you. So, if this discussion you want to have is about that, great. But first I have to say, you are surrounded by people who love and care for you. So, please, stop acting like an ass and let us in." Bonnie's words angered JW, not because they were offensive, but because she was right.

"Look Bonnie, I know for the last couple of months it's been all about me. I'm sorry about that. It's not fair to you and I see that. Getting shot was probably the worst thing I have ever had happen to me. That bastard took something from me. I worked my ass off for thirty years, and in one instant that motherfucker took it away. All those years working to establish who I am, all those years working crappy shifts and holidays, Christmases away from you and my kids. All the time I spent trying to set an example." JW paused and sipped his coffee, trying to decide how to say the next sentence. "Boom, in one moment it's all gone because that son of a bitch gets off a lucky shot."

"First of all, JW, quit feeling sorry for yourself. You know all that self-pity crap is not going to fly with me. No way! You also know it's not true. Second, and more importantly, why? Explain to me how one moment in time erases all of the good you did. Your guys are still out there, doing the job, just like you taught them. They still believe in you, even if you don't. So quit your crying and get off your butt and do something about it. I know that bastard took something from you, so take it back! Now, say what you have to say."

"I am not sure why this cuts so deep on me. Everything you just said is right, but for some reason I feel like a part of me is missing. I don't know how to get that back, but I have an idea."

He paused for a moment, not sure if he wanted to go through with this discussion. "You're not going to believe me; it's going to sound crazy."

Bonnie looked at him with love in her eyes and said, "Yeah, well, I've always known you were crazy."

"Do you remember when Doc Malouf talked to us when we first met him?" Bonnie nodded. "Remember he said I died on the table for a moment." Bonnie was not likely to forget that moment, but again she just nodded. "Well, before I woke up in the ICU, I had a dream, but it didn't seem like a dream to me. It felt too real, but also not real. I woke up on a bench in a park with a stream. There were dogs all over the place, running around and playing with one another. All the colors were so vivid. Everything seemed so beautiful, but a little off. Asko was there, at least it looked like him. He kept bringing me a tennis ball and I kept throwing it, over and over. I thought, 'Maybe I'm dead. Is this heaven?' There was a guy there who told me it wasn't heaven, not really, although it might seem so to me. We talked about some other things, but I don't remember much else. He told me there was something I needed to do, to finish."

She wanted to interject something, but decided to let JW continue, uninterrupted. "Bonnie, I know how crazy this all sounds. I have thought about it a lot. I keep wondering, 'Was it a dream? Was it real?' You're a lot more religious than I am, what does it sound like to you? All I do know is that, after spending a lot of time thinking about what it means, I decided it doesn't matter what it was. It doesn't matter if I spent fifteen minutes in heaven, or if it was a dream, or it was just my body realizing I was dying and trying to help me to accept it all. I don't know and I don't care. What matters is the message. The message was about dogs. It's about me and dogs. That's all that matters. After that, I woke up in the ICU, you were reading and I was exhausted. That's when I knew it wasn't a dream, or at least I don't think so. I went back to sleep and the next time I woke up the nurse came in and drugged me and you said, 'Don't worry. I'll be here when you wake up.' I never told you how much that meant to me."

Bonnie sighed and said, "You're welcome. Now get to the point."

"That is the point. I'm just not sure what's next. I feel like I'm supposed to do something to, what did you say, 'take it back' from that bastard who shot me. I've thought about it a lot—I think it has something to do with me and police work. Now, before you get too upset, I am not talking about going back on the job. I can't do that. It's too much of a grind and I am too old for that. I need to do something that will be part time, but still make a difference. I think it has something to do with dogs. Actually, I know it does. But I also want to do all the things we've talked about, like travel to Europe, SCUBA diving trips to Cozumel and a dozen other places we love. I want to do all that, but I need to do this, too. I hope that makes some sense."

"JW, you know I love dogs just as much as you do. If you want a dog, I am one hundred percent behind that. But what are you going to do with a dog? I don't get the feeling you're talking about going for walks and playing in the park. You're talking about a working dog, right?"

JW paused. This next part was going to be challenging. "Do you remember that study that LBPD was part of about ten years ago? We partnered with the feds and that private school out of Florida to do a formal study. Do you remember what that was all about?" Bonnie shook her head and then made a gesture for him to continue. "OK, well, we were looking at human scent detection and trailing at the time. Do you understand the difference between trailing and tracking? Probably not, most people don't. Tracking is what you see at the K9 trials and competitions. A dog follows a smell on the ground made up of disturbed earth, crushed plant life, human scent, and other things.

"Trailing is more about human scent. Human scent is composed of shed skin cells, oils and such, all things that come from you directly. The dog follows these where they settle, which isn't always right in line with where the person walked. For example, if a person is walking on a sidewalk, the scent may settle in the gutter and not on the sidewalk where there is nothing to hold it. The belief is that scent is as unique to an individual as fingerprints are. That means a dog can trail someone who left a scent days before, even if other people have been through the area. We were working with a couple of different law enforcement agencies and search and rescue groups. Most of them were using bloodhounds, but we were trying to get the same results with a patrol-type dog. Anyway, somebody got wind of it and called us to ask if we would like to participate. Of course, we said, 'yes.'

"There were a lot of parts to it, but Ben Kellum was the most involved. That was about all he did for a couple of years. I had only the big view of it, but the part I remember most was how impressed I was watching those dogs work.

I ran trails with them—double-blind controlled trails—and those dogs nailed them more times than not. One of the major points of the program was to create a scientific analysis of what the dogs were doing and come up with a reliable method to grade them and predict a percentage of reliability. Most people who have seen the movie *Cool Hand Luke* believe bloodhounds can trail someone, but that belief is not enough in court. There's this thing called the 'Frye Rule'; it basically says that, when dealing with scientific evidence in court, the standard of whether it is admissible or not is if it is generally accepted within the relevant scientific community. We were trying to establish that acceptance by doing the studies. Overall, the program was very reliable, but it had other challenges. One was the large amount of time, which translates to serious money, involved in training the dog and handler up to an acceptable standard; and another was the error factor. Lots of things can screw up a trail—time, weather, handler error—and you never know why. Hell, the dog could be dead on and you fail to understand what you are looking at.

"There isn't a lot of work at the local level, certainly not enough to justify a dedicated program. We were always loaning Kellum out to other agencies, including the feds, and the chief finally got tired of it. He wanted to know why he was paying for a police officer who was always away, solving someone else's crimes. I understood, I did, but it also seemed a little short-sighted."

Bonnie listened intently to what JW said. It was an intriguing idea. She wasn't all that excited about him going back out on the streets and possibly being shot again, but she wanted to be supportive. She did think that doing this would be good for him. It would allow him to focus on something positive and help him get past whatever was bothering him. "OK," she said, "but one thing. I want you to go to counseling to talk about what's bothering you. I know you're not crazy, well maybe I do, but I think it can't hurt to talk to someone about it."

JW looked her in the eyes and then paused. He knew something wasn't right with him and thought it couldn't hurt to talk to a professional. "OK, I understand. The police officer's association has a counselor available. I would feel more comfortable talking with him. I think I can get some direction there, but to be honest, I feel like I need to work this out with you, my friends, and by going with this dog idea."

"So, with this dog thing, where do you think you want to start?"

JW already knew the answer to that question. "Ben Kellum. I start with Ben."

9

JW North and Ben Kellum had been good friends for a long time. They had worked together in the K9 unit when JW was the sergeant. Ben was a good dog handler and had taken a special interest in the K9 Human Scent Detection and Trailing Program, alternately referred to as "the program" or "the project." Ben served as the direct liaison to the federal government and university representatives, reporting back to JW so he, JW, could keep his bosses up to date. The program was just too time intensive for JW to be directly involved. He went to as many of the training sessions as possible and spent a lot of time talking to the professor, who was coordinating the academic portion, and his students. There was a great deal of recognition of the importance of the program. If they could provide enough peer-reviewed studies and supporting materials to meet the Frye Standard, scent detection and trailing could become an even more valuable law enforcement tool.

Ben came over to JW's house and was greeted at the door by Bonnie. She gave him a hug and asked how his wife and kids were. She then pointed him to the backyard where JW was sitting by the fire pit, a beer in his hand, looking into the flames. As Ben walked up, JW asked if he wanted a beer and, after receiving an affirmative response, went to the bar and retrieved one for him. JW had briefly explained on the phone what he was considering and how he needed

Ben to help with a plan of action to make it happen. As Ben accepted the beer, he handed JW a one-foot-thick stack of books and paper. "Here's some light reading to get you started. This will give you some background material, plus some of the more interesting studies that came out of the Program. When you finish that, let me know. I have plenty more. LT, let me ask you, what is it you really want to do?"

JW didn't want to tell him about the dream. He wasn't sure he was going to tell anyone else about that just yet. He told Ben about having lost something and needing to get it back. He talked about his desire for something that was not full time but could make a difference. It was then he realized what he wanted, and he told Ben, "I want something that might allow me to find the son of a bitch that shot me."

Ben listened and when JW finished, he said, "We talked about something like this during the Project. We felt it was something that might work, with the right guy and the right dog. I will do everything I can short of getting fired or divorced to help you do this. All I ask is that you carry it through to the end. That you won't quit. I'm thinking, though, this isn't really a part-time job, it will involve a lot of time. And how are you going to pay for this? The Department won't pay the bills and the kind of dog you are talking about is going to be very expensive, plus training, travel, and other expenses."

"That is exactly why I need your help, Ben. I need to put together a plan. It has to make sense to Bonnie, or she may just shoot it down. I have some cash set aside; I think that will get us started with a dog. I'm going to retire, and we can easily live on my retirement income and Bonnie's salary, but she's been putting our surplus cash in a travel fund for when we both retire. The house is paid for, but if I suggest that we take a loan against it, I'm afraid she'll shoot me or lock me up in the loony bin. I'm going to have to make do with what we have."

"OK, first of all, I warned you about teaching your wife how to shoot. Second, I can reach out to my contacts with the local search and rescue and other dog units that were involved. We can follow the basic training protocol we established with the Project if we can get you a dog. I have an idea on that, but I need to hear what you want first."

"You mean breed?" Ben nodded and JW continued, "OK, my preference would be a German Shepherd. I know that may not be the optimal choice, but I love the breed."

"Yeah, we used a few of them in the study. They performed very well, not as well as the bloodhounds, but the Shepherds had their advantages, like not drooling all over you."

JW laughed and recalled a bloodhound shaking off a mouthful of drool that landed on a clean and pressed uniform. "Yeah, I have been slimed and would prefer to avoid that."

They both laughed and Ben said, "I'll talk to Kurt at Vohne Liche Kennels in Indiana. We got several of our dogs from him and he has access to some more specialized dogs." JW knew Vohne Liche was one of the premier dog providers and trainers in the U.S. They not only bred and sold police dogs, but also a lot of the special operations dogs being deployed. If you were looking for something special, it was definitely one of the places to look. "I think we should call him together. I can tell him what you're looking for and you can provide the specifics of what you want. You met Kurt when he came out here with one of the dogs. He's a good guy, and if he can help us out I know he will, but don't expect it to be cheap."

"How much do you think? Best guess?"

"What you want is pretty darn specialized and only a few select dogs are going to meet the criteria. Toss in that you want a German Shepherd and that makes it more challenging. Start at twenty-five thousand dollars would be my guess." JW looked down and swallowed. *Bonnie is going to kill me. Twenty-five thousand dollars to start. Holy cow!*

Ben looked at JW and knew what he was thinking. "OK, LT, you talk with your lovely bride and give me a call tomorrow. If it's a go, I will come by and we can call Vohne Liche together. If it's not a go, I can come by and we can drown our sorrows in alcohol. For now, I am going to get out of here before you tell Bonnie the price tag and she starts shooting. I know she's a pretty good shot, but I don't want to be collateral damage. Let me know how it goes. But one thing I need to say before I go. The last time I did this, it put a lot of pressure on my marriage. My wife was extremely upset about how often I was getting called out or on the road. I want to be involved, but…"

JW nodded and turned back to the fire while his friend stood and made a quick exit.

Bonnie walked out to the fire pit thirty minutes after Ben had left. The fact that Ben had rushed off with barely a "Nice to see you, Bonnie," told her that JW needed some time to think. She knew he would want to talk to her about the discussion and how he would plan the project going forward. She sat down in the chair that Ben had vacated and said, "OK, family meeting."

JW looked over at his wife, gave her a half smile and paused, uncertain how to move forward. "I think my plans have been sent slightly off the tracks."

Bonnie looked at JW, worry crossing her face. *What the hell just happened?* "A little while ago you were all gung-ho about this," using the old phrase she had heard in some old black and white Marine Corps movie, "and now you look like someone just ran over your dog."

"Well, Ben thinks it could cost twenty-five thousand dollars or more just for the dog."

Bonnie laughed. "Twenty-five thousand dollars, is that all? By the time we're done with travel and everything else, I would guess we're looking at fifty thousand, at least."

JW smiled at his wife, this time with love in his eyes. She had done more than just consider his idea; she was well ahead of him in the planning phase. "I'm glad to see one of us has engaged their mind on this problem."

"Yeah well, you didn't really want that Corvette you've been saving for, right?"

JW turned toward his wife, surprised she had so quickly cut through all the drama and come right to the point. "I guess we can redirect those funds toward this project in the short term, although I am reluctant to abandon the need for a sports car completely." JW had owned a Corvette many years earlier and had to sell it when money got tight. The loss had bothered him for a long time and had prompted him to open a specially designated bank account with the goal of saving enough to purchase a slightly used Corvette. "I don't know why, Honey, but I think things are going to turn our way soon. I just can't get that idea out of my head. Something positive is going to happen that will allow us to focus on this plan."

After the meeting, Ben drove home to talk with his wife, Lucy. She was anxious to hear the details, and she needed to get a few things off her chest. After providing a recap of the meeting, he sat back in his chair. He could see the storm brewing on his wife's face.

"Ben, this is exactly what I was afraid of. You are getting roped back into that trailing program. Do you remember how it was for me the last time? You were never home, always on the road chasing one criminal or another."

"I remember you being unhappy and complaining to me about it."

"Well, you get to go off and be the hero and I stay home with the kids and take care of everything else. It's not fair."

"All JW is asking is for some help planning this deal. There hasn't been a mention of anything else."

"Well, I remember how disappointed you were the last time and how I had to pick up the pieces. Tell me you're not going to help JW North make that program work after what the department did to you the last time. You did everything they asked and more, and they cut you off as part of a budget reduction."

"Look, I hear you. To be honest, I'm torn. Part of me wants to see this be successful because I believe it can be a good tool for the police and part of me is jealous that JW might be the guy to make it go, when I couldn't. But JW is a good friend and I feel like I need to help him out on this. As to the future, let's deal with it when it comes." Ben ended the conversation knowing it wasn't done. Lucy had placed a thought in his head though. *How do I feel about JW making this work?*

The next afternoon found Ben Kellum seated in the same place in JW's backyard, except this time there was no fire in the fire pit and no beer in his hands. He had placed a call to Vohne Liche Kennels earlier in the day and spoken with Kurt Steigerwald, the owner, and laid out the essentials of the upcoming conversation. Kurt was excited about the idea and wanted to hear more about what JW and Ben had in mind. Of course, there were still a lot of details to be worked out, starting with finding the right dog.

Ben placed the call and was quickly put through to Kurt. When Kurt confirmed the call was from Ben, he said, "Hey, Ben, I've been thinking about our chat this morning. Is JW there?" Ben replied in the affirmative and Kurt continued, "OK, here is the deal. JW, I like your idea. I felt like this was a good idea when you guys were doing it ten years ago, but there wasn't the political will to continue. I know that you are doing this on your own dime, and to show you how much I like the idea, I'm going to do my best to keep the price down. The dog you are looking for is very specific. Most of my normal suppliers are not going to have what you are looking for, so I reached out to an old friend who is into the more competitive side of things. Most of the trainers are working Belgian Malinois—they're good dogs, but they don't meet the German Shepherd requirement."

JW interrupted, "Hey, Kurt, it doesn't have to be a Shepherd. I can make it work with a Mal," referring to one of the many Belgian Malinois nicknames.

"No need to worry, JW. I think I have this one licked. Besides, I like the Shepherd idea, it's old school. I love old school." Kurt paused, then continued, "My friend in Germany has contacts in a lot of the high-end show dog circuits. Now, you may not know this, but the German dogs are not 'all show and no go.' They have requirements at the national level for a well-rounded working dog to be able to compete and also breed."

JW said, "Yes, I understand most of that. When I was a handler, my working dog was from Germany. He was a pink-papered Schutzhund I." This title indicated the dog was an entry level working dog that was recommended for breeding. "One of the better trainers had him, but he had a minor issue with not letting go on the bite, and boom, they hung a 'for sale' sign on him."

"Well, that's not uncommon at all. A top handler might be working ten or more dogs at any one time. Once they know it isn't going to make it to the next level, the dog is out. They just don't have the time to continue training a dog that can't be the Sieger," referring to the number one dog at the National Show every year.

"When I got my dog, he had been specially imported for me by a family in Georgia. They specialized in bringing working dogs into the USA. I took him to a breed survey and he was rated Korklasse I," JW said, referring to the German for breed class one, or recommended for breeding. "I had to join the S.V., the Verien fur Deutsche Schaferhunde."

"OK, good. You understand some of the complexities of this. I asked my friend to look for a German Shepherd dog, either male or female, since it didn't seem to matter in this situation. I told him I was more interested in tracking scores than in the dog's Schutzhund title or ancestry. Of course, a tracking title would be excellent. Next, of course, would be obedience. I figured you wouldn't be all that interested in the protection phase as it isn't likely you will be doing any apprehension work with the dog. Of course, the dog will bite if it needs to. It must pass all three phases of the trial to earn a Schutzhund title."

JW thought back to what he remembered about Schutzhund. It was the working dog program of the German Shepherd Association of Germany, the S.V. Within a Schutzhund trial, there were three categories: Tracking, following a subject who has recently walked through a field or grassy area; Obedience and Agility, including everything from jumping walls and fences to retrieving heavy dumbbells and basic obedience work; and Protection, in which the dog would work away from the handler, searching and then guarding and barking at a person hiding from them. In Protection, the dog was also required to perform a courage test in which the person would run away and then, when the dog was released, turn and charge the dog. The dog should continue without hesitation and then bite the person's protective clothing. There were three levels of Schutzhund title: beginner, intermediate, and advanced. Each phase was more difficult and challenging for the dog.

Kurt broke into his thoughts with, "My friend says he has a few ideas and he will reach out to me when he finds something. I know you are ultimately looking for a trailing dog, but tracking is a good place to start. My friend has done a lot of tracking work and trained a number of dogs for their tracking certification. He will do a preliminary evaluation there and then I will call you. Relax, JW, Vohne Liche Kennels has this now. Trust us to get you exactly what you are looking for."

JW smiled and said, "Hey, Kurt, I appreciate you helping me do this, on the cheap and all, but what about your friend?"

"Don't worry about him, he owes me a bunch of favors, although I may have to send him a nice bottle of booze as a 'thank you.'"

"Just let me know what he likes. Thanks again, and I hope to talk to you soon."

JW looked over his shoulder at Bonnie. "Well, I guess we're on our way now. Hopefully, this is going to work."

Bonnie laughed and Ben looked at her and then JW with a quizzical expression on his face.

JW answered the unasked question. "I think she is hoping we didn't just sign up to buy a twenty-five-thousand-dollar pet."

Ben turned back to Bonnie. "Oh, ye of little faith. I know Kurt Steigerwald well. He has provided several dogs for us since the Project ended. He also provides a lot of dogs for special forces. Kurt's always treated us great, and if he says he's going to take care of us, then Kurt is going to find us an incredible dog, period. Once we have it, it will be up to us to do the training. I recommend we use the same training and certification process we did during the Project. We worked all of that out in conjunction with the professor and the feds. It will stand up to any judicial scrutiny. By the way, did you take a look at any of the paperwork I left with you?"

Bonnie chimed in, "You mean that stack of papers I found all over the bed last night with JW in the middle sound asleep?"

Ben sent a smiling scowl JW's way and said, "Well, on that happy note, I'm out of here. JW, you need to read and understand all of that, and that's just the start. Remember, it's not only about convincing a judge about trailing, you are going to have to sell this to other law enforcement agencies as we go along. If this goes as I think it will, you're going to become a very busy man once we get this dog certified. It will not be an easy sell; plan on doing a lot of demonstrations. Regardless of what people want to believe, they will need to be convinced."

10

Several weeks went by and JW continued his visits to Monica's House of Pain. She finally gave him permission to hit a few golf balls and then, to play a round of golf. JW had been waiting for this day since before he had been shot. He had a tee time the morning after he was shot that he never made it to. He had a few friends that he liked to play golf with, but for his post-recovery debut, he decided to play with just one other person. He knew this would likely upset his other golfing buddies, but he hoped he could explain to them and they would understand. He decided if he was going to get back on the horse, it should be where he left off—Recreation Park. Some might question this choice as unwise. It was true he was going back to the course just across the street from where he had been shot, and it was the course the suspect likely used to evade the police and escape. That didn't matter to JW. He liked to face his problems directly, rather than avoid them. Sometimes he was a bit too blunt for others' liking, but if nothing else, he was honest. He made a tee time for the morning a few days later and called his friend, Mark Powers, who was the former rangemaster from LBPD, now retired. Mark and JW had shot together on the department's pistol team for over twenty years.

JW had only recently started playing golf and he knew he still sucked at it. When he called Mark to ask him if he wanted to play, Mark had teased him about checking his busy schedule. *Ah, the life of the retired guy.* Technically, even though he was never going back to work, he was still listed on the rolls of the police department as injured on duty. His injuries would have to be classified as stable before he could retire. JW knew he was close and playing a round of golf would be another step in the right direction. Mark agreed to meet him for breakfast before the round to catch up. He knew Mark had wanted to come by and visit him at the hospital but had respected JW's need to heal before being too active. In the meantime, JW decided to go to the driving range and hit a few balls and see how he felt. He wasn't expecting much at all as he had not even looked at a golf club in over five months. JW was pleasantly surprised with his first practice session. He was hitting the ball as well as he had before he'd been shot.

On the morning of his round of golf, JW arrived and entered the small restaurant. As he was greeted warmly by the waitress, he wondered, *Who would have thought she would even notice I have been gone for a few months?* Mark was sitting at a table in the corner reading the local paper. As JW sat down, Mark quietly folded the newspaper, looked him over and said, "You've lost some weight."

Although JW had gained a few pounds back, due to the high rate of cardiovascular exercise he was doing in PT, he was still very slim. "I don't know whether to say, 'thanks' or wonder if I had gotten fat in anticipation of my retirement." Mark shrugged, not sure where to take the conversation. "Well, all I can say is that I have been eating everything in sight and I can't seem to put any weight on. The fabulous 'I got shot diet' does wonders. I heartily recommend it."

"No, thank you. I think I can find a less creative way to keep the pounds off. Besides, with a physique like this, I don't need to diet."

JW turned back to the waitress and said, "Excuse me, ma'am, I would like to order before this man ruins my appetite." Both men chuckled and began the slow process of catching up.

After breakfast, JW and Mark went into the pro shop to pay for their round. As JW walked up to the counter, he was greeted by Terry, who was working check-in. "Hey, welcome back, Mr. North. I had a couple guys who wanted to join your group, but I figured you might want to play just your twosome today."

"Thanks, Terry. Yeah, I wasn't much good at golf before; now with the time off it might be embarrassing."

"No worries, Mr. North. I got them into a group that goes out right after you."

As he paid for the round, he said, "Thanks again, Terry, and call me 'JW.'"

Mark and JW went out to the first tee and waited for the foursome ahead of them to finish the hole. As they walked out to the tee box, Terry announced over the course public address system, "Now on the first tee box, the North and Powers twosome. Welcome back, JW." JW looked back toward the pro shop and saw Terry leaning out the window, a big smile on his face. JW nodded at him with a smile, and then bent to set his tee and place the ball.

Mark looked at his driver and then at JW's bag. "New clubs? I hope you're not expecting them to make a big difference."

JW laughed. "No, I've been waiting almost six months to play these. I just want to see what they'll do."

JW looked down at the ball, checked his alignment and grip, and started his backswing. At the top, he paused and then brought the club down and through the ball. The strike sounded crisp, and when JW looked down to the first green, he saw a nice ball flight that bounced and rolled to a stop seventy-five yards from the flag. After Mark teed off, they rode the cart down to their balls. JW selected his fifty-eight-degree wedge, set his position, and made a nice clean wedge shot. The ball sailed high into the sky, landed on the green, and rolled to a stop two feet from the hole. JW then putted the ball into the hole for a birdie on the first hole. Mark looked at him curiously but didn't say anything.

After parring the next two holes, JW stepped up to the fourth tee. This hole was not particularly long, but it did have a slight uphill climb. He tried to recall whether he had ever made par here. His tee shot was again beautiful, dropping into the center of the fairway. Mark could no longer hold back his curiosity and asked, "OK, what the hell is going on with you? You birdie one, par two and three, and now you have another nice tee shot. Who are you? Where is JW North and what have you done with him?"

"Hell if I know, Mark. You've played golf with me most of the times I have played. I suck at this game, and if I didn't have friends to enjoy it with, I might just give it up. I have no idea why all of a sudden I'm playing well. I'm thinking the guy who fitted me at ClubFix deserves a bigger tip."

Mark looked at JW disgustedly and said, "I used to give you, what, twelve strokes? If this keeps up, you'll be giving them to me."

The play continued until they reached the sixth hole. The sixth green ended near the tee box for the twelfth hole, which was just across the street from where JW had been shot. Standing on the sixth tee box he looked down the fairway and out toward the house he had been dispatched to, the one he hadn't made it to. He was deep in thought, going over the events of that night. A voice reached out to him, but he couldn't make it out. "Huh?"

"Earth to JW, come in JW. Hey, are we playing golf here?"

"Oh yeah, sorry…my mind wandered for a moment." JW aligned himself to his ball and promptly sent it into a beautiful, high slice, deep into the left rough and almost off the course and into the street. His next few shots were OK, but he could tell he was starting to fall apart. Maybe playing golf so soon wasn't a good idea. JW continued his play through the rest of the round, concentration again breaking when they reached the twelfth hole. Although he didn't say anything to Mark, JW's mind was definitely someplace else.

After driving away from the eighteenth green, Marc stopped the cart and turned to JW. "OK, we're friends, right?" JW nodded. "And friends tell friends when they're being a dumbass right?" Not waiting for JW to acknowledge, Mark continued. "With that in mind, I have to get this off my chest. You started off playing as well as I have ever seen you play. At six, you started screwing up, but I chalked it up to fatigue. You got better, and then at twelve you were off again. Golf is a game of focus, it's mental as well as physical, you know that. Well, you went from a tight focus to off into the clouds. What's going on with you? Are you OK?"

JW thought about this for a minute. His friend Mark knew him very well and would see through a lie. "OK, you know the place I got shot is right there, across from twelve, right?"

"Yeah, sure."

"That was my last night at work and I got shot because I screwed up! After all my tactical training and years of experience, I got sniped by some nobody. It fucking pisses me off."

"Well, first off, I've talked to the guys who were on-scene. It doesn't seem to me that you did anything wrong. You know as well as I do that things rarely go perfectly, or even according to plan. That asshole got off a lucky shot. Do not spend the rest of your life beating yourself up over it. Sometimes shit just happens."

"I know, but it's not supposed to happen to me. That asshole took something from me and I want it back."

"JW, what exactly did he take? Your pride?"

The words were like a slap across the face. Normally, something like this would have really pissed him off, possibly caused a violent reaction. But he knew Mark was trying to help, trying to get him to see something he was missing. "You know, when you break it down to its essential elements, yeah. But to me, it feels like so much more than just that."

"OK, I hear you. Have you talked to Bonnie about this?"

"No, I'm not sure she would understand."

"Well, she's your wife, so you probably need to make her understand. Needing to talk about something is not a sign of weakness."

JW laughed. "Yeah, we all say that, but when it's us on the hot seat, we rationalize that we're different."

"OK, I can understand not wanting to talk to a shrink or counselor, but eventually, you are going to need to talk this out with her. But in the meantime, here's my offer—you can talk to me. It will go nowhere else. We can play golf; we'll ride together and talk between shots. Maybe that will help you get your head together, but I think it will probably mess up your game."

"Thanks, man. I appreciate that. Maybe I do need to talk about it."

"OK, problem one resolved. I should do this for a living. Now, the bastard took something from you. What are you going to do about it?"

"You may have heard I am trying to bring back the human scent detection and trailing program."

"I have. I still have my sources."

"I'm hoping I can get that going and maybe do some good. Catch some bad guys, maybe even catch the guy who shot me."

Mark turned to him and looked him hard in the eye. "What are you going to do if you find that guy, JW?"

He returned the same, hard gaze and said, "I'll be honest. I don't know."

"That's honest, just don't screw up the rest of your life because of this guy. He is not worth it. Oh, and another thing—don't expect everyone to be behind your dog idea.

There were a lot of guys that thought it was a waste of time the last time around and were happy the chief dumped it. I always liked the idea, but this time around you have got to achieve real results."

"Thanks for your thoughts on all of this, Mark. I appreciate your help and will take you up on it. The worst thing that happens is we get to play golf and talk. Hard to find the downside to that. I'll keep in mind what you said about the Program, too. Thanks, I really mean it."

After JW said his goodbyes and got in his car, his cell phone rang. *Perfect timing.* He looked at the caller ID, which said "Vohne Liche Kennels," and felt his heart rate quicken; he had been waiting for this call for several weeks. He answered the call through his vehicle's sound system. "Hey, Kurt. You have good news for me?"

"Well, that depends on whether you are in search of a German Shepherd dog who has Schutzhund I, II, and III working dog titles with very nice scores, Fahrtenhund I and II German tracking titles, and a nice-looking pedigree, too. There are some other things here, but I guess the most important thing is a comment from my guy who evaluated the dog. He said that, based on what I told him you were looking for, this dog would be ideal. I have a picture, too—nice-looking dog."

JW did not want to get too excited yet. "Wow, that sounds incredible, but maybe too rich for my blood?"

"I don't think so. My guy, Axel, has some great contacts. I think he can make a good deal for us."

"Alright, so what's next?"

"Well, I assume you will want to see the dog and do some testing before we talk about finalizing the deal. If it's OK with you and your wife, I'll have Axel make the arrangements and we'll put the dog on a plane. We'll want to give him some time to acclimatize and it will take time to get his health papers and such in order. So, I will call you when the dog gets here, but let's plan on two weeks. I assume you'll bring Ben with you to help evaluate him."

"Yes, absolutely. He knows this stuff much better than I do. Thanks, Kurt, this really means a lot to me. What if he doesn't work out in testing?"

"We'll deal with it, but I'm telling you, Axel thinks this is about as sure of a thing as you can get."

Before he hung up, JW asked, "Oh, by the way, what's the dog's name?"

"'Ares,' as in the Greek god of war."

11

JW, Bonnie, and Ben were quiet as they drove to Los Angeles International Airport. They were all thinking about the trip to come and the excitement of choosing a potential candidate for their new trailing dog program. They drove Ben's Chevrolet Tahoe in case they came home with a dog and kennel. Bonnie had handled all the flight arrangements. They were departing at 6:30 a.m. and would arrive four hours later. Bonnie had reserved a rental vehicle at their destination. They parked in the long-term parking lot and took a shuttle to the terminal. They checked in, went through the T.S.A. checkpoint and, once clear, JW immediately went in search of coffee. The trio then sat down and waited for their boarding call. Upon hearing the call for their group to board and entering the plane, Ben commented, "Gee, JW, you could have at least sprung for First Class."

"Well, Ben, once we win the lottery, everything will be first class. No worries."

During the flight, JW talked to Ben about what they would do once they arrived in Chicago. Vohne Liche Kennels was in Denver, Indiana. There were closer airports, but the added flight time and stops made it quicker to go to Chicago. Upon arrival, they exited the plane and went in search of the car rental agencies. JW recalled from previous flights how huge the airport was, and began to second guess their choice. It might have taken longer, but it would have been simpler to fly into a smaller airport. When they finally arrived at the rental car hub, Bonnie presented their reservation and they quickly loaded into a minivan. It was a three-hour drive to Denver, so they decided to go to their hotel and get something to eat. They would go to Vohne Liche Kennels tomorrow morning.

The next morning, the group gathered at a small restaurant next to the hotel for breakfast. JW ranked breakfast as the top meal of the day. He ordered up a large plate since he knew they were going to be busy and would not have time to break for lunch. It had been a long night for JW; he had not slept well. There was just too much excitement and anticipation. He felt like he was on the right path, but was he really, or was it just wishful thinking? Ben and JW continued their discussion from yesterday about their plans for testing the dog. JW did not want to call him by his name until he knew the dog was coming home with him. He did not want to jinx this thing. As the men continued their planning, Bonnie quickly checked her email on her iPad. She was listening to the men while she scanned for anything important. Seeing nothing, Bonnie interrupted JW and Ben, saying, "Look guys, I don't want to be a buzzkill here, but try not to get too excited about this dog. It sounds like you have decided already and you haven't even seen him yet. You're acting like a couple of high school kids going out on a date with the prom queen."

JW smiled at Bonnie and said, "Baby, you're my prom queen."

Ben looked away and cleared his throat as if choking, and Bonnie rolled her eyes and said, "Wow, JW, you are such a romantic." They all laughed and fortunately for them, the waitress brought their meals. Ben and JW finished quickly, while Bonnie ate more leisurely. JW could swear that she was doing it on purpose.

Finally, with everyone finished and the bill paid, the group departed for Vohne Liche Kennels. JW was driving and Ben was navigating. He had been here before and knew the way. After driving for a bit, JW asked, "Ben, where is this place? In the middle of nowhere?"

"Yeah, sort of. Turn right at the next intersection."

As they turned off the road and onto a private drive, they passed under a beautiful gate with the letters VLK on top. JW marveled at the beauty of the place. Trees, grassy fields, and isolated from everything. They drove toward several structures, in front of which was a grassy central area with a large stone monument that read, Vohne Liche Kennels—Specializing in strong, social police dogs. There was a picture of a Belgian Malinois in front of a United States flag cut into the stone. JW had seen the monument in pictures that some of the K9 handlers had taken while he was the K9 unit sergeant. JW knew Ben had been to Vohne Liche Kennels before and said, "Wow, this place is beautiful, Ben. I knew they had great dogs here and fantastic training, but I had no idea."

"It gets better."

They parked at the front office and went inside. Ben saw a woman he recognized and said, "Hey, Jennifer, how's it going? We're here to see the boss. This is my former boss, JW North."

Jennifer smiled and said, "Hi, Ben. Mr. North, nice to meet you. Kurt's inside on the phone. Give him just a minute."

JW didn't want to leave Bonnie out and said, "Jennifer, this is my wife, Bonnie."

"Nice to meet you, Mrs. North. I bet you guys are really excited. I saw your boy a couple days ago. They took him out to one of the fields to let him get some exercise. He is gorgeous." Jennifer glanced down at the phone and said, "Oh, good. He's off the phone. Let me see if he's ready." She stuck her head in and then turned to the group and said, "OK, come on in." As the group filed into the office, Jennifer introduced each of them to Kurt Steigerwald.

Kurt was a bull of a man, tall, barrel-chested, and about as jolly as Saint Nicholas. JW had met him many years ago and the two had hit it off immediately. They all sat down, and Kurt said, "Well, I am sure you guys want to go see Ares, but first I want to show you his paperwork. I've got to say, I haven't seen titles like this on a dog that wasn't going to a major competition or something. Axel, my guy in Germany, found a real gem. You have right of first refusal on him, but if you don't want him for some reason, I know I can sell him in a heartbeat." Kurt grabbed a large folder from the side of his desk, pulled out an envelope and handed the rest to JW. "Here, take a look and then we can walk down." JW started going through the papers. He had learned German in high school and followed up with three semesters in college, but that was conversational German. These documents contained specialized language, some he was familiar with and some not.

He first took the dog's pedigree papers from the folder and began to go through them. The papers were from the S.V., the German Shepherd Association of Germany, and he saw they were pink. That told JW the dog came from excellent breeding stock. All the dog's ancestry had working dog and tracking titles. As JW pointed this out to Ben, Kurt interjected, "I don't get a lot of pink-papered dogs. It's just not a priority for what we do. This dog has a great background. That was important to the breeder/owner." JW nodded, continuing through the pile of papers. He would take more time to read and translate all of it later. Kurt then said, "He's had all of his shots and such, but if you take him, I recommend you take him to a vet and get him checked out. Just to be sure. His hip X-rays look good. I would think they would grade at least good, if not better." Hip X-rays in working dogs are important. The dogs represent a substantial investment and, if they develop a problem that would not allow them to work, it can be costly in terms of training time. For this reason, most working dogs' hips are evaluated and graded either excellent, good, fair, or unacceptable.

JW replied, "This all looks great to me. Bonnie, do you want to look?" Bonnie gave him a look that said, "Don't be stupid, it's all in German," and shook her head.

Kurt led them out of the office, and they walked toward a large kennel building. He said, "I moved him out from the rest of the dogs to the executive suite so he could get some rest. Sometimes the dogs will get excited and bark. I wanted him to look good for you." As they walked to a smaller, separate kennel building, they met up with another man and woman. The man was young, about twenty-five and very fit. "This is Vince Eddington. He is one of my trainers, decoys, and kind of an all-around guy here. He does a lot of our tracking work and instruction." Vince smiled at the group. Kurt continued, "This is Molly. She is also a trainer and she has been babysitting your boy since he got here." Molly nodded at everyone.

Having arrived at the kennel building, Kurt opened the door and the group walked into a room with ten kennels. Each kennel led to a separate outside area to allow the dog to take its breaks there. The kennels were empty, except for the two in the middle on the right. In the nearest was a beautiful, almost all black German Shepherd with red and brown highlights. His eyes were almost as dark as he was. He looked the group over and then jumped up on the gate. The dog had a large head and a powerful body. He was compact, but certainly looked intimidating. Kurt pointed at the big dog and said, "This is Ares." As the group approached, Ares looked at each of them and began wagging his tail.

In the kennel next to Ares was another German Shepherd. This one was slightly smaller and did not look as masculine. JW looked at her and asked, "And who is this?"

Kurt replied, "That is Adeliene." He turned to Vince and asked, "Vince, can you get Ares, take him out to Field Three? We'll meet you there in a few minutes."

Vince nodded and took the dog from the kennel, clipping a lead on his collar and asked, "You want to do some obedience and agility first, right?"

Kurt looked to JW and Ben for the answer. JW said, "Yeah, it will get us used to each other and may help with the testing."

Vince took Ares out of the kennel and, as he did so, Adeliene became agitated and began barking and circling in her kennel. Molly went to her kennel and said, "It's OK, Addy. He'll be right back."

JW looked at Kurt, a bit confused about the exchange. As he did so, Bonnie walked over to Addy. "You guys go on and have a good time. I think I'll stay here for a while and then catch up."

As the men walked out of the kennel, Molly asked Bonnie if she wanted to pet Adeliene. Bonnie had not really spent a lot of time around working dogs and wasn't sure. "Is that OK?" she asked.

Molly smiled and said, "Oh, don't worry. She has all the Schutzhund training and such, but she is a love. She won't bite you unless you put a sleeve on."

"Yeah, I'd love to. She's beautiful." Molly opened the kennel door and Adeliene came out. At first, she went to the door as if to follow Ares, but then she turned and walked back to the women, and then sat and looked at them. "She looks so intelligent," said Bonnie.

"Oh, she is. She is as smart as they come. She learns fast and loves to chase a ball. What do you say we go out to Field One and give her some exercise? They will be looking at Ares for a while and Adeliene could use a break. Her call name is 'Addy.'"

As they left the building, Bonnie asked, "Why do you think Addy was so upset when they took Ares out?"

"Oh, that's because he's her brother. They're litter mates. The Germans name their dogs alphabetically by litter, so all the dogs' names in this litter start with an A. The next litter would all be B dogs and so on. When they get to Z, they start over. Believe me, I have seen some strange names given to dogs."

Bonnie sighed. "Brother? I thought there was a resemblance. No wonder she was so upset."

Bonnie threw the ball for Addy for a while. The dog never seemed to tire; her enthusiasm appeared to be limitless. When Bonnie thought her shoulder might soon fall off, she heard Molly call out to her, "You look like you might be getting tired. Do you want to do some obedience with her? I can walk you through it." Bonnie loved the idea, and her shoulder loved it even more. Molly walked up to Addy and clipped the lead to her choke chain. She handed the lead to Bonnie and said, "The command for 'heel' is fuss—you know, like in 'foosball.'"

Bonnie turned to Addy and said, "Fuss." Addy quickly moved to her left side and sat, looking up at her expectantly.

"OK, but say it like a command, not a request. Addy must learn you are the boss. It is best to start now and establish yourself as her alpha. She is a strong-willed girl and you want her to know for sure who is in charge."

Bonnie laughed and said, "Can I get that to work with JW?"

Molly laughed too. "No, I don't think so. Wouldn't that be nice, though?"

Molly slowly walked Bonnie through a series of commands and Addy obediently responded to each command. The dog moved with smooth confidence. She could tell this was new to Bonnie, but she didn't try to take advantage. The dog had a huge smile on her face. You could tell she had had enough of the kennel and was happy to be outside and working. They worked together for an hour and then Molly said, "Let's give her a break and grab some water. I can give you some more ideas on how to work her. You're doing great, but if you decide you want to take her, we are going to need to compress a week's worth of introductory handler training into a few hours. I know your husband has been a handler and I have seen Ben work, so you will have some help. I expect them to be at it for a while longer, so we may as well put the time to good use."

What Molly said gave Bonnie pause. She hadn't considered getting a second dog. After returning Addy to her kennel, Bonnie reassured her that she was just taking a break and they would go back outside in a little while. Although Bonnie knew Addy had not been exposed to much English, the dog seemed to be happy with her words. Addy took a long drink and then lay down to rest.

Bonnie and Molly went into the kennel office and each drank a bottle of water. The day was not too warm, but they were both thirsty. Molly sat down opposite Bonnie and said, "There is so much for you to know and so little time." She reached behind her and grabbed a notebook off a shelf and handed it to her. "This is the course binder we give to new handlers. It tells you all the basics. It has all the commands and will give you a lot of background information. Some of the stuff in the later chapters may not apply to you, but it will give you some understanding of what your husband is trying to do. From what I understand, the things he is trying to accomplish are going to be extremely difficult. It will help you support him in what he is doing, and help you keep your sanity when you try to understand what the heck is going on. In the back is a list of other resources if you decide you want to know more. Some of them may not still be in print, so they may be a challenge for you to find. If you want to take a look at that, I need to go give some of the other dogs some exercise. By the time I get back, Addy should be ready for some more work."

Bonnie thanked her and started scanning the book. She went to the list of other books in the back and made a mental note to see about finding them. They would make good Christmas gifts and also help JW as he expanded his knowledge base.

While Bonnie was off on Field One tossing a tennis ball for Addy, JW, Ben, and Kurt met up with Ares and Vince on Field Three. As they reached the field, Kurt stopped and said, "Look guys, we need to chat before you go any further. I don't want you thinking I wasn't completely up front about everything with you."

Ben and JW looked at each other and then at Kurt, and JW said, "OK, lay it on us. What don't we know?"

"Well, if you haven't guessed, Ares and Adeliene are brother and sister."

JW was caught off guard and replied, "OK," with some uncertainty, leading Kurt to provide some clarification.

"Hell," Kurt said, "I don't know how to tell you this. Here, this letter is from Axel—it explains better than I can. And hopefully, you won't be too pissed at me after you read it."

12

Mr. JW North,

I would like to take a moment to introduce myself, I am Axel Schmidt. I have been a dog trainer and handler for many years, working both in the German military and law enforcement. I have trained many dogs in tracking and have also judged many at competitions. I have helped my friend, Kurt Steigerwald, locate and purchase dogs for his business for several years now. Never has he asked me for a dog like the one I have found for you. I asked Kurt to tell me about you and he said that you were a police officer and K9 handler also, at one time. He told me that you were shot on duty, but have recovered from that. Thank God for that. He also mentioned that, after your injuries, you came away with a strong desire and need to get back to working a dog. That you specifically wanted a dog that could track or trail, and you wanted to be able to use the dog to help catch criminals, like the one who shot you. He spoke of your desire to help protect those who cannot protect themselves from the evil that exists with us in society today. I consider this to be a calling of the highest order, and I wish I could do something more for you, but I do have a gift for you. Ares. He is a beautiful animal and he has drive and skills like no dog I have ever worked. His tracking scores are almost flawless. He is the dog you seek.

His owner, Josef, is a close friend of mine. He has worked with dogs most of his life and he breeds to achieve only the best. He is known throughout the European Tracking Dog community and many top handlers come to him for his puppies. The story of Ares is particularly interesting and, if you will humor me for a moment, I will share with you what makes him so unique. If you have looked at his family tree and know anything of how dogs are bred in Germany, it will help you understand. The S.V. controls the breeding of dogs in Germany and, to some extent, tells you who you can breed with. They monitor the breed and watch for overbreeding and flaws within the breed. My friend has taken this ideal to the highest level. He has sought to create the perfect dog, and Ares is in many ways as close as he can be. If you look at his Schutzhund scores, you will see his one area of weakness—his protection skills. Ares scores very high, in the excellent range, but this will not allow my friend, Josef, to achieve his goal. He seeks perfection and, as incredible a dog as Ares is, he is not perfect.

The other issue with Ares is Adeliene. She is his litter mate. She is a wonderful dog in her own right, but she and Ares were not separated at an early age as they should have been. They have bonded tightly with each other; they are, after all, family. I believe this bond makes the sum of these two dogs better than they are separately. However, Adeliene becomes upset without him. That does not mean he will not work if she is not there. His drive and desire to hunt are such that they will overcome that. Together, she will allow him to reach his full potential. For her, I have a greater fear. She is so closely bonded to Ares that I worry for her health in the long term. I know this may sound crazy to you, but dogs need each other as much as they need us. I would ask that you consider taking both dogs. I believe you will be able to accomplish the things you want to with both dogs and may not be able to without Adeliene.

I wish you the greatest success in your venture. Your goal is a lofty one, but what you do benefits all of us.

Godspeed,
Axel Schmidt

JW turned to Kurt and just stared for a long moment. He was in deep thought and uncertain what to say. Finally, he said, "Wow, Kurt, what did you tell him? I feel like this giant responsibility has been dropped on my shoulders. I'm not sure I'm ready to be all the things Axel talks about. It's a bit overwhelming. And Bonnie and I talked about only one dog. I'm not sure she'll sign off on two."

"I know, JW, I don't know where Axel got all that. I told him all about you, because he asked. He knew we were looking for a special dog and he knew where that dog was, but he needed to know something about you to convince Ares' owner to let him go. What he didn't say in that letter, but told me on the phone, was that the dog's owner loved that dog to death and it broke his heart to let him and Addy go. But he also knew Ares was not the dog he was ultimately looking for. You have to understand that things in Germany are a little different. There are guys that spend their whole lives working toward that perfect dog. They spend years breeding and training, and most of them never find it. This guy is so close it must be killing him. Axel convinced him that Ares was the dog you were looking for. The rest of that stuff, I honestly don't know where Axel got that."

JW thought for a few moments. *What the hell am I supposed to do with this?* "Well, first things first. Let's run this dog through some tests and see how he does. If he is everything Axel says he is, then I will figure out how to convince Bonnie this is a good idea."

Kurt picked up the conversation after sighing a breath of relief, "OK, I had Vince run a few trails for you guys starting yesterday, separating them by a few hours each. There are a total of six. We can do more if you like, but I think that will give us a picture of what Ares can do."

"That sounds good. How old are the trails?"

"The oldest is a day old, the next is twelve hours, then six, then three, and finally one."

"Wait a minute, Kurt—that's only five."

"You're right, JW. The sixth trail is special. Molly ran it a week ago. If this dog can track a week-old trail, you'd be a fool not to take him. I also had Vince run a trail parallel to Molly's that, after 100 yards, turns and crosses hers. Ares will have been trailing Vince all day, then he'll get someone different, and then someone he knows will cross the trail, and he will have to make a choice. If he continues to follow Molly's trail, then maybe he is the super dog that Axel thinks he is."

At the start of the first trail, Kurt handed JW a laminated three-by-five card with a list of German commands and their English translations, saying, "I know you had a German dog before, but they are not always trained on the same commands. For Ares, 'Zur Spur' is his command to trail."

JW looked at Ares and saw that he had been fitted into a leather tracking harness. "Nice harness, Kurt."

"Oh, yeah. After Axel found Ares, he went to an old friend who is a leather worker. He made a custom-fitted harness and this five-meter tracking lead. There is a ten-meter model back in my office. Don't let me forget that."

JW gave Kurt another questioning look and Kurt said, "I don't know, man. The guy has a lot of friends, and for someone he has never met, he obviously likes you."

"The one-hour-old trail starts out straight, crosses the field, and then goes into the woods. It's fairly straight, but it will give us a good picture of what he can do. We start off here and you will cross the trail at some point up ahead. This will give us a chance to see if he will follow the direction of the trail correctly. Here is your first scent article."

JW gave Ares a "sit" command, unclipped the leash from his collar and clipped the tracking lead to the harness. Immediately, the look in Ares' eyes changed. It was time to go to work. JW allowed Ares to take a good long smell of the scent article and then gave the command, "Zur Spur," and Ares stood and put his nose to the ground and started moving at a slow pace.

The scent was not here, but as they moved forward Ares cast left and right looking for the scent. After ten yards, Ares hit the scent trail and suddenly turned right and started pulling hard up the trail. JW was surprised by the sudden movement and the strength of Ares' drive and was almost pulled off his feet. He jogged behind as Ares pulled him across the field toward the woods. As they entered the woods, Ares stopped for a moment and raised his head, then put his head back down and led JW around some brush to where Vince was standing quietly. Ares walked to within a few feet of Vince and stopped, then he sat and just stared. JW wasn't sure what the dog was thinking, but if he had to guess it was something along the lines of "Go ahead, run… make my day."

It had been a long time since JW had been a handler and he wasn't sure what to do next. Ben said, "Praise him, JW. Lots of love and praise."

JW called Ares and the two performed their version of a happy dance there in the woods. Ben and Kurt looked at one another and grinned. JW was certain if he smiled any more his face would crack. At this moment, his heart was soaring to incredible heights. He had forgotten how great it was to work with a dog, to celebrate their successes. Somewhere deep inside JW North, a small piece that had been missing came back together with his soul. Ben took JW aside and told him the good and the bad of the trail. Most of the good was about the dog and the bad was about his work as a handler.

Kurt handed him a pair of gloves. "You're going to want to get a pair of these. Ares pulls hard on the lead and you'll need them. I will give you some when we get back to the office and I'll tell you where to get more."

Trails two and three went just as well as the first. Ares worked the trail quickly and found Vince with no problems. Ben told JW, "You need to give him some resistance. He works so fast he may blow through a turn and not catch it. He will work it out, but you'll be wasting time and energy. Slow him down by making him pull you along. You have to learn to read him, to know when he is working the trail and when he is off it. You are a team and you both need to be strong to get the job done. Right now, you're not holding up your end. I'll help you fix it, but it's gonna take some time. Even as good as Ares is, it's gonna be a while before you're ready to run real trails."

Trail four had some surprises for Ares and JW. Kurt had told Vince to put some extra turns in the trail to make it tougher for Ares. He had told Vince, "Let's make him work for it." This trail was twelve hours old and Ares slowed himself down to work it. The scent had aged over the time period and wasn't as strong as the earlier scents they had worked. Still, Ares was methodical and found Vince in a relatively short time. Again, JW and Ares did their dance of joy. JW was getting very excited at just how good this dog was, but he had an inkling that Kurt and Vince would have something special for trail five.

Trail five started like the others. Ares found the trail and turned into it. Kurt made a comment to Ben, "Notice how he always turns with the trail. He never goes backward to where it starts. Someone has put a lot of time in on this dog." Ares followed the trail and made all the turns with very little effort. As he approached a turn, he would usually just turn, but on occasion he would cast about and work in a tight circle to find where the trail continued. Ben looked at Kurt and just raised his eyebrows. As they entered the woods,

Ares suddenly came to a stop, lifted his head, and then sat. He was looking at a tree and sat there waiting. JW looked at Kurt, who shrugged his shoulders as if to say, "You figure it out."

JW thought for a moment, then looked up into the tree. The branches and leaves were so thick he couldn't see through the tree. JW continued to look up and said, "Suspect in the tree, make yourself known. Come down and keep your hands in sight."

Vince called out, "OK, you got me, but I don't think I can climb down and keep my hands in plain sight. Keep a good hold on Ares, I'm not sure how he will react to me appearing out of the tree." Vince climbed down and Ares sat and watched, as he had all day.

The final test was going to be tough. A week-old trail with a fresh cross track. JW thought Ares was ready, but wondered if he would be able to do his part and help him work through it. It wasn't a question any longer for JW. He knew he wanted this dog. This was for pride. Of course, in the back of his mind, he was still worrying about how he was going to break the news of the second dog to Bonnie.

First things first. JW scented Ares on a new pad. This time Ares took a long, deep sniff. Before he could give the command, Ares turned his head and looked back at JW. He was convinced the dog was telling him, "No worries, boss. I got this one." The trail started like the others. Ares worked the trail slowly, as he had the previous trails as they aged more and more. This trail was over a week old, but JW was no longer worried about Ares. He relaxed and let himself flow with the trail. As he did, he became more aware of the dog's movements. How his tail would twitch at a turn, how he would lift his head from time to time to take a scent of the air in case the suspect was close. It was amazing to watch. He felt like someone learning a new language. A language that, until this moment, he only barely understood. He drifted so deep into the zone that he missed the point where

Vince had crossed the trail. Kurt pointed out to Ben a small flag they used in training with the dogs to tell the handler where a turn or a cross trail is. It made it possible to give the dog a correction if he missed something. Kurt hadn't bothered to tell JW about the flags or what they meant. It was better that way.

Ares blew by the cross trail like it wasn't there. He kept his head down and didn't even twitch as he continued to work the trail. He made a few turns and then blew past another marker. Kurt whispered to Ben that he had had Vince cross the trail again, but had not told JW. Ben shook his head and said, "Well, I'm a believer. This dog rocks!" Finally, Ares worked through the woods and came out the other side. There, sitting in the open in two chairs, were Vince and Molly. As Ares approached, he gave Vince a "Who are you, buddy?" look and walked up to Molly and sat. JW didn't need to be told what to do. He ran up to Ares and gave him a big hug. He picked the dog up off the ground and did a solo dance with Ares. Ares did not look worried being carried by JW; he looked happy.

Ben walked over to JW and said, "OK, good news and bad news."

JW gave him a questioning look and said, "Bullshit, Ben. He aced that."

"Oh, Ares did great. You, on the other hand, suck. You missed a lot of clues the dog gave you. I have a lot of work to do. The good news is the dog is fantastic. You won't be so hard to fix. I can talk to you. Will you listen?" The relationship between Ben and JW had changed. They had always been great friends, but JW had always been his superior and Ben had to respect that. Now, Ben was the teacher and JW was the student, but more than that, they were partners in this venture.

The group walked back to put Ares in the kennel so they could talk business. Along the way, they talked about Ares' performance. For a dog working with a new handler, the trails had been close to perfect. Everyone continued teasing JW that if they could teach Ares to drive, JW would be unnecessary. JW was reminded of an old K9 instructor he had who liked to say, "Good dog, shit handler." Well, JW could work on that.

When they arrived at the kennel, JW wondered where Bonnie was. He asked Molly and she said, "We took Addy out for a break and she played catch with her. Then we did some obedience work and, finally, she went back to playing catch with her. I told her she could put her back in her run when she got tired." JW thought that she probably had gone back to the van to read and wait for them. He glanced at his watch and realized they had been out working Ares for six hours. *Time flies when you're having fun.*

Upon opening the door to the kennel building, JW spotted Bonnie. She was in the run with Addy. Bonnie was sitting on the floor and Addy was by her side, her head in Bonnie's lap. Both were out cold. The sound of the group entering woke Bonnie from her nap and she looked at JW, smiled, and said, "I've decided. If you get a dog, I get a dog. I want this one."

JW burst out laughing and turned to Kurt. "Well, that problem is solved. OK, now let's get down to business. What is this going to cost me?"

Vince and Molly took this as their cue to leave and exited quietly. "Well, JW, you're not going to like this, but the price is five thousand dollars."

JW's jaw dropped and he shook his head. "No way, that dog is worth a lot more than that and that is not even counting Addy."

"Hey," Kurt said, "I know you are an honest man and I figured that would seem too cheap to you. I told Axel that too. What can I say? Axel talked to Josef. Well, maybe the fact that they are brothers might have something to do with it. JW, listen to me for a moment. Both of these guys love their dogs. They have worked their whole lives and Josef has staked everything he has on what he is trying to do. Axel told him what you wanted to do and told him, maybe he never achieves the level of perfection he is seeking. But you, you are doing something different. It has been tried before, but you are taking it somewhere different, and I think maybe Axel and Josef believe that Ares will give you the success they are both looking for. JW, it's not about the money or the fame for these guys, it's about the dogs.

"Originally, Axel said that Josef wanted to give you both dogs. Axel said you wouldn't accept that and might not even agree to five thousand dollars. They agreed that amount represented Josef's investment in the two dogs, plus having them shipped over. I just threw my part in. I believe in what you're doing too, JW. So does Axel. Now, write me a check for five thousand dollars, take these dogs, and go home. You have a lot of work to do. But before you go, my wife and I are taking you all out to dinner tonight. We're going to 'Bob's Place' at seven. Ben knows where it is. We'll take care of the dogs tonight and you can pick them up in the morning."

13

The drive from Vohne Liche Kennels to the hotel went quickly. As they got out of the car, Bonnie pulled JW aside and said, "I don't feel good about flying these dogs home."

"It'll be fine, Bonnie. Airlines fly dogs all the time."

"Yeah, and every now and then, they manage to kill one by leaving them out on the taxiway."

JW could see he was not going to get anywhere on this one. Bonnie had already bonded with Addy; he could see it in her eyes. "OK, alternate plan on how we get home?"

"Easy, we drive."

JW sighed and said, "Well, you know I don't mind the drive. But what are we gonna do about Ben?"

"Ask him. If he doesn't want to ride back, we still have the flight reservations. We cancel ours and let him fly."

"OK, hang on. I'll ask him what he wants to do." JW knew they had each packed to stay for several days in case it had taken longer, so he wasn't worried about clothing for the trip; worst case scenario, they could do a load of laundry at one of the hotels along the way.

As JW turned to go find Ben, he almost tripped over him because Ben was walking toward him. "Ask me what?"

JW was a little startled by his sudden appearance but managed to say, "Bonnie thinks it might be a good idea to drive back. She's worried about the airline and the dogs."

Ben considered this for a moment and said, "Not a bad idea, actually. Once you have the dog credentialed, he can fly with you in the cabin."

"OK, but what do you want to do?"

Ben looked at JW as if he were insulted. "Well, that's easy. If you want, I'm happy to ride with you. I'll have to call the wife to confirm and the scheduling sergeant to make sure I can get the days off, but I'm with you in this thing. A drive home sounds like fun. Besides, I can help with the driving."

JW responded, "Thanks, buddy, you don't have to do it."

Ben smiled. "Like I said, I'm in."

Ben went up to his room to change and get ready for dinner, and Bonnie made some phone calls while JW showered and changed. "I've cancelled our return flights and contacted the rental car company and arranged to make a one-way trip to California instead of the return to Chicago O'Hare. Ben came by while you were in the shower and said his wife was good with it and his sergeant okayed him for a few extra days off. Maybe when we get back you could talk to the chief and see if he would consider carrying Ben on some sort of a special detail. After all, what he's doing will benefit the Department."

"I'll see what I can do, but no promises."

The phone call to Lucy had not gone as well as Ben led Bonnie to believe. He didn't want to give her all the details and it was something he could talk to JW about later. As he tried to explain his reasons to Lucy, it had not been easy at all.

"Ben, don't you see what is happening? JW is using you to get what he wants!"

"That's not true, Lucy. He asked if I wanted to come back with them, rather than fly. No one is forcing me to do anything."

"Well, you've already been gone for a couple days and now it will be a few more."

"I know, but let me say one thing. Being involved with this makes me feel good. The dog is fantastic and I think this can work. Sure, I'm a little jealous, but this is bigger than me, and JW is the one carrying this. Heck, he's paying for everything, not the City."

"Look, Honey, I'm not trying to be the wicked witch of the west. I just want what's best for us. I remember how you were at the start of the program the last go around, and how you were when they tossed you to the side of the road. I just don't want to see that happen again."

JW thought about what Bonnie had said. He knew he would have to retire to be able to spend the amount of time he would need to train Ares; however, he would need some sort of law enforcement status to be able to do the work he wanted to do. Well, the long drive back would give him plenty of time to strategize on how he was going to convince the chief. Bonnie went in to shower, so JW decided to talk with Ben and solicit ideas on how to approach the boss. He knew Bonnie would need some time to get ready and it would be a productive way to pass the time.

JW knocked on Ben's door and was let inside. Ben had a large notebook open and a few other documents spread out on his bed. He saw JW looking at all of it and said, "I was going over some notes on the protocol we set up when we were doing the Project. I was trying to decide how to approach this training for you and Ares."

Ben continued, "Ares is so much more advanced than the other dogs we worked with, I just can't decide. I think if you are good with it, I want to start at the beginning. Ares doesn't need it, but you do. Also, when we get back, I want to introduce you to a friend, Allen Whelan. You met him when we were running the Project. He has forgotten more about bloodhounds and trailing than I will ever know. He was a lot of help during the Project. He has a lot of knowledge and is great at reading dogs."

Ben looked JW hard in the face. "I have one other thing I need to discuss. Lucy is not a big fan of all this, specifically me being involved." He went on to give JW some of the details of his phone conversation. "What I am saying is that if, at some point, I say no to something, it isn't because I don't want to do it. It's more like I want to keep my marriage intact."

JW was surprised by this revelation and was quiet, thinking for almost a minute. "Hey, Ben, that's the last thing I want, for you to have marital problems. Cops have it rough enough as it is. There is no need for me to add any extra stress on you or your wife. Are you sure you want to do this?"

"I'm in, at least for now. I think she's OK with me helping with training. I just need to be sensitive to what she's saying, you know?"

"I hear ya, my friend. Sensitive huh? Well, if you get that figured out, will you let me in on it?"

"Hell, if I figure that out, I want to find a way to bottle it. I'll be rich."

As the men continued their conversation, there was a knock at the door. Ben answered and stepped back to allow Bonnie to walk in. She was dressed to the nines. JW whistled and said, "Wow. You look great, Honey! You do know we're just going out to dinner?"

She smiled and said, "Yeah, but you know I needed to class things up a little."

Ben laughed and said, "Now I feel underdressed in khakis and a polo."

JW said, "No, don't worry about it, Ben. She likes to dress up and Kurt gave her an excuse." With that said, they all loaded up in the minivan and drove off to "Bob's Place." Ben explained that it was a local restaurant that had great steaks and would probably have a band tonight.

Bonnie chimed in with, "I like the sound of that."

After entering "Bob's Place," JW looked around and spotted a table in the back with Kurt and his wife, Vince, and Molly. As they walked to the table, Ben said to them, "Hey guys," and he looked at Vince and Molly and asked, "When did you guys become an item?"

Kurt laughed and said, "Come on, Ben, try to keep up." They all laughed, and, after introductions, they all sat down. After ordering drinks, the group sat and talked while the band started setting up.

JW turned to Kurt and said, "OK, something's buggin' me and I can't stop thinking about it."

Kurt nodded for him to continue, saying, "I bet I know what it is."

JW was intrigued. "OK, you go first."

"I'm thinking you want to know why a dog like Ares would score so low on his protection testing."

"OK, you read my mind, so why?" Everyone at the table had heard the start of the conversation and they all turned to listen.

"I wondered the same thing, so I looked through the paperwork that came with Ares. Now, all that paperwork did not include the individual score sheets with comments. There was a clue in his breed survey. Did you see it?"

JW shook his head and said, "I saw he was 'recommended for breeding,' but my German isn't that great, so I didn't read the details. I thought I would do that when we got home."

"It's there, in the text. But I wasn't sure, so I called Axel and asked him. He said I was right, that on some of his trials he wasn't clean on his releases from the bite, including on his breed survey. Axel said that was not a disqualifier for breed class one, 'recommended,' but you know how the Germans are. Something like that is less than perfection."

JW nodded and said, "Er last ab nicht."

Ben said, "That's it. Have you seen that before?"

JW nodded and said, "Yes, my old working dog, Asko. It means he doesn't release cleanly from the bite. He had the same issue. He was a pretty damn good dog and I never had too much of an issue with it."

"Yeah, just be aware of it, and if you think it might be a problem, train on it."

With that, the conversation broke up into groups. The waitress came by and brought their drinks and took their dinner order. The band started playing and Bonnie looked at JW and nodded toward the dance floor. Dancing was not on JW's list of things he liked to do, but he knew Bonnie loved it. As they danced and were joined on the dance floor by other patrons, JW wondered, *Is Bonnie really prepared for this project? Is she as sympathetic to everything as she seems?* He realized they were going to have another heart-to-heart sooner rather than later. Dinner arrived and JW said, "Oh gee, Honey, look. Dinner's served. I guess we'll have to go eat."

She smiled and said, "Yeah, you get a break now, buddy, but afterward you're mine."

They rejoined the group and they all started eating. During the meal, JW turned to Kurt and said, "Good call, this is an excellent steak."

"Best in town. Of course, it is a small town."

As JW and the rest were eating their steaks, the Shadow was also dining, less than three hundred miles away. As he did so, in a small diner in Bowling Green, Kentucky, he was busy scanning his laptop. The diner had free Wi-Fi and that was part of the reason he came here. He had come here several times since he had arrived.

After Wyoming, he had stopped in a truck stop in Nebraska. He needed gas and some food and, while there, he had purchased a road map of the United States. He scanned the map and looked at Bowling Green. He found that most of the truck stops had free Wi-Fi for the truck drivers to check their email and such, and he went on the Internet while sitting in his car. He typed in "Bowling Green, Kentucky" and found he liked the description. He also liked that it had only six hundred police officers. It wasn't as big as Long Beach, but it was still big enough for him to lose himself. He decided to go there to take a look and see if Bowling Green met his needs.

The drive there had been incident free. In his mind, the Shadow envisioned a broad net had been spread looking for him. In reality, there had been a lot of interest in California, but once he was out of the state, it seemed no one knew who he was. He thought about that for a while. *Would the Shadow reappear here?* He thought not. If the police were able to link Long Beach to Bowling Green, that would create entirely too much interest for his liking. No, he would need to change things up a little bit somehow. It was hard to argue with success but repeating a pattern over and over could lead to his undoing. That was unacceptable to the Shadow. Perhaps, one day, he would tell the world of his achievements—but not today.

The Shadow liked what he saw when he arrived in Bowling Green. It appeared to be a target-rich environment. He decided he would stay a few days to make sure everything felt right before settling here. Finally, he decided to stay and started looking for a job. He went with what he knew and looked for a night watchman position. It didn't take long to find what he was looking for, since most people did not like working nights. The Shadow loved the night, it was his only true friend. He found a cheap apartment with a small kitchen, but he preferred to eat at the diner he now found himself in. The thing he liked most about it was he could always get a window seat. He liked that because he could eye the locals as they walked by. The waitress brought him his meal. He looked at her and felt something stir. She fit his profile, but he would not touch her. That would be stupid. He frequented this place and taking her when he had been seen here several times would not be smart. He would use her as his inspiration.

The hunger had started to return to the Shadow. Wyoming had satisfied him for a while, but now he was starting to feel the need to hunt. He knew it was a long process requiring a lot of planning; therefore, he needed to start now. He had a campaign to plan. Soon the population of Bowling Green would know he was here, and they would fear him and the night. There was nothing they or their police department could do to protect them. He was hungry and it was time to hunt.

The drive home for JW, Bonnie, and Ben was relatively uneventful. At least as uneventful as possible for three people and two dogs that did not know one another all riding together in a minivan. During the trip, the dogs did what dogs on a trip do best—they slept. Bonnie read, Addy sound asleep at her feet. Ares was sound asleep in the back, seemingly comforted by the constant rocking of the minivan. It was then they discovered one of Ares' few flaws—he snored. Not all the time, but when he did, he was loud. In the hotels they stayed in, the dogs, uncertain of their status, slept next to one another. Ares, unsettled by the constant noise from the highway and other patrons passing by their room, kept a constant vigil. Perhaps that was why he slept so soundly in the car. With both JW and Ben driving, while Bonnie kept an eye on the dogs, the trip to Long Beach passed quickly. They stopped at the Los Angeles Airport to drop off the rental and pick up Ben's Tahoe they had left in long-term parking. When JW returned the minivan, the agent threw a fit when he saw the dog hair inside. He insisted on a cleaning fee. JW considered the demand and relented. The fee wasn't that much considering what it would take to clean out all the dog hair.

On the way from the airport to Long Beach, Ben told JW to just spend the next couple of weeks bonding with Ares. It was OK to take him out for a walk and to play catch, but beyond that, he should relax and let the dogs get used to their new lives. JW hadn't yet finished his physical therapy, so he knew he would need to visit Monica's House of Pain for a few more weeks. He was still not back to his old self. He had found himself getting winded during the trailing tests they had given Ares in Indiana. He was going to need to work on his cardio, and he wondered if he would ever get back to where he once was. That was something he could worry about on another day; for now, he had a dog to train.

14

After Ben dropped them off, JW and Bonnie went inside and unpacked. Bonnie decided to do some laundry. After riding in a car for five days, their dirty clothes stank of sweat and the road. While Bonnie began sorting clothes, JW unpacked "dog stuff." The dogs needed water, so the first thing he did was fill the stainless-steel bowl and place it outside, near the doggy door he had recently installed. He put the other bowls and such in the kitchen, ready for the dogs' evening meal in a couple of hours. Then he sat down and watched as the dogs familiarized themselves with their new home. Kurt had hinted that, although most imported dogs were more used to living in a kennel, he believed that Ares and Addy had spent a lot of time inside Josef 's home in Germany.

The home environment did not seem too foreign to the dogs, but it was still unfamiliar turf. This demanded inspection—a thorough, complete inspection. The dogs worked inside and then outside, then back in, only to go out again. It seemed as if they sniffed every inch of the house but, surprisingly, neither dog tried to mark inside. Ares went outside to the backyard and proceeded to mark the entire yard. Addy watched with interest and occasionally left her mark, too. Although the house was not overly large and the lot was tiny, the dogs took over two hours to complete their inspection. JW sat on the couch and watched with great interest, while Bonnie came and went getting the laundry going. Finally, the dogs seemed to have had enough. JW wasn't certain whether it was from exhaustion or they were satisfied everything was covered. Ares went to the other side of the living room and settled on the floor, his back against the wall and his eyes on JW. Addy came in and walked up to JW. He was on the end of the couch and she simply climbed over the arm of the couch, onto his lap. She settled into a tight ball and rested her head on his knee. Oh great, an eighty-five-pound lap dog! Bonnie walked by, looked at him, and said, "You know, that's my dog. Yours is over there," pointing at Ares.

JW shrugged and said, "I didn't call her. She came up here on her own."

"Yeah, right. Dog thief," Bonnie said with a scowl.

The one thing JW had forgotten in all his preparations was a place for the dogs to sleep. Bonnie went out to the local pet supply and bought more of their dog food and two beds. Ares' bed was blue, and Addy's was red. JW laughed at the idea of her trying to get the dogs to sleep in the right bed. Finally, they all settled in for the night. JW and Bonnie read for a while, a habit they both had to help them relax and get their minds ready for sleep. Finally, they both shut off their iPads and drifted off. JW awoke at 2:00 a.m. to a warm feeling on the back side of his leg.

He was a side sleeper, and something was causing his leg to feel hot. He lifted his head and looked to see Addy there, sound asleep. Apparently, she had jumped up onto the bed while everyone was asleep. JW considered kicking her off the bed but decided it would be impossible to do so without waking Bonnie. When he woke in the morning, not only was Addy still there, but Ares had also jumped up and was asleep at Bonnie's feet. Bonnie was curled into the fetal position and did not look comfortable. Over coffee that morning, Bonnie said, "Well, it looks like I wasted our money on those dog beds."

"We don't have to let them sleep on our bed."

"Yeah, try kicking them out; just try," Bonnie said with a laugh.

The next few days were filled with more mundane tasks around the house. As JW felt better and more able to do things, he got to work on a long list of chores Bonnie had created in a spiral notepad that she had labeled, "JW's Things To Do." He was tired of being cooped up, so he decided to start outside. Long Beach had pretty good weather year-round, so it was unnecessary to start winterizing. JW went through the backyard, clearing out a few weeds and just cleaning up in general. Most of the back was flagstone, outdoor kitchen, or raised flower beds. There was a small patch in the middle that had been grass, but they had removed it and had artificial turf put in. He had been considering turning it into a putting green but decided against it as it was now the dogs' favorite spot to take a break. As JW continued pulling weeds, he heard a rustling behind him. Addy had climbed into one of the raised planters and was digging. At her current rate of descent, it was clear she would arrive in China within an hour. Dirt was flying everywhere. JW gave her a sharp, "Nein," German for "No," and she immediately stopped. She raised her head and gave him the "What? I am only helping" look. Eventually, the tasks in the back completed, JW found Bonnie going over the family budget and said, "Hey, we have a two o'clock appointment with the vet. The dogs are getting the rest of their shots and a check-up."

"OK, almost done here, but tonight we have to sit and talk finances."

It was clear the dogs liked traveling in the car. As soon as JW opened the back of their SUV, he was almost knocked over as the dogs jumped in. Yeah, so much for trained dogs.

Dr. Leigh Ann Harrel had been providing medical care for the K9 unit since before JW had been the sergeant. She had seen a lot of working dogs come and go during her time. JW thought it would be best to use her as their veterinarian even though neither dog was covered by the City contract. He knew she was at ease with working dogs, and if Ares was eventually covered by the City, it would be an easy transition. In addition to her ample experience with K9s, another plus was that this vet offered twenty-four-hour, seven-day-a-week service. It was a bit of a drive out of Long Beach, but overall, the pros far outweighed the cons.

Dr. Harrel came into the examination room and smiled at them all. "Hi, JW, long time no see. Who are these gorgeous beauties?" JW introduced Ares, Addy, and Bonnie and explained what he was trying to do. "OK then," she continued, "let's get this show on the road. Any issues I should be aware of?"

"No, here are their veterinary clearances and history. Unless you read German, there is not much there. They are both well-mannered and not overly aggressive."

She nodded. "Yeah, I love working dogs. Most are not too concerned about you poking and prodding. They have seen it all before. Just the same, hang on to each of them while I give them the once-over. They will need a full battery of shots. They don't do as much over there as we do here."

At the conclusion of the exam, Dr. Harrel said, "These dogs are in fantastic shape and very well mannered. How are you recovering from your injuries, JW?"

"As well as can be expected. Physical therapy is trying to do what the bullet couldn't and kill me off. I think this new project of mine is going to be good for me."

"Well, good luck. I know the original project produced some good results, but they shut it down, didn't they?"

"Yes, they did. Although I believe the reasons behind that were less about the results and more about the cost of having a full-time officer dedicated to it. In this case, I will be retired and working as either a volunteer or a reserve. I'll need some help from the Department, but the cost will be substantially less. The biggest problem the last time was we never had that big splash arrest. I am hoping with Ares on our team, this time things will be better."

"Well, I hope you can make it work. Any bad guy you take off the streets is a plus in my book."

"You should have seen him work when we tested him. I have seen a lot of working dogs, and Ares is almost unbelievable. I need to get down on my knees and thank God for sending him my way."

That evening after dinner, JW and Bonnie sat down at the table, each with a cup of coffee. Bonnie started, "I know you have concerns about the cost of things with our new endeavor. Well, I guess it's time for me to let my little secret out of the bag."

This got JW's attention. He didn't think they had any real secrets between them. "So, when we first met and started dating, I made a decision not to tell you everything in my past. You know my family is well-off—you've been to some of the family gatherings. Well, they're actually very well-off. But the thing about my family is we never really act like we have a lot of money. You know how some people can be, making a big deal about it. We've always been more about what you've done in your life and not how much you have in your bank account. Sure, we all have nice houses and such, but you won't find any of the McClains driving around in Ferraris."

Bonnie continued, "When I was young, very young, my mom's sister, my aunt Susan, died of cancer. She never married, so when she decided how she wanted her money distributed, she decided to give it to her favorite sister's daughter—me. I don't remember any of this, so all I know is what my mom told me. It didn't cause much of an uproar in the family because everyone has their own money. Anyway, she had the family lawyer set that money aside in a trust for when I turned twenty-one. She also had her investment portfolio manager actively manage those funds, investing them in both conservative and aggressive market funds and real estate. Those funds have been invested and growing for over forty years. I know this will probably make you mad, JW, but I just didn't know how to tell you. I didn't mean to keep this from you for so long but, originally, I wanted to make sure you loved me for who I am, and later I just didn't know how to tell you, so I didn't."

Bonnie paused and looked at JW. He could see the first indications of tears forming in her eyes. He certainly didn't want her to cry, but he had some questions. "Honey, we have been married now for almost ten years. You obviously have some money in the bank, so why didn't you want something nicer?" JW asked as he stood and raised his arms in a gesture around their home.

"JW, I love our home and I love our life. I even love my job. It's wonderful how they have been so supportive of me working from home while you were recuperating. I suppose I was afraid that if I brought the money in, it would change things."

JW stood and walked to his wife and said, "Bonnie, I am not going to let a little money ruin our life together."

"Well, it's more than a little money. The last time I looked it was a little over twenty-nine million dollars."

JW nearly collapsed where he stood. The idea of suddenly having that much money overwhelmed him. He sat straight down on the floor and just stared off into space.

Addy, concerned that something was wrong, came over and started licking his face. JW told her, "Thank you, baby. Dad is OK."

Bonnie laughed at Addy and then asked, "JW, are you OK?"

"Yeah, I think so. It is just so much to take in. I'm not mad at you for not telling me. I understand the dilemma you were facing. Frankly, I'm concerned that that much money could change us."

"Don't worry about that, my family has taught me to not let it go to my head, and if I see you going in that direction, I will let you know."

"Well, I guess that means my Corvette is no longer off the table."

Bonnie scowled at him and said, "Maybe you should start by deciding what kind of car you are going to drive your dog around in."

"Good point, I can't keep using your car. Let me think on it for a bit. I just don't want my dream of a Corvette to slip away."

15

The following week, JW had arranged a meeting with Chief of Police Michael Estrada at his office. It was the first time JW had been downtown since before he was shot. It felt a little strange, and his spirits were lifted seeing all the officers and civilian staff greet him as he walked past security at the front entrance and then down the hall on the third floor to the chief's office. As he entered the outer office he was greeted by the chief's secretary, Marilyn. He felt a tap on his shoulder and turned to face another old friend, Javon Hudson. "Hey, Javon, what are you doing here?"

"I'm chief of staff now." JW then noticed the commander stars on his friend's collar.

"Wow, you made commander. Congratulations! When did that happen?"

"About a month ago. You heard Bill Henderson went to be chief over in Arizona, didn't you?" JW nodded and Javon continued, "Well, I got promoted after he left, and the chief moved me in here. I hear you have a meeting with the boss today. Anything you want to forewarn me about?"

"No, I think it's good news. But I only want to have to go through it once. It's kind of complicated."

"Sure, sure," Javon replied, "Let's see if he is ready for you."

Javon went into the chief's office and returned almost immediately, motioning for JW to come in. Chief Michael

Estrada rose from behind his desk and came out and hugged JW. "How are you doing, JW? Ready to come back to work?"

JW laughed and said, "I'm here to talk to you about exactly that."

Chief Estrada said, "Well then, let's sit down and talk." He motioned to a table surrounded by four chairs and said, "I've blocked an hour for you, but if we need more time, let me know and I'll get Marilyn to work rearranging my schedule. Coffee?"

"You know me, Chief, I will always take coffee."

Javon went out the door and let Marilyn know of the chief's request and returned. She came in a few minutes later with three cups of coffee. "Thanks, Marilyn," Chief Estrada said. "Please make sure we are not disturbed."

"So, JW, I hear you now have a wonder dog?"

Not distracted by the chief's sarcastic comment, JW said, "Yes, actually that's what I came here to talk to you about. As you are aware, the night I was shot was supposed to be my last shift. I still plan to retire as soon as the doctor releases me to permanent and stationary. However, something changed for me after I was shot. I can't really explain it, but I have unfinished business—not revenge business, but I feel like I need to do something. The best I can figure, it has to do with dogs. Do you remember the trailing dog project?"

"Yes, certainly," the chief said, nodding for him to go on. The chief's face was impassive and JW could not tell if he was interested in this or not. "I never like having to pull the plug on a program, but I had no choice. The Project was not getting the anticipated results and was a drain on my department. It made us look bad."

"I understand, sir. But the academic portion of the Project was a success, and now we have several peer-reviewed papers documenting the dogs' abilities with scent and trailing. I know the field portion was not as successful as we all would have liked, but we did have small successes, just not the big one I believe you were looking for. I know one of the main concerns was having an officer assigned to your department who was always off assisting another agency. I can't promise that won't happen again. If the FBI or someone else asks for assistance, I am not sure we can or should say no."

The chief interrupted JW at this point. "So, let me make sure I get this right. You went out and purchased a dog with the intention of restarting the trailing dog program?"

"Not exactly, sir. I purchased Ares with the intention of training him to be a trailing dog. I can't restart the Program without your consent. I wouldn't do that, sir. That would be disrespectful. I'm going to train Ares and have him certified as a trailing dog using the standards we established within the original program."

"JW, it seems like you are getting ahead of yourself here. How are you going to do that without my approval?"

JW could see the chief's face was getting a little red and his body language more aggressive. He was a little confused by this reaction initially, but when he paused for a moment, he saw it for what it was. The chief was angry because he believed he wasn't in control of what JW was doing. JW needed to communicate his vision for the trailing program and gain approval. However, he needed to work under a law enforcement agency. He did not want to be a vigilante, but he also needed to assert his independence. This was his program.

"Sir, I had no intention of coming here today to upset you or have you think I am going behind your back. I believe you know that is not my style. Whether I am retired from the Long Beach Police Department or not, I have always had the greatest respect for this organization and its officers. That includes you, too, sir. I'm not here today asking for anything. I am here to offer you an opportunity. You can be the parent agency to the best trailing dog program in the United States or you can choose not to be."

The chief was a little peeved that JW would single-handedly move forward with this project. *Does he think he can go off on his own and do this without my approval?* "JW, let me ask you a question, because I think this goes to the core of my problem here. How are you going to do this without us? And if you cannot do it without us, why would you go out and start something like this before I gave my approval?"

JW was still a bit confused. He wasn't sure what the chief was driving at, and said, "Sir, please excuse me, but I am not tracking you. What do you think I need that you have?"

"Well, to start, money. Money and the infrastructure to support your operation."

JW smiled, handed a folder to the chief and then one to Javon, and said, "Sir, I am not here asking for money. I don't need a budget from you. When you review this proposal, you will see that the program will be self-funded."

Chief Estrada looked at JW like he was out of his mind and said, "How are you going to pay for this? Did the feds offer up some cash?"

"I haven't spoken to the feds, sir. Bonnie and I will be paying for this with our own funds."

The chief was incredulous. "It's none of my business how you got the money, but do you realize how much this will cost?"

"Yes, sir. I think we have it all laid out in the proposal. Perhaps you would like a moment to go over it? I can step outside."

Chief of Police Estrada watched JW walk out into the reception area and turned to his chief of staff. "What just happened?"

Commander Hudson laughed. "I think JW is likely wondering the same thing. I think you both saw this thing was going sideways and wanted to turn the heat down. Let's look at the proposal and see what it says."

They reviewed the document, commenting to each other as they read through it. The chief paused for a moment and then said, "This is certainly a complete proposal. I wish JW wasn't retiring, I would promote him to the next commander slot I get and make him my new chief of staff." Hudson looked at the chief, who finally laughed and said, "Not going to happen, so don't worry about it. What do you think of this?"

"Well, sir," Hudson said, doing his best JW North impression, "I think we need to know a couple things that are not in the proposal, like where the money is coming from."

They called JW back in, asked him to sit down, and the chief said, "I'm impressed. This is a very complete proposal. May I ask where the money is coming from? I know someone else will eventually ask that question."

"Yes, sir, I understand. I'm happy to tell you, but please don't tell anyone you don't have to. I don't want people treating us differently. The fact is my wife received a large inheritance when she was younger. I only recently became aware of this. She has offered to fully fund this project."

The chief's eyes grew larger and all he could manage was, "You're a lucky man, JW."

"I agree, sir, one hundred percent. But money is only a small part of that."

"OK, in reviewing this proposal, it appears that you don't need much from us. So, what are you looking for?"

"Sir, the details are outlined in Appendix C, but basically, I need you to approve the project being under the umbrella of the Long Beach Police Department. I would request, upon my retirement, to become either a volunteer or reserve officer. Reserve officer would probably work better, though. I'd like approval to operate on your radio frequencies and a few other things outlined there. Other questions, sir?"

"No, I think I got it all."

"OK then, sir. I'll get out of your hair and let you get on with your day. Thank you for making time for me."

JW rose and started toward the door, but stopped when the chief said, "I am going to conditionally approve this, JW. And I will approve you going to the reserves—as a lieutenant."

JW started to interrupt the chief at this point, but the chief didn't allow it. "I imagine you weren't looking for a leadership position and it won't be. The existing chain of command within the reserves will continue. You will be in a box off to the side and report directly to my chief of staff. I want you to have the rank so you can say 'no,' should the need arise."

"OK, thank you, sir. You know I'm not shy. I won't let anyone move us in the wrong direction."

"JW, I am counting on your experience and wisdom to do just that. This has the potential to be very high profile and I do not want your actions putting the Department in a bad light."

"Understood, sir."

"It will take me a couple of weeks to run this by the city manager and city attorney. It won't be official until they sign off on it. If you can hold off with anything major for that long, I think we can get this going. I'm sorry things got a bit heated there for a while. You kind of caught me off guard, but regardless, you and I have been friends for a long time. It should not have come to that."

"Sir, there is nothing to be sorry about. I was just surprised you knew about Ares and it threw me off."

With that, JW exited and Commander Hudson said to Chief Estrada, "Sir, it seemed like you agreed to that fairly quickly."

"You're right, Javon, I did. Whether he realizes it or not, JW had us backed into a corner. If we say no, I have no doubt another agency or the feds will pick him up. He may end up with the feds later, anyway. If this works as well as I have been led to believe, they are going to be very interested in him. At least for now, he is with us."

"But, sir, if he leaves anyway, what difference will it make?"

"I've known JW for a long time. He is loyal to this agency and to the officers here. I am sure we can persuade him to keep some kind of link with us no matter what. If we make it too challenging from the start, that loyalty may be diminished when we need it later."

Javon considered this for a moment. "But what if the dog doesn't produce?"

"In that case, we drop the program and ease JW into full retirement."

Chief Estrada paused for a moment and then told Javon, "Give JW a call tomorrow and ask him if he is interested in having Officer Kellum work with him on his project. I know Kellum was a big part of the original venture. I want him involved so that we have a stake in this program. We need something to tie him to us beyond his personal loyalty. Tell JW I will authorize Officer Kellum to work with him a half-shift two days a week. I am not convinced this is going to work, but JW has been a hardworking, loyal member of this department who was almost killed in the line of duty. I am going to make sure we do our part to help him succeed. The rest is on him. The problem for me is to sell this to city hall. Not all of the councilmembers were in office when we tried this the last time, but I'm sure some of their staff were. Not everyone is going to be supportive."

Commander Hudson acknowledged his orders and left to return to his office. The chief sat down at his desk, deep in thought.

16

JW arrived at home confused. He walked in and saw Bonnie seated on the couch. She looked up and smiled at him and said, "The kids are outside sunbathing; they'll come in as soon as they hear your voice."

JW sat down and said, "Well, that didn't go the way I expected."

"How so? Did he say no?"

"No. But I really didn't expect an answer one way or the other. Chief is more of a political job than I ever wanted. I knew he would have to discuss this with the city manager and the city attorney. He kind of stuck his neck out by saying OK."

"He said OK and we're not celebrating?"

"No, we will, it was just weird. A little off." JW then explained the meeting in detail.

Bonnie was the first to figure it out. "I know you didn't go in there intending to do it, but you backed him into a corner. I think he was worried that if he said no, you would go somewhere else."

JW considered this line of reasoning and said, "That's why I married you. You're so smart."

"Well, I did help you put that proposal together over the weekend. Was I right? No questions, no arguments?"

"Oh yeah, Honey, it was bulletproof. It still doesn't feel right. There is something we're missing; I just don't know what it is yet."

Bonnie thought for a moment and said, "OK, enough on that. He gave you a conditional go-ahead. I say we start moving forward on our end. I made a call to the Chevy dealer and set up an appointment for you to meet with the fleet sales manager tomorrow at 10:00 a.m."

JW was excited at this news. "That's great, Honey. You're incredible."

"Thanks, babe. I spoke with him on the phone and told him what you are doing and what you are looking for. He said he may have to order it from the factory, but he is happy to accommodate our needs. I think if you take Ares, you may be able to negotiate a good price."

The following morning Commander Javon Hudson knocked on the North's front door. JW answered, cup of coffee in his hand, and smiled at the sight of Javon. Javon said, "Hey, if you'll get me one of those, I think I have something you may be interested in."

JW stood aside. "Who am I to deny a friend in need? Come on in. Hey, Bonnie, look who's here beggin' for coffee."

After getting his coffee and exchanging pleasantries with Bonnie, Commander Hudson asked JW, "Hey, can we go outside and chat nine-seven-five for a second?" That was the Long Beach radio code for confidential information.

"Sure."

Once in the backyard, Javon was immediately assaulted by Ares and Addy. Javon looked confused and said, "Two? I thought you only got one dog."

JW laughed and said, "Well, my friend, that is a long story best told over a beer, but I guess coffee will have to do. This is Addy and this is Ares." JW then gave him a brief background. The dogs, bored with all the talking, went inside in hopes of finding food or something else to get into.

Javon said, "The chief wants you to succeed and has offered the services of Ben Kellum to you, two days a week for five hours each day, at least until you can get your dog trained and certified."

"Really? That's great! After the conversation yesterday, I wasn't convinced the chief really wanted it to succeed. Tell him I accept and thank you."

Javon paused a moment and looked around to see if anyone was within earshot. "JW, please keep this between you and me, I kind of like my job." JW nodded and motioned for him to continue. "That was a strange conversation. I wondered if the people in that room were the same people I know and am friends with. It just seemed like something was off between you two. Fortunately, the real Chief Estrada and Lieutenant North showed up and common sense took over. Somehow, the chief knew more about your dog than I thought he did. He has a source, somewhere. I just thought you should know. Again, please keep this just between us."

"Keep what between us? I don't know what you are talking about, Javon."

They smiled, shook hands, and as Javon started to leave, he said, "I'll let the chief know you gratefully accept his offer. I will give you a call in a few days after he works out the details with the city manager and city attorney. I'm sure there will be some paperwork for you to fill out."

"There always is."

As Javon walked through the house to the front door, Bonnie said her goodbyes to him. Once he had left and she was sure he was in his vehicle, she said to JW, "It was me. I was listening to you guys. You know me, always nosy. Anyway, I'm the chief's source." JW looked at her, uncertain of what to say, and just motioned for her to continue. "I called his wife—you know we know each other from some of the charity stuff she does. Anyway, I mentioned it to her. I thought it might make it easier if Chief Estrada knew a little about what you had in mind. Hell, I almost screwed up the whole deal."

"You were just trying to help. I don't think it was the information that messed things up, just my lack of knowledge. If you're gonna do Secret Squirrel stuff, let me in on the plan, please."

"Deal. Now get ready for your meeting at Chevrolet and I'll get Ares brushed out and pretty."

"You know Addy is not going to like being left behind."

"Yeah, she's going to have to learn to deal with it. I'll take her on a long walk while you're gone."

JW walked across the showroom floor at the Chevrolet dealership with a large file folder in hand, accompanied by Ares. A quick chat with the receptionist led him to James "Mac" Douglas, the fleet sales manager. Mac stood as they approached and said, "You must be Mr. North, and I bet that is Ares. I asked your wife if you would bring him along—I love dogs."

Soon there was a line of people outside the Fleet Sales Office as other sales reps and office staff came by to meet Ares. JW stood off to the side and just smiled. Dogs were magic. Near the end of the line stood a distinguished-looking gentleman, who said, "Good morning, Mr. North. I'm Derrick Forbes, the owner of this dealership." JW shook his hand and told him how much he loved the dealership. He had purchased several cars there over the past twenty years and was currently driving a Chevrolet Silverado pickup. "Always glad to have your business, Mr. North. Mac told me about your project and I told him to make sure you get our very best service and our absolute best price. I called corporate and asked William Lombard to join us today.

He is a police vehicle specialist out of the L.A. office. He will know about all the bells and whistles available." JW was again surprised by how much support there was in the community for what he and Ares wanted to accomplish. He thanked Mr. Forbes and promised to return and show off the SUV after the police package was installed.

JW and Mac took a seat and Ares settled into a corner. The receptionist, Sally, came in and offered coffee. JW never said no to coffee and gladly accepted that and the offer of water for Ares. JW chatted with Mac while they waited. Mac took special interest in JW's "war stories" of police work. Finally, Mac asked about the shooting. "Are you the officer that was shot earlier this year?" JW nodded and Mac continued, "My God, that was an awful thing. How are you feeling?"

"I'm good. Ready to retire and then go back to work."

"That's a bitter irony, isn't it? You put in your years, do the job the best you can and one incident can throw you off track."

"For me, it's not too bitter. I've always loved working with dogs; there's definitely something special about them and this one is even more so."

"Not to bring up a sore point, but did they ever get the guy who shot you?"

Something changed inside JW; he looked down at Ares and felt a new resolve inside. He looked back at Mac and his eyes shifted from blue to gray. "No, not yet," was all he said.

Mac thought, *There's something about this guy. I sure wouldn't want to be the shooter when he meets up with him.*

As if on cue, William Lombard walked into the room looking a bit harried. "Guys, I apologize. There was a big crash on the 405 freeway. I got tired of waiting and took surface streets for a while to get past it. What a mess." He introduced himself to everyone, including Ares, telling them to call him Bill. "Mr. North, that is one gorgeous dog. Let's see if we can put him in a car that is just as fabulous. If you'll give me half an hour, I have a nice little presentation that will tell you almost everything you want to know about how we outfit police vehicles."

JW said that would be great and that he would take Ares outside for a break while Bill set up. When he returned, they had relocated to a conference room in the back.

The presentation actually lasted closer to an hour. Bill kept stopping the PowerPoint presentation to add his bits in. You could tell the man loved his job. When Bill finished, he took out a notepad and said, "OK, I take it from our furry friend asleep in the corner that this is going to be a K9 unit. Do you know what model vehicle you want?"

JW brought out the folder he had brought with him, saying, "I've been doing some research online. I'm thinking the four-wheel-drive Tahoe Special Service Vehicle, SSV."

"You want the four-by-four, then?" JW nodded. "Great, we have some additions for the K9 that we can do: cage, heat alarm, remote door release and other stuff. If we do that as part of the package, we factor those options in and make some adjustments to maintain your handling, drivability, and pursuit rating. There are a few things that we don't do, like radios and such. We do offer a couple of emergency lighting packages, but those are installed by factory-approved outside vendors, same as the radio."

JW interjected, "This won't be a patrol K9, more of a plain car. It doesn't have to be an 'undercover' unit, but I would like to keep it somewhat anonymous. It will need to be able to run Code Three, though," referring to operating as an emergency vehicle with emergency lights and siren, "potentially outside of California."

"Absolutely, Mr. North. We offer a package that meets the requirements of all fifty states. Now, I would like to be able to put the entire package together for you, ready to roll the day you get it, completely covered and certified to operate as a police vehicle. I will personally deliver the vehicle to you and provide you with a complete overview of all the features. Do you know what kind of radio you want?"

JW wasn't sure of the answer and said, "I'll have to check with the City's radio shop and get back to you on that. Oh, could you do me a favor? I know this is going to be a police car, but I expect to spend a lot of time in it. Is there any way we can upgrade it to make it more comfortable and quieter for long drives? I realize that this is not a grand touring model, but anything you can do to make it easier for me and the dogs would be appreciated. We generally are going to be going to work immediately after we arrive on-scene."

"Again, no problem. I think we can accommodate that. This is going to be a very special vehicle. I'm going to reach out to the boys back at the factory and make sure we get you everything we can, state of the art."

JW opened the folder he had brought with him and went down his checklist of options with Bill. Some features were absolute requirements and others fell into the "sure would be nice" category. He was pleasantly surprised to see that Bill would be able to provide every one of them.

"Now, did I understand correctly that you are going to pay for this out of your own pocket?"

JW nodded and said, "Yes, my wife and I are paying for the vehicle. This is for a special program. I'm going to retire from active-duty police work and become a reserve. The entire program is going to be funded by my wife and me."

"Not a problem. Unusual, but definitely not a problem. Do you think you can get me something in writing authorizing this? We don't normally sell police cars to private citizens."

"Yes, I understand. I'm sure I can get the City to draw something up."

Bill returned to full salesman mode. "OK, I am going to put this all together and get started on getting you a formal quote. You will hear back from me within forty-eight hours."

JW was exhausted when he finally left the dealership, but it was a good kind of exhausted. He finally felt like he was moving forward and making progress. *Dog, check; approval, check; car, check.* It was almost time to start training.

17

In the middle of the night, JW and Bonnie were awakened by two German Shepherds jumping on the bed and climbing all over them. He was startled and wondered, *What the hell has got these dogs so riled up?* Having been a police officer for over thirty years, his mind immediately went to a dark place. *Burglar? If so, then why wasn't the burglar being eaten by his pair of highly trained dogs?*

Bonnie, not used to having an eighty-five-pound dog sitting on her head, said, "JW, what the hell are you doing?"

"Me? I'm not doing anything," he whispered. "The dogs are riled up about something. Stay here and get ready to dial 911 while I go check it out." Bonnie, now more alert to the potential of a threat, grabbed hold of both dogs and reached for her phone. JW got up and hit the four-button release on the small gun safe attached to his nightstand. The door dropped and he reached for his Springfield Armory .45 Operator. He turned to the dogs and gave them a firm, whispered "Bleib," the German command for "stay."

JW raised his pistol to the ready position and began to move out of the room. No need to check to see if the Operator was loaded. He had loaded it personally and then locked it in the safe. Bonnie knew how to care for and operate guns, but more importantly, she knew to leave them in the condition she found them or let him know if she changed something.

Their very lives could depend on things being the way JW expected them to be.

JW used basic search techniques to clear the way. In the Police Academy, he had taught these methods to recruits. Safety depended on using a team to help cover the angles. Nothing drove JW crazier than watching police shows on TV and seeing them get it wrong—in this instance, seeing a two-man team split up to search by themselves. Unfortunately, this time, he would have no backup. He was not going to place Bonnie in jeopardy unless he had to. He used a technique known as pieing to clear the rooms in their house, one by one. This method uses angles to see into rooms. You move side to side, using the angle created by the door jamb to look in, one piece of the pie at a time. As he continued through the house, JW stopped from time to time to listen. The house was quiet, except for the master bedroom. What the heck is wrong with those dogs? JW finished the last room and turned to a window to see if there was something outside. As he started to leave, he heard a loud chirp above him. Say what?

Bonnie was waiting in the bedroom with the dogs, her anxiety rising, worried about JW and what might be going on. Then, from down the hallway, she heard JW laughing. She decided this meant it was clear, released the dogs, and walked toward his continuing laughter. She found JW in the guest bedroom and asked, "OK, what is so funny at three o'clock in the morning?"

The dogs were looking about, concerned looks on their faces. JW merely said, "Wait for it." The loud chirp repeated itself and the dogs ducked like they were being strafed by an F-35 fighter.

JW resumed his laughter and Bonnie looked up. "A smoke alarm? You have got to be kidding me."

"Yep, big, tough German Shepherds, highly trained and fearless, afraid of a smoke alarm low-battery alert."

JW quickly replaced the battery and called the dogs to come with him. "Time to go back to bed. A smoke alarm, you have got to be freakin' kidding me. You two are a disgrace to your breed." Addy and Ares, sufficiently cowed by the admonishment, walked slowly behind JW. If they could have talked, they would have explained to him that they had no idea what a smoke detector was or why it made such a loud noise in the middle of the night. They did know, if they heard it again, they would do the same thing. JW entered the bedroom to find Bonnie already asleep. He got back in bed and the dogs jumped up and were soon asleep. Everyone was asleep, except JW. It would be hours before the adrenaline wore off and he finally dozed off.

JW woke the following morning by himself. He was exhausted from the lack of sleep, but he had a busy day ahead of him. He had his final physical therapy session today and then a trip to the Health Department to talk to the doctor about his return to full duty. Finally, he could go back to work so he could retire and get to work on training Ares. As he stumbled out of the bedroom and walked to Bonnie's office in the front of the house, he was stopped by Addy and Ares who were sprawled on the floor in front of her office. Bonnie heard him and called out, "I'm in here."

"Yeah, I'll be there in a couple, I have to work my way through this 'dogstacle' course first. These two seem exhausted after their trying ordeal last night."

Bonnie laughed and said, "Go get some coffee and come back. I have a couple things to go over with you."

JW stopped at the door. "In here or the dining room?" The dining room seemed to be the place to go for important meetings since they had started this venture. Bonnie started grabbing notebooks and folders and pointed to the dining room.

JW nodded. "You want coffee?" As Bonnie arranged for the morning's meeting, JW entered the dining room carrying a large mug in each hand, and wearing a T-shirt with the slogan, "Coffee saved the world…from me" on it.

Bonnie looked up and said, "You look like a marketing photo for coffee. Well, except for the fact you look like hell from lack of sleep." JW barely managed a smile and sat, waiting to hear the morning's revelations.

"OK, first things first. Bill Lombard called from Chevrolet. He wanted to talk to you, but I explained you were indisposed. He said it wasn't a big deal, but he left me with a bunch of radio names and numbers. Sounded like a very pleasant man as he spoke Greek to me. I have that list for you."

"He's the police vehicle guy, very energetic. I'm not complaining, I think we will have the best they have when we are done, but at what cost?"

"It costs what it costs, but I was hoping the City would take care of that for us."

"Yeah, I had to abandon that idea and tell the chief we were prepared to do this on our own. The good news is he offered up Ben to help us get this going. That is huge and is worth more than we will pay for the car."

Bonnie realized that was probably caused by her miscalculation of being the chief's source for some intel. JW had been blindsided, but had forgiven her, so no need to bring it up again. It did reinforce the need to have better communication between them. That would be a bit of a challenge as JW did not place a high priority on talking.

"Alright, that's one item off my list. I've been working on a budget, but right now there are a lot of unknowns. I don't want you to skimp when it comes to the project. Your and Ares' safety are number one; however, just because we have money, doesn't mean we should spend it. Let's keep our personal spending under control until we get a better idea of what our operating costs are going to be." JW nodded in understanding. "So, here is what I have so far," she said as she handed him the first notebook. "I need a couple things from you, such as vehicle and other equipment costs. For now, let's assume the Department is not going to cover anything. I need to factor in fuel and maintenance. We will SWAG those until we have a better idea. How long do you think the car will last?" JW recognized the term from his days in the military—scientific wild-ass guess. They discussed budget items for a couple of hours until JW had to get ready for therapy. There was still plenty to discuss, but JW hated being late for anything.

After therapy, JW made a few calls and got some solid recommendations from the radio shop. When he explained his concept for the project and the need to communicate with other agencies, the director of communications told him that could be a challenge due to the variety of frequencies and the possibility of encryption. He told JW the best solution currently available was a mobile radio and portables by Motorola. These would work well within the Long Beach system and offer the flexibility he needed. JW looked down at his list from Bill Lombard and there was the make and model at the top. JW smiled. This guy is good.

The release back to work was effortless and soon JW was back at the house. He made a quick call to the personnel department to start arranging his new retirement date. He and Bonnie then decided to take the dogs to the local park to get some exercise. They loaded up, and five minutes later they were at El Dorado Park. JW picked an area away from other people and opened the back hatch for the dogs. No sooner had Ares and Addy jumped out of the car than they were swamped by a family with five kids. "Can we pet your dogs, sir? Please!"

JW liked kids well enough so he said, "Sure." He watched cautiously, as he didn't know if these dogs had had a chance to interact with young children. His worries were for nothing, Addy started licking the kids as they petted her. Ares was enjoying the attention.

"Mister, are these police dogs?"

The question surprised JW a little. "Well, the big dog there is going to be. His name is 'Ares.' The other one is 'Addy' and she probably won't be."

A little girl, particularly enamored with Addy, asked, "Why? Isn't she good enough?"

Bonnie smiled and asked, "Yeah, JW, isn't she good enough?"

"She certainly has the potential," he said as he looked at Bonnie with a question in his eyes. *What is going on here?* "But she is my wife's dog. I'm not sure she wants her to be a police dog." The answer seemed to satisfy the little girl and she went back to fussing over Addy.

The father asked, "Can we get a picture of my kids with your dogs?"

JW thought about it and said, "Sure, go ahead." The five kids were arranged around Ares and Addy as carefully as if this were the family holiday portrait. JW took out a tennis ball and brought it to eye level. A quick "Bleib" was issued and JW said they were ready. The dogs' eyes were fixated on the green ball. *Target lock.*

As the family left, Bonnie said to JW, "See, they're celebrities already. I am OK with you giving Addy a little training. I don't want you putting her in harm's way, but as you often say, 'Always have a backup.'"

JW thought this was a good idea. *Why waste her talent?* "Good idea, Bon, but I want to get Ares done first so we can get rolling. I'll bring her along afterward when we have more time."

The dogs were then released and had a fun couple of hours, chasing their balls, and playing in the isolated area. When everyone was tired, they loaded up in the SUV. It had been an enjoyable day, but soon the work would begin.

18

It took JW longer to get all the approvals than he would have liked, but he understood that these would be important in the long run. He did not want to be a vigilante; therefore, he needed to operate under the umbrella of a law enforcement agency. Although he was anxious to get going, the delay allowed more time to get his vehicle ready. JW had arranged for permission to use the K9 training area located at the police academy next to El Dorado Park, an expansive park located on the east side of Long Beach. It had areas ranging from picnic grounds to more natural settings including a nature center, an eighteen-hole golf course, and the site of the 1984 Olympic archery competition. Once they got going on running trails, it would be a great place to train.

The K9 training area included a large kennel complex as well as an obedience field and K9 obstacle course. JW knew the K9 sergeant, Jason Plein, and most of the current K9 handlers. Sergeant Plein had no issue with sharing the facility with JW and Ares, but JW could tell he was a bit unhappy about having to share Officer Ben Kellum with him. JW would have to think about how to make amends. Ares worked through the obstacles and obedience exercises easily. A lot of things about dogs that JW had forgotten were slowly coming back. He understood on a subconscious level that he needed to be able to read the dog, to understand the subtle clues he would give off while trailing. This would come with practice and time with Ares, but his timing on corrections needed some work. This was as much about JW learning to work with Ares as it was about Ares. It gave Ares and JW an outlet for their energy and provided JW with a sense of moving forward. He was frustrated because he wanted to have Ares trained and certified, but he realized it was important to take their time and get it right. They would probably only get one chance at this before the chief retired them both.

While training one day, JW received a call from Communications Supervisor Sunny Gabrielle. "Hey, LT, how's it going?"

JW remembered Sunny from his many phone calls to the center over the years; she had been a shift supervisor then. Now, he had heard, she was in charge. "Hi, Sunny, I heard about your promotion. Congratulations!"

"Thanks, LT. Hey, I heard a rumor you might be coming back with a dog?"

"No rumor. I'm going to give it a go and see how it works."

"That's great, LT. I guess we'll be talking more often then. Is this number good for you for call-outs?" JW remembered being called out for a variety of reasons over the years. Calls at 3:00 a.m. typically do not deliver good news.

Fortunately, this call was during normal business hours. "Yeah, this number will work for now. The Department hasn't given me a phone or email yet, but once I have them, I'll update your roster."

"Excellent, sir. I got a call from on high to issue you a radio call sign. I have earmarked 'King 99' for you, if that's OK." All K9s in Long Beach are issued a call sign based on seniority, starting with King One. There weren't ninety-eight other dogs, but it was not uncommon for reserves and support units to be issued call signs from the bottom of a sequence.

"Yes, ma'am, that works."

Sunny decided it was time to give the new guy a little hazing. "Now, LT, you do recall how the radio works?"

JW decided to play along. "Well, I remember you push the button and then talk, but I can't remember what to say."

Laughing as she said it, she replied, "Well, LT, we have a couple of dispatchers in training, so if you need a refresher, we can get you into a class." JW laughed and thanked her for the call. King 99. He liked the sound of that.

Before JW could put the phone away, it rang again. "Mr. North, this is Bill Lombard. I have your vehicle here at the dealer and want to know if you'd like to take delivery of it today. I know you're excited to get going, so I brought it down here as soon as it rolled into L.A."

Wow, this is the day for good news. "Thanks, Bill. I can be there in about forty-five minutes." As he was leaving the Academy, JW called Bonnie and told her the car was in. "Hey, why don't I swing by and pick you up so I can drive the new car home? We can take Addy—she'd probably like to get out." Bonnie agreed; she was tired of staring at budget spreadsheets and could use a break herself. Besides, if she got bored, she could come home and leave JW there.

JW and Bonnie arrived at the dealership with Ares and Addy. The two German Shepherds again garnered attention from everyone, including several staff from the dealership next door who wandered over. JW introduced Bonnie to everyone and then met with Bill. JW thanked him profusely for speeding his car along as quickly as he had. He told Bill, "I think if I had to appropriate my wife's car one more time, she might divorce me."

"Well, we can't have that," replied Bill.

Before they started the tour, JW noticed how shiny the black paint was and how clean the car was. He commented, "Bill, this car glows."

"Yeah, I might have had the guys do a full detail. Don't tell anyone." Then he started the Tahoe with the key and said, "This feature keeps the car running after you remove the key. Press this button here and then rotate and remove the key. This way you can keep the AC running, but the car won't go into gear if someone tries to take it. Helps keep the dogs alive in hot weather. This button overrides the heat alarm. If, for some reason, the car gets too hot, it will set off a very noisy alarm. That works whether the car is on or not, thus the override. You don't want it going off during the day when you are parked at home. The override resets at each restart, so no need to worry about permanently disabling the alarm. There's an app you can put on your smartphone that will alert you, too."

JW realized that the walkthrough was going to take a while. He saw Bonnie walking over with the dogs and told her, "This may take a while. Maybe you want to go home and sit this one out?" She agreed and told him she was going to leave both dogs with him. JW opened the back door of the Tahoe and both dogs immediately jumped in without command. A K9 enclosure was now housed where the backseat had been removed. They both decided it was nap time and dropped off, ignoring Bill's talking.

Bill continued on, providing detailed instructions. "One cool thing they did, since this wasn't a patrol K9, they integrated the emergency lights and radio into the infotainment display. You can access them by using either the menus or verbal commands. Take the driver's seat and push that button on the steering wheel and say 'Police Radio.'" JW did as instructed and the display changed to a custom screen with several selections.

"Since your radio shop is going to program the frequencies for you, it doesn't show anything right now. The system will load those into the infotainment display automatically. It's made to be as user friendly as possible. OK, now say 'Emergency Lights.'" Again, JW did as instructed and the screen changed to an emergency lighting control display. "Now, you can give verbal commands for a lot of stuff like, 'Police Radio Channel One' or try this one: 'Emergency Lights Position Three.'" JW repeated the command and then got out. Bill pointed out the lights to him as they walked around the vehicle. JW was impressed. Bill told him, "This has the full Christmas tree package for you."

JW paused and looked at Bill. "Bill, this seems to have a lot of features we didn't discuss."

"Yeah, I might have told the folks back at corporate about you and what you are doing and they might have done just about everything they could think of. Mr. North, this Tahoe has every feature available and everything they have in the planning stages. Oh, and I might have mentioned to corporate that you were paying for this personally, and they might have given you a special price. What can I say, they all have a soft spot for police dogs."

"I'm not sure I follow all this Bill. I don't want to seem ungracious; it is just a bit overwhelming."

"Mr. North, let me put it this way. When I tell people that there is a guy in Long Beach that is funding his own K9 unit, well, let's just say that gets their attention. You might be surprised how much people want to support something like this."

"Yeah, it seems like every time we have a dog injured here in Long Beach, the community gets together and donates money to our K9 unit. I guess I just thought it was a Long Beach thing. Please tell everyone how much I appreciate what they have done."

"Sure thing, Mr. North."

The orientation lasted over two hours. At the end, Bill gave JW a pile of papers and the keys. JW went through it all and wrote out a check. "Mr. North, it has been a pleasure doing business with you. If there are ever any issues, call me, any time, any day. Here's my card with my cell phone number. If you need anything, call me."

JW thanked him and said, "Bill, I believe I have asked you to call me 'JW' once or twice. If you don't start, I'm never calling you again."

"Yes, sir, JW."

JW drove to the radio shop and they quickly programmed his radios using the Panasonic Toughbook mounted in the car. It was a straightforward process, but the tech told him they knew he was coming and had done a quick review of the instructions they had received from Chevrolet. Bill thinks of everything. Before he departed, the tech also told him, "This has a couple of cool features; we program it here on the laptop and you can send that programming to the two handheld radios in the back. Once we get the correct equipment, we can reprogram your radios while you are on the road and just transmit it to you."

Once JW was done and had made it back home, he was swamped by his neighbors. They all knew who he was and were surprised to see the new vehicle. One neighbor commented, "JW, I thought you were retiring."

"Well, not exactly," he said and then explained the new project. His neighbor seemed surprised but simply said, "Well, alright then. Good luck. We're all behind you."

19

The next available training day, JW and Ben met at a more isolated area of El Dorado Park. Both were wearing the unofficial training uniform of the project—tan 5.11 trousers and a white LBPD polo shirt, as well as ballistic vests worn on the outside of their shirts. Seeing the new Tahoe, Ben proceeded to give him some serious crap about the SUV.

Ben then reintroduced Allen Whelan. Allen had been a part of the original project and had an extensive background in trailing dogs. Ben had asked him to help teach JW everything he knew about scent and trailing. Allen was a tall, lean man, who appeared to be very fit. He was significantly older than JW, with a full head of gray hair. While JW and Allen became reacquainted, Ben began crawling over every inch of the Tahoe. After playing for fifteen minutes, Ben rejoined them. JW could clearly see the jealousy in Ben's eyes and told him, "Hey, if we can make this work and you retire, I can see one of those in your future."

Ben nodded and said, "Food for thought."

Allen said, "Well, let's see this boy of yours." JW let Ares out and Allen immediately proclaimed, "Oh my Lord, he is certainly a pretty boy. Ben tells me he tested very well and has a very comprehensive German tracking background. All of that is great, it makes a great foundation. We're going to start out slowly. I am sure Ben has told you this is as much for you as him. I expect him to have to work harder once we start transitioning to city work on streets and sidewalks. He is used to working off-road and I expect the change will be a bit challenging at first. OK, let's get to it."

"Before we get started with Ares, I want to give you a present. I called a friend from the original Project and got this for you." Ben handed JW a black Pelican box. JW set the box down on the bench next to their training area and opened it.

Allen then picked up the narrative. "This is a Scent Transfer Unit or 'STU.' You are probably more familiar with the original models that were developed; they looked like dust-busters on steroids. The government took that concept and one of their research and development units came up with this streamlined, rechargeable, battery-operated unit. You will remember the basic concept is that we use the vacuum to suck the scent of our suspect from an item he has had contact with. In this case, it will be the seat of Ben's car. Ares probably hasn't trailed using a scent pad collected with a STU, but we need to start off doing this as we will do it in the field. As the army says, 'Train as you fight and fight as you train.'"

Ben handed JW a box of plastic bags, a box of four-by-four gauze pads and a box of sterile medical gloves and said, "You're going to need a lot of these. Have Bonnie buy them in bulk online."

"Next is this GPS tracking unit. Attach it to his harness and we will use it to grade his trails. I used it when we marked them yesterday, so together we will have a 'verified' trail. Since I am the suspect, Allen will act as your backup and he will grade Ares' work. He's going to evaluate how well he follows the trail, how he works, and how he does on the turns. This will all go into a computer-based training and trailing record. You will enter every training event you attend and every trail you run. This is all part of the package we will begin to assemble on the two of you. A portion of it includes all his German records, but they don't use a system like ours, so you will keep that separately in a section at the front. When you go to court, all your records will be subpoenaed. You don't want to have to explain why something is missing. I have added the trails you guys ran at Von Liche, so you are already developing your resume."

Ben pointed toward the open field to their left. "I'm your bad guy for the day. I've laid out five tracks with varying lengths for you." Ben then walked off to hide in some trees while Allen showed JW how to properly perform scent collection.

"Remember, JW, always do this the same way and exactly as I show you. You will be called on to testify as to procedure in court. If everyone does it the same, then it is easy to remember what to say." JW nodded and assembled the machine and then proceeded to collect five scent pads from the driver's seat, following Allen's instructions exactly.

Once JW was done with this, he let Ares out of the back of the Tahoe. The big dog stretched and walked over to a tree to leave his mark. JW then slipped on the tracking harness, but not before Allen had inspected it and said, "Very nice. From Germany?"

"Yes, along with two tracking leads of five and ten meters."

Allen smiled and said, "Nice, first class all the way. OK, let's see your boy work." He pointed at Ben's car and said, "This is a stolen car. Officers report the suspect ran from it, but they are uncertain of which way. Run a trail from the open door and locate the suspect."

JW went to the open car door and placed Ares on a down stay. He clipped his five-meter lead on and then opened the bag and scented Ares, giving him the command, "Zur Spur." Ares immediately stood and began a slow cast until he hit the scent on the trail. He then pulled into the trail with JW close behind. JW had been paying attention to Ben in Indiana and now wore gloves and provided some resistance to Ares to slow him and help keep him focused on the trail.

The trail crossed over the open ground and into some trees. Ares continued trailing, moving easily between the trees until he came across Ben, sitting at a picnic table. Ares looked at him for a moment, his head raised, scenting the air, and then sat. Allen said, "OK, lots of praise, JW." JW grabbed Ares and patted him and told him he was a good boy. It felt good to be successful, but not the same as in Indiana. JW guessed the next time he felt that way would be when they captured their first suspect.

JW, Ben, and Allen walked back to the cars, Allen critiquing along the way. He seemed very pleased with what he saw, but he critiqued every little detail of the trail. JW was fairly certain that only perfection would bring a smile to Allen's face. JW was OK with that.

"One more thing, Lieutenant North. You gave the German command for trailing, 'Zur Spur'; I am not fond of it. What do you think about changing it to something some of the American handlers use? It's an old Native American word for hunting, 'Geo-say.' An old friend and mentor used it and I would consider it an honor to him if you could also."

JW looked at Ben and he shrugged.

"Why not?" JW knew he would have to give both commands for a while until Ares adapted to the change.

The next few trails went about the same. Ares continued to perform as expected for a dog with a lot of tracking experience. These trails, although more aged than Ares was used to, were not much of a challenge for him. The last trail set up like the first four. Allen gave JW the scent pad and, after Ares sniffed the scent, he started off and picked the trail up immediately. After many twists and turns through the woods, they finally reached Ben. Ares stopped and looked at him for a moment and then turned hard and went back to the trail. JW started to correct Ares, but Allen stopped him. "Not yet, JW. Let him work it a bit." The trail led out of the woods and back to the road, but in another area of the park. Ares stopped at the road and did a few circles, working out the trail. Eventually, Ares started down the road and continued. After almost half a mile, Allen stopped them and said, "Give him lots of praise, JW. That was damn impressive. Let's go back and Ben and I can explain what you just did."

JW nodded and started walking back with Allen. As they walked along the road, JW said, "Allen, you are at least ten years older than I am, yet you run like a deer, don't sweat at all, and never seem winded. How the hell do you do it?"

"Clean living," was the only explanation he offered.

When they made it back to the cars, JW gave Ares some water and a short break. He started the Tahoe, put Ares back into the air-conditioned SUV, and addressed Ben and Allen. "OK, please explain to me what just happened."

Ben started with, "That was a bit of a test for Ares and you. The trail was laid by one of the K9 handlers three days ago. It was longer than the rest, with more turns and certainly rougher terrain."

"Yeah, I noticed. It kicked my butt and Allen isn't even breathing heavy. Clean living my ass." They all laughed.

Allen continued, "Well, JW, I've been working dogs for a long time. When you spend as much time as I do looking at the south end of a northbound dog, you'd better be in shape or die. The last trail was tricky for both you and Ares. Ben was on the trail, like he has been all day, except Ares knew by the scent that he was not trailing Ben. What you didn't know was I switched out the scent pad for another one.

"So, when Ares got there, he gave him a 'what are you doing here?' look and then he continued. At that point you wanted to pull him off the trail and correct him, but you would have been wrong and that would have hurt his training and set him back. You have to learn all the subtle clues he gives you. They are there. It's easy for me, I know what is going on. Today, we were testing you. In the future, it will be a mix of testing and teaching. When we are teaching, I will point things out to you to help you learn. Every dog is different, and Ares is certainly different from what I am used to with bloodhounds.

"So here is where it got interesting. Ares was doing a good job and worked out that Ben wasn't his target and then he continued, which is exactly what your suspect did. When Ares got to the road, he circled and worked the trail, like he would a turn. Then he started up and we went for a half-mile jog. I called it at that point because I had seen what I needed to. I can tell you, I am a believer. This dog is something special and he is going to be one hell of a man trailer when we're done. You'd better get used to the idea, JW, you are going to be in big demand. Not many dogs are as good as he is, period. You just don't see it, even in bloodhounds. Here is what happened at the end. Your suspect got in a car. One with the windows closed, but the ventilation on.

"I know you know about scent. It is a real, physical thing. It has weight and substance. That is what allows it to stick around over longer periods of time. How long depends on the conditions present. On most cars with some form of flow-through ventilation, that scent is going to pass through and out, unless the suspect has it on recirculation. That scent collects, just like it would normally, just not as much comes out and it can disperse a little more due to the speed of the vehicle. A lot of this is theoretical, and many people don't believe a dog can do it, but you just saw it. Hell, if I had let him, I bet Ares would have gone up to that guy's house and knocked on the door. We saw it work today, and we are going to do this a lot when we get further along in training. Everything is documented and we will submit that to the academics. They won't give it a lot of gravity because they weren't there to control the testing, but it can still be added to the body of information. Hopefully, we can get some interest like we had ten years ago and put together another series of studies, this time focusing on car trails. If we can do that, then we are on the way to gaining general acceptance. Great work today, gentlemen," and then turning towards the Tahoe, "You too, Ares."

With that, training for the day ended. JW and Ares returned home and, upon arrival, Addy began barking at JW and jumping around him. He guessed she was saying, "Oh you think you can go off and leave me all day. Where have you been, mister?"

Training continued over the next few weeks at the same pace. JW was officially retired and sworn in as a reserve lieutenant. All the agreements with the City were signed and sealed and the program now existed officially.

JW was invited to speak at one of the monthly Management Training Days for all the Long Beach officers, lieutenants and above. He explained what the program was about, how it would work once he was certified and where he hoped it would go eventually. The training was really a sales job. The people listening to his presentation would help determine the fate of his program because they would be the ones to encourage their officers and detectives to use JW and Ares.

The good news was many of the people in the room were his friends and had a favorable impression of working dogs. Those who weren't, well, they might look stupid if the program worked and it was discovered they weren't utilizing him. Their call. JW could feel a bit of tension in the room. Clearly, not everyone here was open to the idea. A good sales pitch was one thing, but these guys would want to see proof. Cops are definitely 'Doubting Thomases.'

Things were going well, and everything seemed to be on track. A firm believer and victim of Murphy's Law, JW started looking over his shoulder. Things had been going too smoothly. Something had to happen, he knew it. He just didn't know what direction it was going to come from.

20

Murphy's Law struck in a manner JW was not expecting. It wasn't the disaster he feared, but instead a complication with the potential to throw his program off track. He was home, sitting in his living room reading a book by a new author, Jack Carr. Bonnie was in the kitchen, working on the beginnings of the evening meal. As she was working with food, she had the undivided attention of both dogs. JW's cell phone rang but he didn't recognize the number. He did, however, recognize the 703 area code—it was Quantico, Virginia, site of the FBI National Academy, where he'd spent some time early in his career. He didn't usually answer his phone when he didn't know who was calling, but decided that perhaps he should answer this time. The National Academy, often referred to as the NA, served as a multi-jurisdictional training program for middle and upper police management.

"Is this Lieutenant North?"

"Yes, JW North here." He instantly feared it was a telemarketer and started thinking of ways to get off the phone.

"Hi, Lieutenant North. My name is Dr. Lauralynn Gaurdia. I'm with the Federal Bureau of Investigation here in Quantico."

Having been to the National Academy, JW wondered if Lauralynn might be connected to it. "Hello, Dr. Gaurdia. By any chance, are you with the NA?"

"No, Lieutenant, nor am I soliciting a donation."

They both laughed at her joke and JW asked, "OK, well how can I help the FBI today?"

"Right to the point, I see. I like that. I have been made aware of your current work by a mutual friend who has asked to remain anonymous for the time being. I know of the work your agency did in the past with human scent and trailing. You are probably aware that your agency assisted the FBI on a few cases during that time, with some interesting results. We were rather disappointed that your leadership decided to discontinue the work."

"Sorry, Doctor, such decisions are made at a level much higher than JW North."

"I am aware of that, Lieutenant North. I'm going to be in Los Angeles next week and I was hoping that we could get together and discuss your current project. I would be very interested in seeing your new partner, Ares, work. Do you think that would be possible?"

"I am always happy to be of any assistance to the FBI, Dr. Gaurdia. I just want to warn you that Ares and I are still in training and are not ready for prime time right now. Of course, you are still welcome to come; just know that we won't be certified and ready to work for at least a few more months. We will be training on Tuesday morning. I can get you the particulars later this week when I have the details. But first, would you do me a favor, please? Would you call the Long Beach Chief's office and make the request through him? He gets kind of touchy about things like this."

"Certainly, Lieutenant. I understand the political realities and am happy to do so. I will send you an email with my contact information. I'll have a couple of colleagues with me. Perhaps you can make arrangements for all of us to go to lunch Tuesday afternoon."

"Yes, ma'am. I can do that," said JW, and they ended the call. As JW disconnected, Bonnie was standing in front of him. She definitely had a nose for when there was information she should know. "That was the FBI. You didn't call them and drop a hint in their ear, too, did you?"

"Really? Come on, that was one time and you know I admitted it was wrong. Besides, I don't know anyone at the FBI. What did they want?"

"Hang on a minute, Hon. I want to call Ben and see if he contacted someone."

JW was off the line in a few minutes and went to find Bonnie.

"Ben doesn't know anything, either. He knows the agent who called, though. He worked with her on the old project. She is some kind of academic, obviously has her Ph.D. She works in the Behavioral Analysis Unit, which is kind of a think tank that studies serial criminals—think the Scott Glenn character in *Silence of the Lambs*. Anyway, she is very interested in our work and is going to be in Los Angeles next week with a couple of her colleagues. She wants to see Ares work and then have lunch with us. I have no idea who is talking to the FBI about us. I know one thing for sure, Chief Estrada is not going to be happy about this. I'm going to call Javon Hudson right now and let him know about the call coming in. Maybe I can head off some of the shitstorm that may be coming our way."

There it was, the Federal Bureau of Investigation. JW had considered their involvement with his project, but had hoped to put it off until later, when he and Ares were both ready. He was very concerned that this Dr. Gaurdia would not be sufficiently impressed, and it could lead to the program either stalling or failing altogether. He knew that ultimately the program would need to go national, there just wasn't enough work locally to justify it, even if he was a volunteer. He just wasn't ready for it so soon.

It was a typical Monday morning for Commander Javon Hudson. Everyone wanted a piece of the chief's time and part of his job was to work with the rest of the staff and make sure they could fit everything in. The chief of staff never had a lot of downtime and today was certainly no exception. It was early and he was the only one in the office. He had woken up without the alarm clock and could not get back to sleep. Finally, he gave up on the idea of sleep and got up, being quiet so as not to disturb his wife. Now that he was at his desk, the fatigue of his early wake up was hitting him hard.

His mind wandered, back to a time early in his career. He was new to the job and ready to conquer the world. All rookies were—it took years before they began to lose their innocence. He was working Central Long Beach in a black and white. His beat was known for its poverty and crime, particularly the heavy drug use and sales.

He had been dispatched to a disturbance involving a man possibly under the influence of drugs. He heard several units chiming in on the radio, advising dispatch that they were also en route. When he arrived, he parked out front and walked into the courtyard of a two-story apartment building. Young children lined the upper walkway looking down at him. He felt like a gladiator in early Rome in the coliseum. *Those who are about to die salute you.* There was certainly something happening here, and they would probably start passing out the popcorn soon. His eyes and ears scanned, seeking out the bad guy. Where the hell was he? He glanced at his audience again and saw their eyes move from him to the rear of the structure, toward the opening that led to the carports and alley.

A large man came toward him, naked and sweating profusely. His eyes were glazed over and he walked as if uncertain as to where the ground was. He was sweating like crazy, yet the day wasn't even warm. *PCP!* PCP was a powerful drug; it had been immensely popular before he started working as a cop. An analog of PCP, Ketamine, was used in medicine for its anesthetic properties. It had the benefit of relieving pain, but also elevated vital signs. On the street they called it "Angel Dust" and users were known as "Dusters." The old timers talked about having incredible fights with people under the influence of PCP. They were superhero strong and felt no pain.

Javon ordered the man to stop as he reached for his handheld radio to update dispatch. *Two men enter, one leaves. Thunderdome. Oh shit!* Hudson keyed the microphone on his radio, but before he could say anything the man charged. All he managed to say was, "Duster! Help!" before the man knocked him to the ground, his radio skidding along the hard concrete that was the courtyard of the apartment complex. *Nice landscaping.*

Javon felt the man, astride him, pulling at his pistol. *Fuck, I am going to die today!* The man couldn't get the gun out of the holster; it was a well-made model by Safariland that offered Level III retention. A Level III holster offered three different types of retention in order to draw the gun from the holster. The man pulled so hard he literally almost tore the gun and holster from his belt. *This guy was so fucking strong!* Javon knew he was fighting for his life, and he began striking the man in the face with his fists. The blows served as a distraction and the man left the gun and started choking him. Javon kept striking him as hard as he could, but then started to tire of the fight. He heard sirens and knew he only had to stay in the fight for a few more minutes. *The boys are coming for you, motherfucker!*

Over the man's shoulder, Javon saw another man, bigger than the suspect. He was wearing a uniform. *It's a brother in blue. Thank God!* His uniform was a little different than Javon's, more like a tactical uniform. *K9 handler?* The officer reached down to the man, hooked his hand under the man's chin and pulled him up and off Javon. He slid an arm around the man's neck until his elbow was centered on the front of his neck, and he began to squeeze. This wasn't the infamous choke hold, but rather a carotid restraint. There was no pressure on the delicate windpipe. Pressure was applied to the carotid arteries on the sides of the neck, reducing blood flow to the brain and rendering the suspect temporarily unconscious. Having pulled the man up and off Javon, the officer now applied downward pressure, forcing the man to his knees. *Textbook, just like I was taught in the Academy.* Javon saw the man's eyes roll up and he was out. The officer lowered the suspect to the ground and, as he reached for his handcuffs, five more brothers in blue arrived.

Before the officer could get his handcuffs on the man, his eyes opened again; PCP can be like that. Normally, the carotid restraint would keep someone unconscious long enough to apply the handcuffs, but PCP changed the rules. The man was back and now he was really angry. Before he could get back up, the officer was on him, forcing him back to the ground. Several other officers grasped his arms, trying to force them behind his back. The man continued to fight, still strong. Finally, the officers got a handcuff on each wrist and were able to pull the man's arms together. One of the officers told Javon they would transport the man to L.A. County Jail for him. No way they would take him in our jail, too violent and high. The initial officer reached down and helped Javon to his feet. He said his name was North, JW North. "Hudson," was all he could squeak out. His voice was almost gone from being choked. Javon was exhausted and could hardly breathe. The time of the fight from beginning to end was only one minute. That could be a lifetime.

They began to walk out of the complex and were confronted by a group of young children. The first one said, "Hey, Police, you got any stickers?" Javon knew they wanted the adhesive Junior Police Officer stickers available from Community Relations. He forgot to get any and could only shake his head.

North said, "Hang on, I have some." He reached into his shirt pocket and pulled out a handful of stickers. He reached into the other for some baseball-style trading cards with pictures of a police dog. Javon watched North interact with the kids—he was kind, but not patronizing. These kids grew up hard here and North knew it. "OK, guys. You want to be police when you grow up?" Some responded "Yes," but not all. "OK, then put your stickers on and repeat after me, 'When I grow up, I promise to be good and not an asshole like that idiot,'" pointing to the suspect now being carried to a waiting police car. Javon knew that if someone complained, the language would get North a trip to Internal Affairs and a letter of reprimand. Yet, somehow it all seemed appropriate.

The kids looked at the trading cards and one asked, "Hey, Police, you a K9? Can we pet your dog?"

North said, "Sure, hang on." He turned to the senior officer of a two-man training unit, and asked, "Billy, can you have your rookie drive Hudson's car to the station? I'll take him to Community Hospital and have him checked out."

The officers conferred for a moment and the rookie said, "Officer Hudson, I got your ride. I'll park it downtown near the back steps."

North got his dog out of the car; it looked more like a wolf than a dog, raw power and strength. The dog turned toward the kids and wagged his tail. Javon lost sight of the dog as the kids swarmed over him. North turned back to him and said, "Hudson, get in the car. Let's go get you looked at." He put the dog in the back of his unit, a big Tahoe SUV, and opened the rear hatch. He handed Hudson a sterile gauze pad and said, "Hold this on the back of your head, I don't want you bleeding all over my car." As he sat, the dog put his head out of the K9 cage behind him. Its head was massive, intimidating. *This dog scares the crap out of me.* The dog licked his face. "Hudson, meet Asko," said Officer North.

They went to the hospital, had X-rays taken, and did all the things that hospitals and doctors do. He talked with North to pass the time, pointed at his holster, and told him the man almost tore it from his belt. North looked at it and told him, "That's a good holster. I had one of the early models and it saved my life."

A young nurse flirted with him while she checked his blood pressure. They shaved the back of his head and gave him two stitches. The nurse said she thought he would look good with a shaved head. All the while, JW North stood to the side watching him. A sergeant came and talked with North and then did a stack of paperwork to document his injury. Finally, the doctor said he was fit to go. As he left, the nurse hurried up to him and handed him a piece of paper. She shook his hand and said her name was Alesha. He looked at the paper and saw her name and a phone number. He smiled at her as North walked him out. Later that night, he shaved his head. It would remain that way for the rest of his life. A few days later, he called the nurse. Two years later they were married and JW North was the best man at the wedding.

JW told him, "Stop calling me 'sir.' 'JW' is just fine." JW explained that the doctor was putting him off work for the day. He needed to go to the Health Department the next day to get cleared for work and not to come to work without the pink "Return to Work" form. They wouldn't let him back without it. They drove to the station and, while Hudson changed, JW arranged for another officer, Donald Harrison, to drive his car home. JW didn't want him to drive. When they got to his apartment building, he thanked

JW for everything and said goodbye. As he started to leave the car, JW said, "Javon, next time you wait for your fucking backup." His eyes were cold and gray and Javon knew he meant it. JW pulled away without another word.

Hudson paused for a moment, reflecting on the mistakes he made that night. His TAC officer at the Academy had told him, "Mistakes are your friend, recruit. Learn from them and be better as a result, but don't repeat them." A small piece of the innocence in Javon Hudson chipped away that night, but the next day he was back to work on the same beat, doing the job. It seemed right; he was born and grew up in this neighborhood, he should be the one to protect it.

The next day he went to Community Relations to pick up some Junior Police Officer stickers. The receptionist greeted him and said, "Oh hi, Officer Hudson, here are your stickers." Javon looked at her, confused; he hadn't asked yet.

"Officer North said you would be coming by."

Javon snapped out of the dream as one of the staff came in. "Hey, Javon, you're here early. Are you OK?"

"Oh, yeah, I'm good. I guess you caught me daydreaming there for a second."

"Well, OK then. I think I'll make some coffee. You look like you could use some."

Javon paused for a moment and thought about the daydream. It had been like he was watching a movie, a participant and a viewer at the same time. Why are you thinking about that now, Javon? Easy answer. JW North had called on Friday and given him a heads up that the FBI was coming. JW was his friend, a good friend, who had looked out for him, and he needed to do the same.

21

Chief Estrada arrived at his usual time and asked Javon to join him in his office. "You want some coffee, Chief?" Javon started walking to the coffee pot, knowing the chief would say yes.

He went inside and they sat in the small seating area. Time to go over the calendar for the day. "OK, so what do we have today? First thing, I know we have the City Council meeting tomorrow night. Is everything in order for that?"

Javon said, "Yes, we're good. Nothing on the agenda for us."

"OK, so who's first?"

"Your first meeting is at nine a.m. with Dr. Lauralynn Gaurdia with the FBI."

"Yeah, I saw that on the calendar. Who is she and what does she want?"

"She didn't say much. Lieutenant North called me to give us a heads up. He said she's from Quantico, somehow involved in the old trailing project, and she wants to come out and watch him work his dog. He said she reached out to him directly and he told her the request would have to come through the chief's office. JW told her that he and the dog are not very far along, but if she wants to watch, he is OK with it if you are."

Chief Estrada thought for a moment. "Boy, that didn't take long, did it? Remember? I told you the feds would be after him. Do we know how she found out about the new dog?"

"JW said he didn't know. He says it wasn't him and I believe him."

"OK, good. It will be interesting to see what she has to say. Tell JW thanks for the heads up."

Javon made a quick note and continued with his briefing.

At 8:50 a.m. Dr. Gaurdia entered the headquarters of the Long Beach Police Department. Her escort from the front desk told the secretary who she was and she was promptly ushered into Commander Hudson's office. Hudson greeted her and offered her coffee, which she politely refused. Commander Hudson looked her over, evaluating her. Dr. Gaurdia knew that he was wondering why she was here. He and the chief would be concerned any time the FBI came on their turf. Most officers in law enforcement liked working with the feds, some more than others, but all were wary of the FBI. They had a bit of a reputation for wanting to know everything and sharing very little. When she had met with the director of the FBI prior to her trip to California, he had warned her and given her a couple of favors she could throw their way if she needed to. She had dressed up a little bit today, wearing a beige business suit. Always important to make a good first impression.

Commander Hudson probed a bit, trying to gather some intelligence from her. She played a bit coy, not because she had to, but it was fun to experiment from time to time. She had a Ph.D. in psychology and a law degree. She was smart and she knew it, and she knew how to maneuver in rough waters. Not that she was expecting any trouble, at least not yet. At 9:00 a.m., Commander Hudson took her into Chief

Estrada's office. The chief greeted her warmly and offered her coffee. She declined with a smile, then commented, "You guys seem to drink a lot of coffee."

"Yes ma'am, it flows freely through our veins." He seemed honest; she liked that.

She decided to play her best card first. "The director sends his greetings from Washington." She paused, giving them time to process that. "He says good things about the Long Beach P.D. and would like to extend our gratitude for the work your detectives have done with the Joint Terrorism Task Force."

"We are always happy to maintain good working relationships with our federal partners. I look forward to continuing and possibly expanding our ties," Chief Estrada replied.

"The director mentioned that there was a new position, funded through a grant, that would be opening up soon. Perhaps you would be interested?" She could tell the chief was interested, just by his body language. People were always interested when you invited them to the big game and offered to pay, too.

"That certainly would be of interest."

"Well then, I am sure you are aware that I would like to view some training exercises involving your new scent dog program." She knew JW North would have called and warned them that she was coming. "The FBI had an excellent working relationship with your agency several years ago when you were doing something similar."

The chief nodded and said, "Yes, I do recall that. Are you looking to use Lieutenant North on a case?"

"Not at this time. I know he isn't ready yet, but I am interested in what he is doing. We had some positive results with the previous project."

"Yes, we had some good and not-so-good results. We were forced to make a decision concerning the cost of a K9 officer that was frequently away from our city."

"Well, that is the nature of these things. Scent evidence is always going to be only one contributor to solving a case. The courts will not allow us to make a case based purely on scent evidence. As for the cost, the director indicated that, should we have a use for the dog and you were willing to partner with us, he would be willing to pay for the position with some form of grant."

The chief smiled, he thought he had her here. "You may not know this, Doctor, but Lieutenant North has retired. He is working for us as a reserve officer. He has paid for the dog, his car, everything, out of his own pocket."

Of course, she knew this. Lauralynn Gaurdia always did her homework and she had excellent sources. "Oh, in that case, if we did use him, there wouldn't be a huge negative impact for your department." *Boom! Now toss the bone.* "The director also mentioned that there are some new technology initiatives—you know, SWAT things—that are coming up. I believe one of the initiatives involves training with our Hostage Rescue Team in Quantico. Perhaps Long Beach would like to evaluate some of their toys. Of course, you would be able to keep them after the evaluation period."

Chief Estrada shook his head, as if he was clearing it, and said, "I am sure my SWAT lieutenant would enjoy working with your HRT and looking at new technology. And you are certainly welcome to attend training with Lieutenant North. As a matter of fact, I was planning on going out to observe myself."

She saw Commander Hudson look at the chief out of the corner of his eye and then make a notation on his steno pad.

"Well, Chief, I thank you for this opportunity to visit. I don't want to take up more of your valuable time."

"I am always happy to make time for the FBI."

As she walked out of the office, she smiled to herself. *That went well, just as I planned.*

Her next meeting was in fifteen minutes with the local FBI office. It was nearby, but parking would be a challenge, so she decided to leave her car in the City parking structure and walk. The downtown police station was near the waterfront. The walk would be refreshing, and she would enjoy the smell of the ocean.

"Javon, have we just been played?"

"I have to say, sir, she is good. It was highly instructive observing that conversation. It was like watching a well-choreographed dance with Ginger Rogers and Fred Astaire."

"Well, I think we came out alright. We got some promises from them and she doesn't even know whether JW's dog will work."

"Oh, Chief, I think she knows a lot more than we think."

"Yeah, Javon, you may be right. But I gotta say, if she had mentioned 'THE DIRECTOR' one more time, I might have screamed."

Javon laughed a little. "I think she was doing it on purpose."

"And why do you say that, my young Padawan?"

"Two reasons, sir. First, she is letting us know she has friends in high places and, therefore, she carries a lot of juice. Second, I think she was trying to irritate you a little. I think she wanted to keep you off balance because it would make it easier for her to get what she came here for: JW."

Chief Estrada pondered this for a while and finally said, "Very astute, Commander. We will have to be cautious around her in the future."

"JW North? Oh, he is a good guy and a great cop!"

Lauralynn was now in the Long Beach office of the FBI talking with local Special Agent in Charge, Dareena Jones. She had worked with Dareena in the past. The FBI was like that; it was a large organization, but if you stayed long enough, you developed good working relationships all over. "Why is that, Dareena?"

"Oh, I could give you a hundred reasons—he's just a great guy. But let me tell you a story. We were working a case in Long Beach, serving a warrant, a low-profile deal. Suspect is supposedly non-violent, so it should be an easy arrest. Bad guy grabs a gun and shoots one of my agents in the leg before we light him up. He was D.R.T., dead right there. Our guy is down, so we call paramedics. JW North is the watch commander. He shows up, gets us everything we need. When the paramedics are ready to roll, he orchestrates a full escort with a black and white stopping traffic at every intersection. At the last intersection, just before the hospital, there's JW himself, standing in the middle of the street, blocking traffic for my guy.

"I am telling you, Lauralynn, he is one of the good guys. A lot of the agents in the office like him; they think he can do no wrong. When he got shot, I about cried myself sick worrying about him."

Lauralynn nodded her head and could only manage a "huh." She thanked Dareena for her time and left. She had several other meetings today before attending the training session tomorrow.

22

The following morning, JW was up early. He was excited about the day's training exercises. He was also a little apprehensive since he knew that Dr. Gaurdia from the FBI would be there. *Ben, I will kick your ass if you embarrass me in front of the FBI.* Of course, he doubted Ben would do that; he wanted this program to work just as much as JW did. It was just his nerves getting the best of him. The reality was, having to work for multiple bosses was a pain in the butt. If this panned out, he would have two masters, Long Beach P.D. and the FBI, and that could get complicated. After a quick breakfast, he loaded his equipment and both dogs in the Tahoe and left.

Ben had told him to meet him at the former Olympic archery range. Somehow, Ben had arranged with the local archery club that used and maintained the range for them to use it today for training. When he arrived in the range parking lot, it was empty except for Ben's police K9 vehicle and Allen's pickup truck. JW got out but left the engine running for the dogs. The training scenarios were an unknown for JW, but he and Ben had a little surprise for the feds too. Bonnie had offered Addy for them to train. They had started two weeks ago, and she showed promise. She was already almost as good as Ares. She seemed to enjoy running trails and showing off in front of her brother. Today, she was going to run one trail. She would be proof that they could replicate Ares' results.

JW walked up and Ben immediately offered coffee. He had a table set up beside his vehicle with a disposable urn of coffee, and donuts. JW looked at the donuts and said, "Ben, you're going to give us a bad image." Ben and Allen laughed and JW continued, "So, what do we have planned?"

"All in good time, JW. I would like to have to give this briefing only one time." JW demurred to Ben as he was in charge of training.

JW let both dogs out to give them a break before training. When they were done, Ben asked, "Hey, can you keep Addy under wraps until her trail? I want to surprise Lauralynn; she doesn't know about her."

"OK, but she doesn't strike me as someone who likes surprises."

Ben nodded enthusiastically. "Oh, she hates surprises. All the more reason to do it."

"OK, you know her better than I do."

"When we ran the original program, she wasn't in charge of the fed team. She wasn't much more than an analyst, so I don't know her well. I do recall that she does not like surprises, but this will be a pleasant one."

"OK, Ben, you are in charge of this circus, I am merely the clown with the performing dogs. Did I tell you Chief Estrada and Commander Hudson are coming out?"

"No, but no big deal. We got this." Contrary to his words of confidence, Ben was as worried as JW about the day's presentation. He knew if it did not go well, it could derail the entire project, or at least set them back significantly. They could not afford any missteps, even small ones. He couldn't think of something much worse than embarrassing the chief in front of the FBI.

As they finished talking, a few vehicles pulled into the parking lot. As the guests arrived, Ben greeted each and offered them coffee. After everyone had a cup of coffee, except Lauralynn, and they all gathered around, Ben said, "Oh, I'm sorry, Special Agent Gaurdia, you don't drink coffee. But I came prepared and brought you tea." Lauralynn gave Ben a smile, but one that said, "I know you are trying to mess with me," and took the tea. Ben looked at her, frowned, and said, "Sorry, Lauralynn, I am just giving you a little grief."

Lauralynn smiled and said, "I know, Ben, so am I. Thanks for the tea."

Ben then took charge of the group, saying, "OK, everyone, let's do some quick introductions here."

JW knew all the people there except the two men with Lauralynn. She introduced them, "This is Dr. Michael Feldman from the University of Southern California; he is doing some remarkable work with human scent. And this is Special Agent Rick LeClair; he is with HRT and is on loan to me as the second in command of my little unit. For the police officers here, I think he is what you would call a 'door-kicker.'"

Ben introduced himself and Allen, noting, "I will be coordinating today's trails and guiding you through the exercises. There are a total of six trails.

"Allen is going to act as JW's backup and will provide him with the instructions for each trail. This is a double-blind exercise today. Neither JW nor Allen know where the trails go or who they will find when they get there. Assisting us today are several members of the Police Department's Explorer post. They have not volunteered with us before today and are unknown to both JW and Ares. I have given them careful instructions, so they don't give anything away. We are doing our best to make this a valid scientific test and we are recording the results on a GPS. The trails were all run three days ago and were recorded on a GPS then. We will have the results available on my computer for you to see afterward. Are there any questions?" Ben scanned the group for a moment. "Seeing none, JW please get Ares and introduce him."

As JW walked to his vehicle, the chief pulled him aside. He looked at JW's brand-new K9 handler uniform and said, "Looking good there, King 99. Knock 'em dead."

JW felt a great deal of pride at that moment. He had been knocked down and then gotten back up. He wasn't back all the way, but he was getting closer. "Thank you, sir. I appreciate that," he told the chief before he jogged off to get Ares. As he left, he blinked his eyes to clear them. *Must be some pollen in the air this morning.* Another piece that had been lost slipped back into place. *Control your emotions, JW. They flow right down the lead to the dog.*

JW went to his Tahoe and opened the back door. Ares jumped out and JW closed the door quickly so Addy would not get out. She immediately started barking. She wanted to come out too. Bonnie, who had been hiding behind the tree by JW's Tahoe, now stepped out and said, "I'll keep her quiet. I wanted to come out and watch the big show but didn't want you to know I was here."

"Thanks, Hon, I appreciate the support." *Holy cow! Nothing like a little more pressure.* JW took a deep breath. He knew that his stress could travel down the lead and affect Ares. *Knock it off and just do as you have trained, dumbass.*

JW brought Ares over to the group. His arrival was met with several oohs and aahs. Lauralynn bent down to rub behind Ares' ears and said, "Aren't you a gorgeous big dog? Are you going to show off and make your daddy look good today?" She stood up and smiled at JW.

Ben began the demonstration. "JW, you and Allen go out to the marker on the Olympic archery range and wait for my signal."

As they walked away, JW could hear Ben telling them all about Ares, his family tree and titles. *Laying it on a little thick there, Ben.* "OK," Ben continued, "The first trail is a bit different than anything we have done so far. This trail involves both trailing and scent discrimination. There are six trails, laid by six different individuals, who are now downrange, behind those bales of hay. They went there by a different route than they took three days ago. Allen has six bags with him, one for each subject. In each bag is an envelope containing a name and a scent pad. He will pick one at random and give the scent pad to JW, who will then begin the trail. Questions?"

No one asked any questions and Ben gave the signal to Allen. JW looked over Allen's shoulder and could see members of the local archery club standing on one of the side ranges. They were all watching with great interest. *NO PRESSURE, JW.* Allen handed JW the scent pad. JW knelt by Ares, who was sitting waiting to begin. He whispered into the dog's ear, "Ares, please don't screw up. If you love your dad, please do not embarrass us." Ares looked into his eyes for a moment, calm and confident, and then licked JW on the face. JW scented Ares and gave the command, "Geo-say." Ares, having adapted to the new command, moved quickly, first with a smooth cast and then walking forward. They worked about halfway across the field. JW was beginning to wonder if this was a negative trail, one where the scent he was given was not on any of the trails. Negative trails were important for training but didn't look good for a demonstration.

As JW pondered this, Ares made a hard turn. He was on-trail and pulling hard. JW gripped the trailing line firmly with his gloves, applying the brakes and slowing Ares down. Ares was as pumped as JW was. *Gotta keep cool so he will stay cool.* Ares covered the 100-yard trail in no time and stopped when he reached the explorer. It was a young lady, and her face was impassive. Of course, she didn't know if she was the right one, either. Ares sat and stared at her. Allen reached into his pocket and pulled out the envelope. JW could hear Ben in the background saying, "And the envelope, please." He was definitely going to shoot Ben when this was over.

Allen fumbled the envelope and JW could swear he saw a little mischief in his eyes. *Damn it, he is screwing with me too. I guess I forgot to check my calendar and see that it is "Screw with JW Day."* Allen finally opened the envelope and asked, "Are you Emily Estrada?" JW paled. *OH MY GOD! That's the chief's daughter. I recognize her now. I haven't seen her since she was about two years old. This is a blind test; what are the odds?*

The explorer nodded her head and JW exploded, "YES!" He pumped his arm and yelled "Yes!" again. He heard cheering behind him and looked—it wasn't the guests; it was the archers. *Amazing!*

Emily dropped to her knees and called Ares to her and gave him a big hug. She looked up at JW and said, "Congratulations, LT."

The next three tests were a bit more straightforward, but still challenging. They involved multiple turns, cross-trails, and moving from grass to the road and back. Ares performed perfectly. The last trail was like the others, except three-fourths of the way through it, they came to a small stream. Ares worked back and forth and then just leaped in. JW had no choice but to follow. The water wasn't deep, about knee-high on JW. *Really, Ben? You are going to pay for this.* Ares got out on the opposite side and shook off. He worked the side of the creek until he regained the trail and began pulling hard again. The trail continued until they had worked their way back to the parking lot. An explorer had worked his way into the group and was standing with them, silent. As JW approached from 100 yards out, he thought, *Too easy, Ben. I don't need Ares to figure out who it is.* But then he remembered Allen's training. *No preconceptions, JW. Let Ares do the work.* As they got closer to the group, the rest of the explorers worked their way into the group, crowded all together in a tight ball. *Nice, Ben...very nice. I'm still going to kill you.*

When Ares and JW made it back to the group, Ares wormed his way inside the cluster. He took scent on each person in passing and then moved on, in search of his target. He practically knocked the chief off his feet as he moved by. Finally, he sat in front of an explorer within the group. It wasn't the one he had seen earlier as he approached. Allen opened the envelope to confirm that Ares had located the correct individual. Ben smiled and said, "Congratulations, this concludes Ares' testing." JW left to put Ares back in the air conditioning of the Tahoe.

The chief interrupted and said, "Wait a minute, Officer Kellum. You said six trails and I only counted five."

"You are correct, sir." He motioned to JW and then said to the group, "We have a bit of a surprise for you all. As you can see, Ares is doing a great job and will be ready to certify soon. But first, we will have to transition from all this grass to more concrete and asphalt. That will be a challenge, but we believe Ares is up to it and will become the number one dog for the Long Beach Trailing Team. However, any team is only as strong as its weakest link. In this case, our weakness is that we have no backup for Ares.

"JW always told me you need to have a backup, no exceptions. What happens if Ares is hurt or sick? Who are we going to call? Well, we will call Adeliene, or as we call her, 'Addy.'"

JW then marched out with Addy. Lauralynn looked at Ben and said quietly, "I believe you know I hate surprises, but I think I am going to like this one."

Ben sent JW and Addy off with Allen to the start point. When they arrived there, JW brought out a new harness for Addy. It was handmade from leather just like Ares', except this one had her name on it. She had been using Ares' harness, sized down to fit her, but it was time for her to have her own. JW had ordered it from Germany after reaching out to Axel for the contact information of the leather craftsman. "Here you go, Addy, your own harness." She seemed excited at the gift and gave him a quick lick as he put it on her. Allen handed him the scent pad and he gave Addy the search command, "Geo-say." Just like her brother, she began to cast, moving forward slowly and side to side to pick up the trail. When she hit the trail, she also turned hard and began pulling JW along. He applied back pressure to slow her down as she worked. As the team moved out of sight, the rest of the group remained behind. Ben gave them some background information about Addy, including the fact that Bonnie had offered her up for training, and how little training she had actually completed.

JW and Addy worked through the park, over and under benches, and around several turns. JW picked up that she was working some cross-trails and smiled when she continued, having worked them out. Finally, they came out of the trees to the park road. Here she began working in tight circles. *Oh, Ben, you have got to be kidding me. A car trail, no way. She is not ready.* JW looked at Allen and said, "Car trail, huh?" *This demonstration has been going well so far. Ben, I hope you know what you are doing.*

Addy began pulling down the road, a little more slowly now. After several intersections where Addy had to make decisions on which way to go, they returned to the parking lot. Addy worked her way to a parked car and raised up, putting her front legs into an open window and startling a woman inside. It was Officer Joan Smithers, the explorer adviser; she was here to supervise her young charges. She looked at Addy with curiosity but smiled when Addy sat in front of her. *Good alert!* Once again, the envelope confirmed the correct identity of the target.

Ben picked up his narration again. "OK everyone, that was a half-mile trail through the park with six turns and two cross-trails. Then Addy picked up a one-mile car trail with four intersections. Obviously, she worked her way back here and gave us a proper alert. JW is probably going to shoot me, and I have seen him shoot with the pistol team, so I have every reason to be concerned. That trail was very advanced for Addy. Normally, a dog would not see a trail like that until they had completed several months of training. She has been doing this for two weeks."

Everyone came over and congratulated JW and petted Addy. Ares was brought out to receive his recognition too.

The demonstration complete, JW told everyone he would need to clean up before lunch, but Ben would take them to the restaurant. Bonnie told JW she would take the dogs home in her car. She gave Ben a dirty look as she said, "I guess I'll be giving Ares a bath, too." JW asked her if she wanted to join them for lunch and she said, "No, thanks. You're going to be talking business and I have some work to catch up on at home. You know, ddoing double duty with this project and my real job is starting to wear on me."

JW hugged Bonnie and told her, "Honey, I could not have done this without you and your support."

Ben gave everyone directions to a local favorite barbecue place. They served buffet style, which would make it easier for a large group. Fortunately, Bonnie had brought JW a backup uniform and pair of boots to change into. He stopped off at the Academy located nearby and did the quick-change routine, arriving at Andy's Barbecue about fifteen minutes after everyone else. Andy, the owner, greeted him and said, "Ah, the guest of honor. You know, you never did have that retirement breakfast you planned with your guys. Something about getting shot?"

JW smiled and said, "You're right. We're going to have to fix that."

23

Before JW arrived, Special Agent Rick LeClair pulled Dr. Gaurdia aside and asked, "Impressed? I was. What can you tell me about this guy?"

Lauralynn answered, "That was phenomenal. Especially for a dog that's not fully trained yet. As far as I can see, Ares is ready for certification, and I think Addy has even more potential than Ares. JW just needs to be able to read them better and get in tune with them."

"What can you tell me about him, boss?"

"Smart, good education, former Marine, thirty years as a cop, six as a K9 handler and three more as the unit supervisor. Tactically sound, good leader. His guys love him."

"Are you thinking of adding him to the team full time or as an asset?"

"To be honest, I don't know. I can see where he could fit, but I'm not sure I could get him to Quantico full time. So, for now, we wait and see, and let this develop some more."

Rick said, "Good copy," and went to get his food.

JW arrived and joined the group in line around the food stations. The large buffet area offered a variety of barbecued food. The aromas were overwhelming. *It's a good thing Ares isn't here; his nose would be on overdrive. He'd probably be jumping on tables stealing food.* He was waiting in one line where a chef was cutting and serving fresh barbecued pork ribs when he was joined by Dr. Feldman. JW said, "Dr. Feldman, I didn't get a chance to speak with you earlier. I'm JW North. It's a pleasure to meet a fellow USC alumnus." Dr. Feldman asked with interest, "You attended USC?" "I did, in the eighties on a Marine Corps scholarship. I was in the NROTC program." "Are you by any chance a football fan?" JW's face lit up. "I am a huge fan, Doctor. You and I should talk football sometime. My wife isn't all that interested."

"You know, as a member of the faculty, I have access to season tickets. Would you like to go to a game with me sometime? I have the same problem getting my wife interested in football."

"You bet. Here's my card. Anytime you can't find someone to go with you, call me. If I'm not chasing the south end of a northbound dog, I will be there."

Dr. Feldman thought about the reference for a moment and laughed. "Lieutenant North, sometime when you aren't too busy chasing dogs, I would like to talk to you about setting up some tests to help validate my work concerning human scent. I think Ares and Addy would be perfect for the job."

"Please call me 'JW.' Anything I can do to help with your work, let me know. I'm building my little team of experts here in Long Beach and we will be happy to contribute."

"Thank you, JW, and please call me Michael."

JW approached the open seat next to Dr. Gaurdia. "Mind if I sit here, Doctor?"

"No, Lieutenant, I don't mind. Actually, it's perfect as we need to talk. I am very impressed with what you did today. Ares is incredible and Addy shows great promise. You have a natural ability with them, and I think you could be a great asset to law enforcement."

"Thank you, Doctor. This has been a challenging journey. I have a great team supporting me and could not have done this without them."

"That's very humble of you Lieutenant, and speaking of teams—I'm assembling one at the FBI and I think you could be a part of it. But first, I need you to get these dogs certified and ready to work. Once that's done, I can go into more detail. I need to get my boss's buy-in on this idea, and to do that, I need results that I can show him."

"That sounds very interesting. How does my team fit in?"

"We are approaching the problem from a different perspective than we normally do, but it seems as though something is missing. I think human scent detection and man-trailing could be that missing link we need. So, when you are certified and ready to start, reach out to me."

"Sure thing, Doc. May I ask what it is you are hunting?"

Lauralynn smiled to herself, *Line baited, nibble, set the hook.* "Oh, I'm sorry, I forgot to mention that. We're hunting serial criminals, specifically serial killers."

JW smiled at her, but his eyes weren't smiling. They were gray and hard. All he said was, "I'm in."

JW decided to go grab seconds; it had been a busy morning and he had worked up an appetite. As he walked to the buffet line, Rick LeClair stopped him. "Going back for more, cowboy?"

JW was confused by the reference and LeClair continued, "Sorry, no offense. I thought your initials were a John Wayne reference."

"Oh, that. They are, in a way. It's a long story. I'll be happy to tell you over a beer sometime."

"Deal. So, what do you think of all this?"

JW looked the man in the eye, wondering if this was another sales pitch or if it was another brother in blue reaching out in friendship. "Well, it is a bit overwhelming. I'm still figuring it out."

"Fair enough. What are your concerns? Is it the doc? If you're worried about her, don't be. She is much better than she thinks she is, and she has a very high opinion of herself. Always the psychologist, she plays her little mind games. You'll get used to it. But, at heart, she is still the farm girl from Iowa who believes in good and evil. She's like you, a true believer."

JW tilted his head to the side and questioned, "True believer?"

LeClair smiled and said, "She told you what we do, I saw your reaction to it. I can see it in your eyes, you're definitely a hunter. I bet there's one thing she didn't tell you, though."

LeClair let his words linger in the air for a moment. "There are some things you should know, JW. Here's my card." LeClair wrote something on the back and then handed it to JW. "We'll talk more later, but one thing, brother. You haven't gotten the offer yet, but it is coming. This is hard work, it can be boring, it is definitely meticulous, and it is nothing like what they show you in the movies." JW took the card and looked at the back. LeClair had written, "Bellam, Iowa." It meant nothing to JW. He put the card in his wallet, making a mental note to research it later. LeClair walked back to his seat on the other side of Gaurdia and said, "Mission accomplished."

That night at home while Bonnie was relaxing and watching one of her favorite TV shows, JW was at his computer, in his office. He reached into his wallet and removed the card Special Agent LeClair gave to him. He flipped it over and read, Bellam, Iowa. *What are you and why are you important?*

A quick Internet search gave him a broad list of hits. Scanning, he saw nothing of note. He tried again, this time adding Lauralynn Gaurdia to the search. This time he received several specific hits. He clicked on the first, then the second. *Wow. Holy cow.* He left his office and poked his head into the living room. "Hey, Honey, pause your show and come take a look at this."

Bonnie followed him back to the office, saying, "I hope this is important. I know you're not a big *Walking Dead* fan, but I am. They were getting ready to kill Negan, again."

JW pointed to the screen with a somber face. "Read," was all he said.

Bonnie scanned the article and looked up to JW. "Wow."

"That's exactly what I said."

"That's scary, but it explains a lot."

The training continued for the next few weeks at a rapid pace. Ares continued to develop and Addy worked hard to catch up. It wasn't long before she was running the same exercises as her brother. Ben and Allen determined that the dogs were ready to start working in a more residential environment. JW reached out to the police department's Community Relations Division, specifically the Neighborhood Watch representatives. He asked for a variety of neighborhoods, all around the city. He wanted strong neighborhood watch programs, where the team would be welcome to work. Because they would be doing more work on city streets, he enlisted the help of other members of the police reserves to assist with traffic control and site security. JW went to the local police uniform supply company and had them create some custom traffic vests imprinted with "Police K9 Training In Progress." He also asked the City's sign shop to create similar signs. People would see officers and cars and wonder if there was a SWAT call-out. A few well-placed signs would hopefully prevent a lot of questions. Ben and Allen were pushing the length of the trails out to two to three miles. Both dogs absorbed the extra work without a problem; JW, on the other hand, was getting worn down. He had not completely recovered from his injury, and the addition of Addy doubled the training workload. The group discussed this problem over coffee one morning. Allen brought forward an interesting idea.

"OK, here is how I see it. We are training two dogs and our handler can't hang with it." JW shot him a cold stare and Allen laughed at him. *JW bites the hook again.* "I know, JW, I was where you are a long time ago, so relax. Anyway, the answer is easy, and I think it will benefit the program and the dogs. We add another handler to the mix. JW, you still need to run with them, but it is a lot easier being on the backside, plus you may see more. I will be there to point out the small things. A good thing about this change is it will allow the dogs to work with someone else. That way if JW can't go for some reason, the other handler can fill in. So, the only question I have is, who is the other handler?" As he said this, he emphasized the last few words and looked directly at Ben.

Ben laughed and said, "I should have seen that one coming. More importantly, I should have called in sick this morning."

Allen said, "It makes sense. You've done this before, you know how to work the dogs, and it benefits the dogs and gives us more flexibility."

JW added, "Look, Ben, you're getting close to retirement. I know you want to do this; I can see it in your eyes. We've talked about this before; *if* the program is successful, it will need to grow. I don't want to put any extra pressure on you, but I can't do this all by myself, so quit your whining and grab a leash." JW pulled Ben away for a moment. "If this is going to cause problems at home, I don't want to put that on you."

"Thanks, I appreciate what you're saying. I think we are OK with this. I'll run it by Lucy and see how she reacts."

The plan worked wonders for them all. JW learned a lot from being in the backup position and Ben picked up his old trailing skills as if he had not stopped ten years ago. JW was inspired by the self-revelation that he was still out of shape. He started going to the gym when he wasn't chasing dogs or reading. After a few months, he was in the best shape he had been in a long time, if not ever. *Not bad for an old guy.*

One morning as JW sat drinking coffee and mentally working on the schedule for the week, his phone chimed. It was an email from Javon Hudson. Chief Estrada was requesting the pleasure of his company at his office at 3:00 that afternoon. *Well, that doesn't sound too friendly. I wonder what bucket of crap I have stepped in this time?* JW quickly typed "Happy to be there" and added it to his calendar. Bonnie strolled in, cup of coffee in hand, with both dogs following her. She watched JW finish the email and looked at him quizzically. *How is it she always shows up when something is happening?*

"More good news?"

"Probably not. The chief wants to see me at three o'clock. I would say that ninety-nine percent of the times I was ordered into the chief's office, it was usually bad news."

"OK, what did you do this time?"

"If I only knew," he said with a laugh.

JW arrived early for his meeting with the chief. One of the many things he had learned as a Marine was "if you are on time, you're late." He had not been in the Marines very long, just four years active duty. He had made plenty of dumb mistakes which, of course, provided him with plenty of opportunities to learn. He hoped he had not made the same mistake more than once.

JW was hoping he could get five minutes with Javon to help him prepare for what he feared was likely an ass chewing. He had no idea what he had done wrong, but he was prepared to receive his punishment. Unfortunately, the chief's secretary told him that Javon was in the office with the chief.

At 3:00 p.m. exactly, the door to the chief's office opened and JW was called in. He quickly scanned the room. It looked the same, he did not see a guillotine or any instruments of torture. The chief greeted him warmly, as he always did, and started with, "How is the training going?"

"Very well, sir. Both dogs are progressing rapidly. The transition from urban, mostly park for us, to suburban and urban has been remarkably smooth. Each dog has adapted to the changes very well."

The chief seemed a bit reserved today, which JW found unusual. "That sounds great. How long do you think it will be before you certify?"

"We're looking at next week for Ares and two weeks for Addy."

"Excellent. I would like to attend, if you don't mind."

It wasn't really a question, but JW treated it as such. "We'd be honored to have you there, sir. I'll make sure Commander Hudson gets the details."

"Great, thank you. Now, for the reason I asked you in today. You have done a fantastic job with this program. You're getting some nice press, which is always a good thing. Your recovery from your injuries is a great story in itself. I want to congratulate you and thank you at the same time."

JW interrupted, saying, "Sir, if you will forgive me, I think there is a large 'but' at the end of that sentence."

"You are correct. I am concerned. Concerned about you and what is going to happen with this program. I know the FBI has their eye on you. I am willing to bet the minute you certify, you will receive a call and an invitation. I want you to know that whatever you decide to do, I support you. I just want you to be careful. Make sure that you want that before it comes. You may not be given a lot of time to consider their offer. Working that job full time can put a lot of pressure on you, on your marriage. JW, even though you are working for free, the department has made a substantial investment in this program and I would hate to lose it as a resource."

JW considered the chief's remarks for a moment. He had a great deal of respect for the man, even though they had not always agreed. JW restarting the program was not an easy choice for the chief to allow. After all, they had tried this before and ended up cancelling everything due to the lack of the big capture. But the chief had given him all the things he needed to get it done.

"Sir, I don't want to get all misty-eyed here. I do want to take this opportunity to thank you. Without your support, without the loan of Officer Kellum, I would not have been able to do this. No way. I am honored to have you at certification. It means a great deal to me to know you have my back. I understand your concerns. I have some, too. Just know that I am going into this with my eyes wide open.

"I'd like to share something with you, and I would appreciate it if you would keep it in confidence. When we were at lunch with the FBI a while back, I had a chat with Special Agent LeClair. He told me a little about this unit of theirs. He said when you get down to it, they chase serial killers. He said he thought I was a 'true believer' and he thought Dr. Gaurdia was one also. I didn't know what he meant that day, but he gave me a card with the name of a town on it—Bellam, Iowa. I looked it up and found a news story from over thirty years ago. The story told of two young girls who were out playing in the woods, hide and seek. One girl just disappeared and wasn't heard from for days. Then they found her body. She had been molested and brutally killed; her body just left there in the woods for the animals. The other girl was her cousin. Her name was Lauralynn Gaurdia.

"Chief, you and I have been chasing bad guys for a long time, but you know there is something else out there. We don't see it often, but sometimes we see things that are so sick, so disgusting that it can only be Evil with a capital E. I don't know how to characterize it other than that. I have met evil on a few occasions and it has affected me. It has changed me into the man in front of you now. I am sick and tired of evil fouling the streets of our cities. I'm still gathering my facts, but if I am right about this group, then I believe I will sign on, in whatever capacity they need me." JW's eyes took on a very serious look. "I am a true believer and it's time for me to get back in the fight.

"You know that I've been working with Ben Kellum; he's been doing some handler work with me. He is going to retire before too long and, if this program goes where I believe it can, I will set him up with a dog. I don't see Ben leaving the area. He has too many family ties to go too far. Sir, know that if Long Beach calls, we will be there for you. I want you to know I will always be LBPD to my core." The chief thanked JW and told him he would see him the next week.

Once he had left, Commander Hudson said, "Holy shit, Chief, did you see that?"

"Oh yeah. That was somewhere in between awe-inspiring and scary as hell, with a little bit of cheesy to go with it. But I can forgive the cheese, he believes it. Man, I wouldn't want to be on the wrong side of him."

"Sir, I have seen the wrong side of JW, and it was not pretty."

24

After his meeting with the chief, JW decided to drive home. It was time to have a heart-to-heart chat with Bonnie. The chief was right, the call from the FBI was probably right around the corner. Of course, that depended on certification. There was a lot of pressure piling up on JW and he had never really mentally recovered from being shot.

As JW walked through the door, he called out, "Family meeting."

"Be right there, Hon. Let me hit save and I'll meet you in the dining room. Can you grab me a cup of coffee?"

"Coffee? I'm beginning to think I might be a bad influence on you."

"JW, you've been a bad influence on me since the day we met." He stared at her, a look of hurt and dismay showing. "Love you, Hon, mean it," she said, smiling.

"OK, well now that I forgot what I came in here for, what do you have?"

"Me, not much. Everything is going OK so far."

"OK, now I remember. We need to talk." JW's confusion concerned Bonnie for a moment. Was something wrong, something she didn't know about?

"Is something wrong?"

"Yes, no, maybe. The chief wanted to warn me that the FBI is going to call if everything goes well at certification."

"OK, well, I thought that is what would ultimately happen," Bonnie replied.

"Yeah, me too. I think it's the natural progression of something like this. I just want to make sure you're on board with it. That you have no reservations."

"JW, we've talked about this. I understand it as well as I can at this point. You know the law enforcement world better than me. So, what's bothering you?"

"When Ben was involved with the trailing program before, it ultimately led to problems with his wife. I didn't know that before, but Ben opened up to me recently. He has issues at home and who knows, after certification he may drop out. We may be on our own. But, more importantly I don't want the same thing to happen between us. As important as the program is to me, I just want to make sure you're OK with everything. Ben mentioned that Lucy hated how often he was gone from home."

"Well, if you need to go on the road, that's OK with me. Heck, I could use some 'me' time," she said with a short laugh. "Seriously, JW, you think I haven't thought about it? You and the kids out on the road, away from home. Not to mention the potential danger you might be in. That's all I think about."

JW smiled. "Well, if it helps, all of my reading on serial killers indicates that when confronted, they are not likely to resist violently."

"All I ask is you be as safe as you can and make sure you and the dogs come home. That and keep me in the loop."

The rest of the week flew by for JW. Training was still challenging; Allen and Ben always managed to come up with some new twist. Allen had a lot of friends in the trailing community and he was reaching out to them, asking for their mistakes so he could incorporate them into the training. Allen always told a story after these trails about how someone else had inspired that day's work. The trails were tough now, tougher than certification would be. One day after JW complained about the ridiculous difficulty of a trail, Allen countered with, "You can't make it too tough. The real deal should feel like a vacation. Well, at least that's what they say."

JW pondered this for a moment and said, "I can take it, I just don't want to wear out the dogs."

"OK, JW, I hear you. But do you hear the dogs complaining? Do they look worn out to you? What is it the SEALS say? 'The only easy day was yesterday.'"

Finally, certification day arrived. JW woke early that morning. As usual, the stress of the upcoming test was too much to allow him to sleep. Other than performance anxiety, JW could not understand why he was up at 3:00 a.m. He did know he always put more stress on himself than any one supervisor ever had. He was a perfectionist, plain and simple. *Failure was not an option.*

As Ares walked into the room, JW asked him, "You want a cup of coffee, big boy?"

Ares looked at him and JW answered for him, "No, thank you. I really don't like the stuff. Makes me too jumpy."

JW laughed to himself as Ares came to him and rested his head in his lap. "You are a lot smarter than people give you credit for, huh, boy?"

JW and Ares had bonded easily. Dogs and humans often do. The training had brought them even closer; they were a team now and a team is only as strong as its weakest link. JW hoped he wouldn't be the one to ruin certification. JW scratched Ares behind the ears and let his mind wander.

At 8:30 a.m., JW's phone chimed with a text message from Ben: "10-19 Downtown Station in thirty minutes." *Gee, Ben, nothing like giving me plenty of time to get there.*

JW went to find Bonnie. She was in the bedroom, dressed, sitting on the bed. Both dogs were sprawled out on the bed and Bonnie was petting each of them slowly. She was talking to Ares, but he couldn't make out what she was saying. She looked at JW and smiled. JW's heart filled with love for her.

"Honey, I want to thank you for supporting me in all this. I know it hasn't been easy."

"Oh, don't be getting all mushy on me. You don't do mushy well. I love you. Now get your butt in gear. You need to get downtown. Oh, and Ben suggested you stay off the freeway because it's backed up."

"OK, if I could just borrow my dog." JW looked at Ares, who was almost asleep and said, "Ares, you want to go to work?" The dog was up in a heartbeat, racing to the front door. He looked back at JW as if to say, "Well, hurry up!"

Addy raced behind them, eager to go, too. "I'm sorry, little girl, you can't go today. Mom will take good care of you." With that, JW was out the door with Ares. He navigated the streets of Long Beach in the black Tahoe, taking streets he had learned from years of driving would not be thick with traffic. The closer he got to downtown, the more nervous JW got. *Why are we meeting downtown? Hopefully, Ben isn't going to have me trail on the busy streets of downtown Long Beach for Ares' certification. Oh, if he does, I am so gonna shoot him.*

Ben Kellum stood before a rather large gathering in the community room of the Long Beach Police Department. There were several invited guests, including Dr. Gaurdia and Special Agent LeClair of the FBI, Dr. Michael Feldman from USC, Chief Estrada, and all the deputy chiefs and several commanders. Several members of the city council were also there.

After introductions, Ben took a deep breath and said, "Wow, that's a lot of introducing. First off, I would like to thank you for attending this morning. When I first mentioned to Chief Estrada that we could do this downtown, I did not anticipate this level of interest." There was standing room only, with a spillover out onto the patio.

Ben told the backstory of what they had been working on for the past six months and what they would be doing today.

"OK, now I have to swear you all to secrecy. JW does not know where we are trailing today. He cannot." The overhead projector lit up and showed a map of the downtown area. "The trail will begin at the foot of Chestnut Avenue, next to the station.

"From there, we will go through the parking structure and out into Lincoln Park. We'll go across Pacific and down Pine Avenue to Ocean Boulevard, across and up onto the Promenade. We'll go through the birdcage stairwell and into Shoreline Village. Then we'll go inside the Aquarium of the Pacific and out into another parking structure. We'll cross the roller coaster bridge, go back through The Pike shopping center, through another parking structure, and ultimately end up here in a small park in front of the Harbor View condos."

The chief interrupted, "Officer Kellum, that covers quite a distance, how far is that?"

"With all the twists and turns and stairs and such, that is just at four miles, sir."

Dr. Gaurdia asked, "Ben, how old is this trail?"

"We wanted to really push Ares on this one; the trail is two weeks old."

The chief asked another question. "Who is he looking for?"

Dr. Feldman said, "I can answer that. Lieutenant North is trailing one of my grad students. Someone he does not know and has never met. She has a rather extensive criminal history of being late to my class. She is volunteering today for extra credit and to get out of my doghouse." The last comment drew a few laughs from the audience.

At that moment, Bonnie North worked her way through the crowd. She had Addy with her on a leash. Ben picked up the narration, "Here is one of our guests of honor, Bonnie North. She is the CEO of this project and has with her 'Addy,' who will be certified next week as the backup dog for Ares. Bonnie, by your arrival, can we assume JW will be here soon? Because I am running out of stuff to talk about."

Bonnie nodded and Chief Estrada stepped up to the podium. He took over from Ben and gave a short speech, as chiefs usually do at such occasions, speaking of JW and Ares in glowing terms. She smiled to herself as she listened. *He means it, I can tell. Good thing JW isn't here yet. He would hate this.*

JW pulled up in front of the police station behind a line of black and whites. *This must be the place.* He got out of the car, leaving Ares for now, and walked up to a group of uniformed and bicycle officers. JW smiled at them and said, "Hey guys, what's going on?" He recognized all the faces, men and women he had worked with over the years. He saw Don Harrison and asked, "Isn't this your day off, Donnie?"

"We're all off, LT. We heard you were having a parade downtown and thought you might want an escort. We'll block traffic and try to keep people from interrupting you during the trail. Ben has briefed us, so we know what to do."

JW looked the group over. He knew time off was precious to cops, and he said, "You all came in on your day off to watch me walk the dog? Boy, you guys and gals must live boring lives. Thank you."

Don smiled and said, "Oh, Lieutenant guest of honor, I think you are needed inside." Don laughed and started getting the group organized.

JW walked into the community room and was immediately overwhelmed by the turnout. *Damn, no extra pressure here.* He smiled at Dr. Gaurdia and SA LeClair; somehow, he knew they'd be here. He greeted the chief, saw Bonnie, and hugged her. She whispered in his ear, "You do a good job and you might get lucky later." He laughed to himself, *Oh, the freeway's backed up, huh?*

He smiled and bent down to Addy and said, "Now don't be jealous, little girl. Your turn comes next week." The attention earned him a quick lick to the face.

Ben said, "OK, JW, I have already briefed everyone on the certification. I need you to go to the foot of Chestnut with Ares. Allen and your cover team will be there waiting. Allen will give you the trail brief."

"Cover team, Ben?"

"Just go with it, JW. If we were doing this for real you would have somebody making sure you didn't get yourself shot again."

JW scowled. "Ouch, Ben, that hurts in so many ways." With that, he went to get Ares.

With Ares on leash, JW walked up to the group of officers, now on Chestnut where it dead ends in front of the Police and Fire Departments' Memorial. He could hear the helicopter overhead and wondered if something else was going on downtown. "Hey, Donnie, what's up with Fox?"

"Nothing, they're here training. They're going to watch and record your trail and send it back to the community room. That way everyone can watch you and Ares." Don continued, "OK, I am going to be your cover officer and will run with you. Allen there is going to observe. The bike guys are going to ride parallel and help keep the area clear, but I will direct them based on what Ares does. The guys in the cars are going to help us get across streets and through intersections. I have cleared channel six for the operation to help with coordination. There will probably be one or two people who get upset; tune them out and let us deal with it." Don looked down at Ares. "So, you ready to go, Big Dog? Oh, you too, LT."

Allen stepped forward and handed him a scent pad and said, "The suspect abandoned his vehicle over there. I have taken the liberty of collecting a scent pad for you. You may begin your trail when ready."

JW looked around for a moment at his friends and co-workers. He smiled at them and bent down to Ares and gave him a one-armed hug around the neck, whispering quietly, "I know you got this, buddy. I know we can do this, so let's get to it."

He walked to the suspect's car and put Ares on a sit, clipped his tracking lead to his harness, had him sniff the scent pad, and said with authority, "Geo-say." Ares put his nose to the ground and began working. He picked up the trail quickly and worked his way out into the street and then into the parking structure. The bike officers moved ahead to help clear their path, but not knowing where they were going, they moved in fits and starts. Ares worked well, pulling hard on the lead, but slow. *Old trail. Well, you knew that was coming.* They moved across the structure, then up a stairwell and back across, finally down the stairs and out. They moved across Lincoln Park and out onto the street. The patrol vehicles blocked traffic like they had been doing this all their lives. JW could hear Donnie talking on the radio in the background, setting up the cars and bikes as they moved along.

JW stopped the trail to wait for the escort team to set up a block as it appeared the trail led across Ocean Boulevard, a major east-west thoroughfare. Cars flew by them, people on their way to work, home, out to eat, you name it. A bike officer moved into the street to block traffic as the black and whites were trapped behind other cars.

JW restarted Ares and they stepped off the curb together. They had only gone a couple of steps when JW heard the scream of tires. The driver of a red import had been texting his girlfriend, looked up and saw the police officer in front of him, and slammed on his brakes—but it was too little, too late. The car went into a locked-wheel skid that hit the bike and threw the officer over the hood, sending him into the gutter. The bike flew through the air, knocking Ares down and striking JW in the lower leg. Lieutenant North fell to the ground, grasping his left knee. As he shook off the impact, he felt Ares licking his face. "You OK, big boy?"

Back in the community room, the gathering had a front-row seat to the accident, courtesy of the camera on the helicopter. There was a collective gasp as they watched the bike officer fly over the hood of the car and JW and Ares go down. "K99, can you confirm you are Code Four there?" Ben asked over the radio. They could see JW on the screen, looking Ares over, checking his legs and torso.

"K99, it appears we are OK. Give me a second to see if we are still a go."

JW started to stand, but almost collapsed, a strong pain radiating from his knee. "Oh crap. Donnie, give me a hand here."

Donnie helped JW get to his feet. "You OK, LT?"

"No, my knee is killing me. I can't walk. Probably just as well at the moment, as I have a strong urge to drag that idiot out of his car and strangle him. I think he just screwed up this whole deal." One of the other escort officers had called dispatch and asked for paramedics to check out the bike officer and JW. They arrived in a few moments, as Fire Station One was co-located with the downtown police station. As they checked out the other officer, JW began trying to walk, but it was difficult, and he had a limp.

Outwardly, there was no injury to North, but he was feeling pain from the trauma of the impact with the bicycle and then falling. Ares seemed to be fine, but he was definitely concerned about JW's condition. Finally, the bike officer was cleared and the paramedics came to look at him, only to be waved off. "Thanks, guys, I think I'm OK, at least as good as I'm gonna be for a while."

Donnie looked him hard in the eye. "OK, boss, this is your decision. You wanna call it, or keep going?"

JW was torn. He knew this trail would be a long one and they had barely started. He still wasn't one hundred percent sure that Ares was OK. It would be the smart thing to call it a day. The problem was, there were a lot of people watching. If he cancelled the rest of the trail, would all of the support he had seen so far just evaporate? "Give me a sec, Donnie." JW started walking with Ares, then went into a slow jog. Ares looked OK, but JW was hurting. He walked over to the paramedics and asked, "You guys got any vitamin A?"

The first paramedic looked confused, the second laughed. "How much you want?"

"Oh, about 1,200 milligrams should do it."

JW took the Advil and a bottled water saying, "Thanks."

"That's gonna take a bit to kick in. You sure you're OK?"

"I'm afraid I need to be OK. Sucks to be me."

Donnie walked back to JW and asked, "Hey, LT, what's it gonna be?"

"Let's give it a go."

"You sure?"

"What? Are you getting tired, Donnie?"

"Hell, no. If you can go, there's no way I'm falling out." Donnie took charge of the escort team and within moments everything was ready to go. JW restarted Ares, who then led them across Ocean Boulevard without further incident. Donnie watched JW carefully as he worked behind Ares. JW applied more back pressure than usual. He didn't think he could jog far the way his knee was hurting. He still wasn't convinced he would be able to finish.

"Damn it!"

"What's that, LT?"

"Nothing, Donnie. I'm cussing Murphy, bad drivers, and anything else that seems to want to stand in the way of this project."

JW had paused at another intersection, waiting for his escort to block traffic so he could continue. "Hey, LT, I know it sucks, but that's the way it is. Everyone is here for you, everyone is watching you and the dog. Remember what that famous Notre Dame coach, Lou Holtz, said—'Quitting is a permanent solution to a temporary problem.'"

"Really, Donnie, you're gonna quote Lou Holtz to an SC guy? Really?" He smiled at Donnie and said, "Let's get going, time's a-wasting."

Back in the Community Center, the group relaxed as they saw the trail start back up. "Ben, JW is limping a lot. How much farther is this trail?" Bonnie asked, concern in her voice.

"They've barely gotten going," replied Ben. His face looked troubled.

"Do you think they'll be able to finish?"

"I don't know. The good news is Ares looks OK right now." He didn't comment on JW, who was limping worse with every step.

To JW, the trail seemed to go on and on, and the Advil was only dulling his pain. Ares seemed to be working well, but it was getting warm. He hoped the dog wouldn't suffer too much from the heat. JW chuckled as they made it down to Rainbow Harbor; the offshore breeze here was refreshing. So far, they had weathered their first visit by Murphy. *Was that it, or were there more surprises in store?* When the trail took them through the Aquarium of the Pacific, JW smiled. *Ben, really, the Aquarium?* The employees were lined up and cheered as they went past. *Everybody loves a parade, I guess.*

They exited quickly and started to cross the road. A motorist was angry about being delayed and honked his horn. A bike officer rode up and handed him a piece of paper. By the time he was done reading, the team had moved on. Ares went into the stairwell of the Aquarium parking structure, working slowly. JW asked Donnie, "What's on the paper?"

"It's a note explaining what we're doing and why, it apologizes for any inconvenience. It's signed by the chief." JW shook his head as Ares pulled him back to reality.

They followed the trail all over the area. JW felt like they were on a walking tour of downtown Long Beach. JW let Ares do the heavy lifting while he tried to relax and enjoy the beauty of the day. Finally, the team worked their way back to Ocean Boulevard and Ares turned in to a small park in front of the Harbor View condos. *Is this it or is there more?* He looked at the building and hoped Ben wasn't taking them up that stairwell. He was getting tired and his leg was killing him. He couldn't imagine how Ares felt, but to look at him, he seemed to have plenty of energy. The dog was in the zone.

JW tuned back into the real world and noticed that Ares was sitting in front of a young woman seated on a park bench reading a college textbook. Ares was looking intently at her as if she held the key to all the tennis balls in the world. JW turned to Allen and Donnie and said, "I guess that's it, guys."

Donnie laughed and said, "About freakin' time, LT. I was about to have a heart attack waiting on you."

Allen walked up and shook his hand. "Congratulations, JW. You and Ares are certified."

Don turned to JW and said, "I think Bonnie has arranged a little reception down at Barney's Fish House at Rainbow Harbor. I had one of the guys follow in your truck so you could ride down."

"Thanks, Donnie, but I think I want to walk. This has been a long journey and I'd like a few minutes to let it all sink in. Please make sure everyone who helped today knows they are welcome to attend."

"Are you sure, LT? You're not looking good."

"I'm OK, Donnie. Hell, I'm pretty good right now."

JW unclipped Ares from his harness and let him take a break. He thanked his trailing suspect and invited her to the reception too. He put his equipment in the back of his Tahoe and nodded to the driver. He didn't know her. He walked up to her and said, "Thanks for helping. I'm JW."

She smiled and said, "It was my honor, sir. This is one nice ride! My name is Leandra Gonzalez, I was training with Officer Harrison the night you were injured. I wanted to be here today to see you make it all the way back."

"It's a pleasure to meet you, Leandra. Thank you, again, and make sure you come down to Barney's and get some chow."

JW limped back down to Rainbow Harbor with Ares. He loved Long Beach and wondered if this might be the last time he would do this. No, he thought, he would be back. He loved it here. Don Harrison walked quietly behind him. He didn't want to disturb JW, but more importantly, he didn't want anything else bad to happen.

When they arrived at Barney's, they went into a large private room overlooking the bay. Addy was off to the side with a small crowd of her own. JW took Ares over to be with her. He spotted a water bowl nearby and a couple of pads for the dogs to rest on. A reserve officer, one of the many who had helped him during his training, said, "I'll keep an eye on them for you, LT."

Everyone in the room wanted to congratulate JW and pat him on the back. He worked his way through the crowd and finally found Bonnie. She hugged him and told him how proud she was. "How is your leg?" she asked, concerned.

He hugged her back, told her he loved her, thanked her for everything she had done and said, "I'm OK, but some ice for the knee would be great." She nodded and went toward the kitchen in search of ice. Chief Estrada came by, and JW made sure to thank him again. "I couldn't have done it without your help." JW was pleasantly surprised to see Bill Lombard, the Chevrolet rep who had taken such good care of his vehicle needs.

Suddenly, the crowd quieted and JW laughed when he saw a section of the USC Spirit of Troy marching band come in. They started playing music and finished with the USC fight song, "Fight On!" Before JW went to thank each of them personally, he turned to Bonnie with a questioning look. "Well, you know the owner is an SC alum and it only took a small donation to the band to get them here." JW laughed, hugged her, and went off to continue to thank those who helped make this happen.

JW walked forward to a podium that was set up for them and took the microphone. "Could I have your attention for just a moment, please?"

From the crowd Don Harrison called out, "No, Ben! Don't let him have the microphone, we'll never get out of here alive. I have never heard such long speeches from a man of few words."

JW scowled at him and said, "Someone please gag him. Now, first, I have a lot of 'thank yous' to say." He pulled a paper from his pocket and went down a long list of names and their contributions. At the end of his speech, which did in fact run a little long, JW said, "If I missed anyone," and Don called out, "You didn't," and everyone laughed. "Please accept my apologies for the oversight and my thanks for what you have done. Bonnie and I have a little gift for each of you." JW reached behind the podium and pulled out a small box and opened it. "Challenge coins seem to be a big deal nowadays. The first time I saw them, I was in the Marine Corps. There's quite the custom of having your unit's coin with you or having to buy drinks at the bar.

"Each of you here today will receive the first challenge coin from the Long Beach Police Trailing Unit. One side of the coin has the unit name and the Long Beach PD badge on it. The other side has a silhouette of a man and a German Shepherd working a trail in front of the U.S. flag. Along the outside is our unit motto. It reads 'Potes Currere Sed Te Occoulere Non Potes,' which translates to 'You can run, but you can't hide.'"

As the party wound down and the guests started to leave, JW was approached by Dr. Gaurdia and SA LeClair. "I was wondering if you guys were going to come over to chat."

Dr. Gaurdia replied, "Well, the line was long and distinguished. We waited our turn. I have to say, very impressive today. Oh, and you were good, too." JW laughed; it seemed the polite thing to do. She continued, "Well, you're certified. Now I need you to go out and catch someone. We'll be in touch."

While JW and Bonnie celebrated, the Shadow was at work as a security officer. Although he enjoyed the new position, he had considered that this job was not going to work well with his new plans. He needed to find something that would give him more mobility.

As he pondered this new problem, his mind wandered. He enjoyed going over his past hunts and reveling in the mastery of his prey. He could remember every detail, although he did not know the names of all his girls. He continued down the neural pathways of his mind, wandering into dark corners he had not visited in a long time.

He recalled being a teenager in his hometown of Portland, Oregon. The teen years are always challenging, but they helped shape John into the man he would become. He grew up with his mother alone; his father having abandoned them right after his birth.

Dropping deeper into his dream-like state, John recalled getting up early for his paper route. He paused for a moment and thought, *That's where I learned to love working overnight. It's so quiet and still...perfect for hunting.*

He liked delivering papers; it provided money for his experiments and he had little to no interaction with anyone. Even at the newspaper depot, where he would pick up his morning load, he had almost no contact with the other delivery boys. He thought it was because he intimidated them. In reality, they thought he was strange and did not like being around John.

Being a paperboy allowed him to wander the streets as he made his deliveries, but also to examine other aspects of the human condition. He was such a natural part of the background that he was almost invisible. He liked the freedom to watch people as they began their days. Their lives had no similarity to his and this made him angry. Why did they get to live their lives in comfort and prosperity?

One morning, it seemed especially cold and the cool air flowing over his hands on the handlebars of his bike gave him a chill. While he paused in the shadows under a tree to warm his hands in his jacket pockets, he glanced at a house to his left. There was nothing special about this place except that a second-floor light was on. His curiosity piqued, John took a quick look and saw a young girl, partially dressed. She was brushing her hair while walking back and forth, into and out of his view. It was like she was teasing him. *Wait, I know her.* She went to his school but was a year younger. He had seen her in the halls walking to class. She was one of the popular girls.

He watched her for a while as she moved back and forth. He thought she was incredibly beautiful here in her natural setting. He thought that if he had a girl like that, his whole life would change. All he had to do was talk to her and she would see what an incredible guy he was. He would talk to her at school the next time he saw her, maybe even ask her out. He rode off to finish his route while planning how he would make it happen.

With the difference in their class schedules and the normal interruptions of school life, it took a week for their paths to cross in the hallway. There she was, right in front of him. As he approached her, she looked right at him and smiled. She said, "Hi," but then walked off in the direction of her next class. She had smiled and talked to him. But there was something else. He knew, he saw it in her eyes. He had seen it before—pity.

Realizing all his plans had been for nothing, he became angry. She was just like all the others. She didn't deserve him. That bitch felt sorry for him!

A week later, the girl's father found a dead cat in their front yard, its neck broken. He didn't recognize the cat and thought perhaps it had been hit by a car and the impact had thrown it into his yard. He placed the cat in the trash can and thought nothing more of it. He never knew it was a tribute to lost love, a gift from the boy who would grow into the Shadow.

As the Shadow returned from his trip down memory lane, he realized there was something there. An idea began forming in his mind that would give him the freedom to hunt. It would take some work from him, but he knew the answer now. All he had to do was make it a reality and his campaign of terror could begin.

25

After the party, JW and Bonnie took the dogs and went home. The dogs were exhausted from a full evening of petting by just about everyone there. At one point, JW had looked over and the band was taking a photo with the dogs. JW laughed at the memory of it. Bonnie came into the living room with two cups of coffee and sat down. JW looked at the coffee curiously and Bonnie said, "Mine is decaf; I know caffeine doesn't keep you awake, so you have leaded. We should talk." JW tightened on the couch, sensing one of "those" talks. Bonnie sensed his apprehension and said, "Relax, it's not one of those talks. It's just that it finally hit me tonight just how big this could be. Dr. Gaurdia approached me and we had a nice chat. I like her, but there's something mysterious about her."

"Yeah, she's a shrink, they like to play mind games."

"OK, I can see that. The funny thing was, I didn't feel like she was playing games. It was almost like she was telling me she would take care of things; take care of you and me and the dogs. I got the feeling we would be under her protective umbrella and nothing bad would happen."

JW was silent for a long while, thinking about what she had said. "I guess I don't let my guard down around her. It's hard for me to do that."

"Yeah, I know. You rarely do it around me."

"I know, I'm sorry."

"No worries, JW, I knew who you were when I married you."

JW looked at the dogs and laughed. They were side by side on the floor, sleeping. "Those two are out. They both had a busy day."

"You know we were watching the trail on TV? The helicopter was filming it and broadcasting it back to us. That was maybe the most amazing thing I have ever seen. It seemed to go on forever. I was so worried when you got hurt and so proud when you finished."

"Yeah, I'm going to have to have a chat with Ben about his Bataan Death March trails. The dog had no problems, but it almost killed me. When we finally got to the end and Ares ID'd that student, well, let's just say I almost lost my breakfast right there."

"You've been under a ton of pressure. I know this whole thing has been hard on you, but somehow you made it through. I am so very proud of you, and Ares, too."

"Thanks, Hon. Next week we get to do it all over again with Addy."

"Will that be as big of a production?"

"I don't think so. Today was all about showing off Ares with a trail that, I'm sure when Ben first told them about, they were all saying, 'No freakin' way.'"

"Yeah. I was worried, but then I thought about all the times you told me about the crazy trails that Ben and Allen came up with, and I said to myself, 'Ares has this.'"

The two sat side by side, holding hands in the dark room. They both fell asleep there on the couch. Sometime after midnight, Addy climbed up beside them and burrowed in next to JW. Ares stayed on the floor, watching from a ways back, just like a cover officer would watch another officer's back while out of the car talking to suspects. At 2:45 a.m., JW's phone rang. He clicked it off his belt and answered with a hoarse, "JW North."

"Hey, LT, this is Janie in the Comm Center. Sorry to wake you, but I have a request for you and your dog at a command post at Eighth and Freeman."

JW laughed and said, "Well, that didn't take long."

The dispatch supervisor laughed. "To tell the truth, we heard about you certifying and started a pool to see how soon you would have your first call-out."

"Who won?"

"I don't think you know her. She has only been here about a year. Her name is Cynthia Hewitt."

"Yeah, I don't think I know her. Well, congratulate her for me. I will be en route in five."

"Five minutes? You sleeping in your uniform, LT?"

"Something like that. Please give Ben Kellum a call and let him know I am responding to this. He may want to tag along."

"Roger, LT. I called him first since he lives farther out than you. He's on my screen and shows en route. I'll have the dispatcher log you, so just let us know when you are rolling."

JW asked one last question. "Janie, what is this call?"

"It started as a dead body call, found in the alley. The first unit on-scene said it looked suspicious and called a supervisor, who then called Homicide."

As JW ended the call, he felt Bonnie's eyes on him, questioning. "Well, Dear, that is our first call-out. Possible homicide over near Rose Park."

"How is your leg? Can you do this?"

"Surprisingly, the leg feels OK. I guess the ice really helped. Besides, I don't think we can afford to say no. We need officers to call us and if we start off saying no, well, they just won't call. Worst case, I'll ask Ben to run the trail."

"Sure you will."

JW laughed and hurriedly pulled on his boots and grabbed the rest of his gear. As he and Ares stepped out of the house, Bonnie wished them good luck. The night was typical for Long Beach, cool with a bit of a marine layer overhead. There was not a lot of air movement at all. *Good, should make it easier to trail.* In many ways, this trail was more important than the one they ran the day before. It was nice to be certified, but if he couldn't convince his brother officers it worked, it wouldn't matter. Police officers were like the original "Doubting Thomas." Show me.

JW arrived at the command post and checked in. He saw Ben was already there and walked over to him. Ben was talking to one homicide detective and the other was on his cell phone. JW recognized the first detective as Alex Brennan. He was another old friend; he and JW went way back. They had played Little League baseball together.

"Hey, JW, welcome back. So, here's the deal. My partner thinks this is BS and is afraid it will screw up any case that may come out of this. I'm not sure about it myself, but I think this is a drug overdose, so what do we have to lose? We go way back, so I'm willing to give you a shot. Personally, I think my partner was asleep during the class you gave. I think we have nothing to worry about either way."

JW nodded and waited. Finally, the other detective got off the phone and said, "Hey, LT. OK, the bosses say if we are good with it, then go ahead."

JW looked at Brennan, who said, "You're a go." Brennan then looked at his partner and said, "Quit being a worrywart. This is gonna be fun. OK, JW, let's see what the pup can do."

Ben and JW went back to his car and Ben got the scent transfer unit out of the back while JW prepared Ares. They walked along with Brennan and his partner to an alley. JW could see some activity partway up the alley and asked Brennan, "Any issue with how we go into your scene?"

"No, we don't see any evidence of how she got there. Just try to stay to the center in case we missed something."

The alley was dark with very little lighting. As they approached the scene, he made out a shopping cart off to the side with a body in it. There were two patrol officers there, lighting up the body for the coroner. JW didn't recognize the coroner, but he said, "Hi, JW North. Are you done? Is it OK for me to collect some scent evidence?"

"Can you explain how that works? I don't want to mess up any trace evidence on my victim." JW nodded and provided a quick explanation while Ben set up the STU. "OK then, but please don't touch the body."

JW stood back while Ben collected several scent pads. He looked at the woman, whose body had been dumped in a shopping cart and pushed here. She was probably about twenty-five, but her obviously heavy drug use made her look much older. Her eyes were open, staring toward the sky. *Sorry lady, no stars out tonight for you.* There was a crust of powder around her mouth. *Brennan's probably right, overdose.* The night air was still not moving much, and the odor of death hung in the air.

Ben finished the scent pads while the coroner set up a gurney to transport the body. As Ben handed the pad to him, JW heard the coroner ask the officers to help her lift the body out of the shopping cart and onto the gurney. Ben looked at JW and asked, "How's your leg? You OK running this?"

JW nodded, took the scent pad, and moved a few steps away. He brought Ares to his side and clipped his tracking lead on while unhooking his leash. He scented Ares with the pad and commanded, "Geo-say."

Ares began to cast a bit, looking for the trail. He hit it quickly and worked back past the officers and coroner working with the body. Ares worked past without even a glance their way. They, on the other hand, were very interested in the big German Shepherd. Ares continued down the alley. So far it was an easy trail. Hopefully, whoever dumped the body hadn't gone through a yard. The search team exited onto the street and made a quick right. Ben had a couple of officers staged in black and whites to assist with traffic control, if needed. The trail continued mid-street and made the first turn possible. Ares was still pulling hard and JW had to apply strong back pressure to keep his speed down. Fresh trail.

The team worked the streets, left and right, for several blocks. Occasionally, JW could see a mark on the street's surface where it looked like the shopping cart wheel had stuck and marked the asphalt. After about a half mile total, Ares stopped in front of a one-story, eight-unit apartment building. These were relatively common in this part of Long Beach and dated back to long before JW was born here. Ares worked the street and the sidewalk until he finally stopped in front of a gate. A modern security fence and gate had been placed across the front to help keep trouble outside, but looking at what was in front of the gate, JW thought perhaps it was to keep the illicit activity inside.

In front of him stood a six-and-a-half-foot-tall mountain of a man. He had to weigh at least 280 pounds, but there wasn't much fat on him. He was covered with prison tattoos and looked down at Ares with mild interest. JW was willing to bet there was a dealer inside and this guy was the equivalent of a doorman. Right now, he was blocking their way. JW looked at the man for a moment, considering his approach to the doorstop. He could hear Ben on the radio requesting additional units to the front and rear of the place. JW told Ares to "Sitz" and he promptly sat. He never took his eyes off the man in front of him. He was not giving what JW would call an alert, it was more of a target lock.

JW walked up to the man and said, "Nice night."

The man looked at him and said, "What you doin' out so late?"

"Oh, walking my dog. You?"

"Me, I'm just standing here enjoying the night."

"It is a lovely evening to be out. You didn't happen to see a woman go by earlier in a shopping cart, did you?"

The man looked at him and asked, "What you want, Mr. Policeman?"

"Well, right now I would like to come in with my dog and look around, but you seem to be in the way." As JW continued his conversation, he could hear the sounds of multiple cars stopping behind him. He really didn't want this to end in a fight, but the man didn't seem inclined to get out of his way. JW looked at the man's face. It was hard from what appeared to be many years in prison. The man had a prominent nose ring on the right side of his nose. JW said, "Hey, I'm curious about something. That's a nice piece of jewelry there on your nose. But I was wondering, when you pick your nose, do the boogers get stuck on it?"

The man looked at him for a moment. JW was convinced he was going to attack him. He was big—JW would probably end up in the emergency room again. Bonnie would not be happy. The man continued to stare at JW and then looked at the big German Shepherd by his side. He laughed and said, "OK, Mr. Policeman, you and your big dog can come in."

The man stepped aside and JW walked past him. As he entered, he said back to the man, "Thanks for your courtesy, sir."

Once inside the gate, Ben and two more officers moved inside with them. Two other officers walked up to the man and started asking him questions.

JW looked at Ben and said, "A bit claustrophobic in here."

Ben nodded and said, "Yeah. You remember when we talked about problems with a suspect's neighborhood?" JW nodded. He remembered Ben telling him that trailing isn't the hardest thing for a dog, but it could be difficult when you went into an area where the suspect lived and moved around a lot, because the suspect's scent would be all over. Ben had told him that, on occasion, they had to bring in a different dog to isolate the scent, that the trailing dog just couldn't do it.

"Well, I guess we get to see how he does, then, don't we?"

"This is my fault. We should have done some training exercises on this."

JW shook his head and said, "No fault, brother. We can try, but we can't train for every eventuality."

JW gave Ares the scent again and restarted him. Ares worked as they both thought he would. He covered the courtyard, back and forth. He was almost frantic to isolate the scent, but there was just so much here. JW was getting uncomfortable, moving in front of all these windows, not knowing if there was a gun inside pointed at them. Finally, after a good ten minutes, Ares isolated the scent, sitting in front of unit five. JW looked at Ben and he nodded.

"OK, let's get out of the way and let the patrol guys do a knock and talk."

JW and Ben walked out and went back to JW's Tahoe, which had been driven to the apartments. On the way, he stopped and talked to one of the officers, who was busy interviewing the man who had been guarding the gate. He let Ares in the Tahoe, praised him, and gave him some water while Ben spoke with the detectives. JW overheard, "OK, we'll work on getting a warrant."

JW handed Ben a bottle of water as he walked up. Ben said, "OK, we can roll out of here. It will take them a while to get a warrant. Patrol did their knock and talk. Guy answered the door and talked to them. Claims he doesn't know what we're talking about. He's full of it. They pulled a couple more addicts out and then backed out to wait for the warrant. My guess is our victim died of an overdose and they just dumped her body to get her out of there."

"Yeah, makes sense to me. Let's get out of here."

Before he left, JW went to the detectives and said, "Hey, guys, thanks for the call. I appreciate the work."

Brennan said, "Hey, I'm impressed. Dog took us right here. Now, this is probably nothing big, but success is success in my book. I'll shoot you an email later if we get any more information."

JW looked to the side and noticed the man who had been guarding the gate was still there. As JW walked up, the man said, "Hey, those other cops told me they could have arrested me for interfering with a police investigation, but you said unless it was a big deal to let it drop. I appreciate that, man."

JW nodded at him. "How long you been out?"

"Two months, man. Look, I'm just trying to get some money together and get home."

"I hear you. You using?"

"Naw, man, I was never into that shit. Just fucks your body up."

"I hear that. I had knee surgery once. They gave me some good stuff. I got off it as quick as I could. There's a whole week of my life I can't remember. So, where's home?"

"Tulsa. Tulsa, Oklahoma."

"Tulsa, huh? What's it like there this time of year?"

The man smiled, a far-off look in his eyes and said, "It's coming off the really hot season. Soon it's gonna be great."

JW said, "Good luck to you," then turned and walked away. JW scanned the black-and-white cruisers, looking for a training unit. He found one and motioned for the driver to hang on as he walked up. Officer Johnny Hanover called out to him, "Hey, LT, that was pretty cool with the dog and all."

"Thanks, Johnny. Can you and your partner do me a favor?"

"Sure, LT. What do you need?"

"What do you think a bus ticket to Tulsa costs?"

Hanover looked at him with a question in his eyes and said, "Dunno. Rookie, fire up that computer and get the LT an answer to that question."

A few minutes later, the young officer said, "Sir, it looks like it's $150.00."

JW said, "Hell, that sounds like a bargain to me." He reached into his wallet and pulled out ten twenty-dollar bills. "Here's the favor, Johnny. See that big guy over there? Take him to the Greyhound station and buy him a ticket to Tulsa."

"That's it? Does he want to go to Tulsa, LT? Because he looks awful big to make go anywhere."

"I believe he does."

"OK, LT. What do you want me to do with your change?"

JW smiled and said, "Let him have it. A man that big must eat a lot." They both laughed and JW walked to his Tahoe.

"Rookie, go ask that rather large gentleman if he would come over here."

The rookie looked out of the car and said, "Sure thing, sir."

A few minutes later the big man walked up to the black-and-white cruiser. Hanover looked him over and said, "You're even bigger up close. What's your name?"

The big man stared him down and said, "Julian."

"Well, Julian, get in, we're going for a ride."

Julian looked concerned and asked, "Where we going? Am I under arrest?"

Hanover laughed. "Arrest? No. You're going someplace worse than jail. You're going to Tulsa. Lieutenant North just bought you a ticket to Tulsa."

Julian smiled. "Really? Tulsa's not bad, man, that's home. I got a girl there."

"Well, OK then. Let's get you on your way. Climb in, I know it's tight back there. These rides are not built for comfort."

26

The following morning JW woke feeling hungover, but he hadn't had anything to drink; he was just tired. He wasn't as young as he used to be. Even after spending most of his career working the graveyard shift, staying up all night was getting harder as he got older. He had adjusted to more of a day shift routine, plus he was not one hundred percent back from the shooting injuries. He felt fine, but tired easily. He stumbled down the hallway, through the ever-present "dogstacle course" toward the kitchen. *Coffee. Need coffee. Now.*

As he moved slowly past Bonnie's office, she called out to him, "Good morning. Your coffee cup is in the dishwasher."

"Why?" was the only word JW could muster.

"Simple. Your cup was dirty and it got washed, along with the rest of the dishes. Now it's nice and clean."

"I keep telling you that the cup is not dirty. It is pre-flavored."

"Well, your pre-flavored is my dirty."

JW continued to the kitchen and dug around inside the dishwasher until he found the cup. "Did you have to hide it?"

"If by hidden, you mean on the top rack, up front, then yes," she answered. The dogs were sitting up, their heads turning back and forth watching the verbal tennis match.

JW filled his coffee cup and sat down with his iPad to check his email. He scanned through the hoard of overnight arrivals and found what he was looking for, an email from Alex Brennan. The email said:

JW,

We got our search warrant and went back into that apartment. We didn't find much other than some dope. We did find a pool of puke that we think came from the victim. We called Narcotics and they came out and worked with us. They took the dope lead and we worked the dead body. We interviewed the witnesses and had to sweat them a bit, but they gave up the dealer and told us the victim OD'd. They told us the dealer gave them some dope to take her out of there and dump the body. He didn't want her stinking the place up. After you left, the coroner gave us an OD as a preliminary cause of death. Since we have the dealer and some witnesses, we thought we might go chat with the district attorney to see if there was anything we can use to file a case on him. Then Narco asked us to hold off. They were going to use that on the dealer to sweat him. They want to work their way up his chain a bit. Who knows, maybe something big will come of it. Can you come by the office today and file a follow-up for us on your trail? We probably won't use it, but Narco may. Either way, we need the paper to close out the dead body case.

Thanks again for coming out and helping. It was great seeing you, and your dog is incredible. Are you thinking of going to the Nationals this year? I haven't shot much, but I am thinking about it myself.

Talk later,
Alex

There was another email from the Narcotics lieutenant also asking him for a follow-up report. He thanked JW for the lead on the dope dealer and was hopeful something might come out of it. JW wrote out quick replies to both emails, thanking them for the work and asking for the Department Record or report number so he could file his follow-up for them. Fortunately, he did not have to go downtown, he could file the follow-up from his Tahoe in the driveway using the laptop computer.

As he finished his correspondence, Bonnie came into the room with both Ares and Addy in hot pursuit. "Alright, you two. It is not breakfast time yet. You have thirty minutes more to go." Both dogs looked like they had lost their favorite tennis ball and quietly walked away. A half hour could be a lifetime when you are starving.

As JW was clearing out the rest of the junk that had arrived in email overnight, Bonnie sat down, a pile of paperwork with her. JW decided he would forget to mention the two hundred dollars he had given away last night. It had seemed like a good idea at the time. There was a quick email from Johnny Hanover telling him that Julian Sanchez had been happy to get on a bus and had thanked JW for the money. The last time Johnny had seen him, he was boarding a bus that would take him home.

Bonnie asked how the previous night's work had gone. "Well, the trail was good. Ares worked well, but it was a fresh trail, not real challenging. It looks like an overdose, but we ran a trail anyway, back to where we think the victim died. They put together a search warrant, found some dope, but not much else. Narcotics thinks they might be able to work the dealer. That's about it."

Bonnie nodded. "A small success is better than failure."

"That's what I love about you; always the optimist. But I agree. It seems like there is interest by the Department and that's a start. We knew that selling this to the line officers and detectives was going to be a big challenge. Last night was a good start, but I don't think it was the big splash that Dr. Gaurdia wanted."

"I agree. Now let me put on my CEO hat and give you an update on other things. First off, moneywise, we are still well below budget. We got lucky with the car and the Department stepped up more than we expected with the loan of Ben. Do you have any major unplanned expenses planned?"

"You mean besides the Corvette?"

"Good, no new expenses. Now I'm having trouble with one detail." JW looked at her and raised his eyebrows, silently asking her to elaborate. "I don't know what line item to put that two-hundred-dollar expense under."

JW laughed. "Not much gets past you, huh?"

"So, what was that about?"

JW decided not to ask how she knew and said, "Let's just call it an investment."

Bonnie then continued giving JW a full status update. "Oh, and one other thing. We're gonna need a bigger boat."

"Say what?"

"If this program takes off, we may need to get a bigger place."

"I thought you loved this house."

"I do, but it got a lot smaller with two big dogs."

JW laughed and said, "Well, it wouldn't be quite so crowded if these two dogs weren't always right in front of everywhere you want to go."

"Yeah, no kidding. But seriously, I know I signed up for this and all. I knew the job was dangerous when I took it, but I just need you to know there is a part of me that worries when you go out and play policeman. I almost lost you once and it scared the hell out of me. I'm with you on this wherever it takes us, but I want you to know I worry. I have worried about you since I met you and I just don't want to lose you or the dogs."

"I hear you. I can't say I understand because I haven't been where you are. I'm always in the thick of it, so there isn't time to worry, but I do hear you. I will be as safe as I can be and still do the job."

The next two months crawled by for JW. The temperature cooled as it moved later into the year. Soon the holidays would be upon them. The stores were already full of Christmas decorations, wrapping, and gifts. JW continued to train both Ares and Addy. Addy's certification went off without a hitch. This time there wasn't a big gathering. It was a private affair with a few witnesses from search and rescue groups. The FBI did not attend. Addy was, in some ways, better than Ares, but in others she didn't match him. Ben started working what he called neighborhood trails into the training. These simulated the problem they encountered while trailing the dead narcotics overdose victim: isolating scent in an area that the suspect frequented, where there was a lot of scent present. This was an area in which Addy excelled while Ares was just OK.

One day, at the end of training, JW and Ben were chatting with Allen and some others. JW threw out the idea of running a dual dog team. "What do you think about running two dogs on a team? One to do the hard trailing work, the other to work the neighborhood problem."

Allen thought a moment and said, "Plus you would have a backup dog. If you're running a long trail or it's really hot, having a backup right there is a huge positive."

JW added, "You know me, I am always good with a backup."

Ben decided to rib JW. "Yes, we know, JW. You have two of most things and three of everything else. Your car is sitting pretty low from the weight."

There wasn't much work for the team during this time. JW began to worry that the program would just fade into disuse. On Thanksgiving weekend, JW was again awakened in the middle of the night. The communications supervisor told him there had been a pursuit of a stolen car in the East Division. The pursuit had ended with the suspect vehicle crashing into a row of parked cars and finally coming to rest against a block wall where Bellflower Boulevard ended at Loynes Drive. The suspect had failed to make the turn, but was able to flee on foot before police units could establish a perimeter. JW asked the supervisor to call Ben out and she replied, "Already done, LT. Kellum is at the top of the call-out list for your program. He said it was more important that he respond quickly than you."

"Well, OK then," was all JW could say.

Ben was already there when JW arrived at the command post. He had collected a scent sample from the driver's seat of the stolen car and had a traffic team ready to go. JW asked, "How far behind were the guys when he crashed?"

The incident commander replied, "Hard to say exactly, I would guess maybe a minute or two. The helicopter was down for the night because it's so late. Plus, we had a shooting on the west side and most of our units were deployed there, so we didn't have as much out east as usual." JW nodded; he had experienced many a night just as had been described.

JW put Ares in his harness and clipped on his trailing lead. He gave the command, "Geo-say," and they were off. The car had crashed into a high wall surrounding a private residential area. The suspect's vehicle came to rest against the wall but had not broken through. *Well-made wall.* Instead of the trail starting eastbound as he imagined it would, Ares moved back and forth about the car, finally jumping on the hood and looking up at the wall. JW saw some footprints on the hood and said, "Looks like he may have used the car to get over the wall." Rather than climb the wall themselves and possibly injure Ares, Ben and JW walked around to the other side. They went into the backyard of the first house, re-scented Ares and worked through it until they came out on a street. As they moved along, it was apparent the suspect was moving close to the trees and plants, obviously trying to hide from someone. As they continued eastbound, it became clear who he was hiding from: there was a guard shack near the entrance to the private residential area.

When he got to the shack, JW stopped to speak with the guard, who told him that he had heard the crash and then the police sirens. When he didn't see anything after a few minutes, he stepped out and looked around a bit. He came around to the front entrance and stopped a police officer and asked what was going on. Hearing there was a criminal in the area, he decided to get back to his post. JW believed the suspect used the few moments the guard was away from his post to sneak past. The trail continued eastbound until they came to another entrance, this one unguarded. The trailing team went out and turned right, southbound on a side road that paralleled Pacific Coast Highway.

The trail continued until they reached a small park. Here the trail went up and onto Pacific Coast Highway. JW and Ben continued along the road, while their escort had to turn around and go back. They crossed the bridge over the channel, and JW hoped the suspect had not gone further east, into the oil fields.

JW's fears were unfounded as the trail continued south past Second Street. JW could hear Ben on the radio to dispatch asking them to notify the Seal Beach Police Department that they were getting close to the border. Sure enough, the trail continued and JW wondered, *How did we not see this guy? He's right out in the open, hiding in plain sight.* As they crossed another bridge, this time entering Seal Beach, JW could see a police car a few hundred yards down the way. It was stopped by the side of the road and appeared to be waiting for them. As he got closer, JW could see that the Seal Beach officer was talking to someone sitting on a bus bench.

The parade stopped at the Seal Beach police car as Ares walked up to the man on the bench and sat, looking at him. JW smiled to himself and the Seal Beach officer said, "Nice morning for a jog. Getting some exercise?"

JW laughed; he knew the officer had been advised by his dispatch of what they were doing. "Yeah, you can't get enough exercise. My dog was bored, so he came along. So, what's this guy's story? Is he waiting for the bus?"

"Yeah, we got a call from West Comm, that's our dispatch, that you guys were out for a stroll, so I thought I would come by and say 'Hi.' This guy was just sitting here waiting on the bus."

JW nodded and said, "Did you tell him the bus doesn't run at this time of night?"

"No, as a matter of fact, I thought I would let you do that."

Ben walked up to the man sitting on the bench and asked, "How come you have scratches on your arms and face? Is that from where the airbag got you?"

JW tuned the conversation out and turned back to the Seal Beach officer. "Hey, good catch. You don't mind if we take this guy off your hands, do you?"

The officer smiled and said, "No, I don't mind at all. I was with LA County Sheriffs for five years. It felt like I was never going to get out of the jails, so when I heard about an opening here in Seal Beach, I jumped on it. I love it here. Nice quiet town, except when some interloper from Long Beach comes down and messes our stuff up."

Laughing, JW said, "Well, we try to keep our criminals at home, but you know, the grass is always greener."

As Ben put handcuffs on him, the suspect became visibly upset at being arrested. "This is bullshit. I didn't do nothing, and you guys can't prove it anyway."

JW turned to him and said, "I'm sorry, sir, but I find it difficult to prove a double negative. You seem unhappy about something, certainly it can't be your arrest?"

The man glared at JW, who stared back and said, "You're going to have to work on that hate stare. It isn't having the desired effect."

Ben looked at JW and said, "No matter how hard you try, you can't please all the people all the time." Ben handed the suspect off to one of the follow vehicles and then updated Long Beach dispatch that the suspect was in custody. JW gave Ares a lot of praise and petting and said goodbye to the Seal Beach officer. They got in the Tahoe, which another officer had driven to them, and returned to the command post to update the incident commander. Before getting back in the car to head home, JW turned to Ben and they gave each other a high five.

"Before we head back, I have a couple things I need to say," Ben said, looking down at the floorboard of the car. "When you first started the program back up, I have to be honest, it bothered me."

"I'm not sure I follow."

Ben hesitated; what he had to say was not easy, and he felt uncomfortable saying it. "Look, I was crushed when they cancelled the program the last go round. Everyone worked so hard on it and the way the department quit on us, kicked us to the curb. It hurt."

"I can see that." But what JW didn't see was what Ben was getting at.

"Then you come along, the great JW North and everything just comes so easy to you."

"Ben, you know I couldn't have done this without you. I think I have made that perfectly clear to everyone.

I understood you were getting grief from Lucy, but I didn't know there was all of this."

"I know. You see, that's the hard part. Explaining. I am jealous. I know that sounds stupid, but it is what it is. I hate that saying too. BUT—I love doing this. I love working with you and the dogs. But I don't think Lucy sees that."

"Would it help if I asked Bonnie to have a chat with Lucy? They're friends. I can engineer a get-together and we can give them some time to talk. Maybe if she understands, she will be more supportive."

"That might help, I dunno."

"Look Ben, I owe you a lot. More than I can ever repay. If I can help out, you know I will. Now let's get out of here. All this sharing of feelings is making me hungry. Let's go grab a bite to eat before we call it a night. I'm buying!"

27

JW sat in a chair in his backyard. It was a typical February day in Long Beach—sunny, with temperatures in the mid-sixties. The smoker was filling the air with the scent of burning wood from an apple tree, the ribs were halfway through their six hours of cooking. JW loved cooking on the wood pellet smoker they had recently purchased. The food was excellent, and the company provided great recipes for the would-be chef. It was the weekend and he and Bonnie had organized a little barbecue with Allen, Ben and Lucy. The party would give everyone a bit of a break and also allow them some time to brainstorm their next steps. JW had a small glass of Clase Azul, one of his favorite tequilas from Mexico. He liked how the tequila flowed over his tongue like warm butter and then went smoothly down his throat. Bonnie and JW had discovered it in a tequila bar on one of their SCUBA diving trips to Cozumel, Mexico.

Ben wasn't much of a drinker and had a Diet Coke in his hand, while Allen was drinking a Coors light. JW was more of a beer man himself, but the tequila was a treat and he felt like he deserved something special. Bonnie and Lucy were off in a corner sipping wine, the dogs lounging at their feet, while they were in deep discussion. The program was shaping up nicely. It wasn't yet the big success he was hoping for, but that was more about opportunity than ability. Ares and Addy both trailed well. It had been proven in certification and on real street trails. They had participated in several arrests, but so far none were "the big one."

JW thought back to when he had first applied to be a police officer. He was in the final stages of the hiring process and was doing the last interview. The interviewer asked about his other interests and JW had told him about dogs. He didn't know about K9 then, but he had always had dogs and he liked them. There was just something about a dog and how it could make your day special or take away your pain. Afterward, as the interviewer walked him out of the police academy, he asked JW, "Have you ever thought about working K9?"

JW had answered, "No," but admitted it sounded interesting. The idea intrigued him, so he went home and started doing some research.

After completing his field training work, he had volunteered to work with the K9s as the bad guy. He did everything from hiding in trees to putting on the protective sleeve and taking bites. He recalled his first bite—it came from a Rottweiler. He remembered looking at the dog as it charged him and thinking his heart was going to burst right out of his chest. He was scared to death, but the dog did as it was supposed to and bit the sleeve. JW thought about how strong the dog had been as it pulled and twisted, and imagined if the bite had been without a sleeve. He thought about how one question, one man could make such a difference in your life. If the interviewer had not asked him that one question, how different things could have been.

Ben snapped him back to the present. "Earth to JW, come in, JW."

"Sorry, Ben, I guess I was daydreaming."

"I have heard tequila can have that effect on you. What I said was, have you heard anything from the FBI?"

"FBI, no. I know Dr. Gaurdia has her sources, so I haven't been reporting to her. I think she's waiting for something big to come up, and we won't hear from her until then."

Ben nodded and said, "OK, you've had more recent contact with her than I, so I will trust your judgment. The FBI was so hot on the program, and we have done everything they asked and then some. I guess I thought they would have reached out by now."

Allen joined the conversation, saying, "Have you thought about a Plan B? What if they don't call?"

JW considered this for a moment and shook his head. "Allen, to be honest, no. I never considered that the FBI wasn't going to ask us to participate. Just like I never doubted the program would work. I have always had a feeling that things would work out; that they would be fine. I guess I am surprised that it has taken as long as it has, but I still believe it will all work out. But what do I know?"

Allen answered, "You've done well so far. I think you're right, but if not, you have something special here. Los Angeles and Orange Counties are pretty big; I'm sure there is more than enough work here for you. The question will be, where do you draw the line?"

JW gave him a questioning look and Allen continued, "What I mean is, you are right to be happy about that stolen car suspect arrest the other night, but Ares and Addy and you are a limited resource. If you chase every small-time crook in the area, you won't be available when something big comes up. I believe you need to start putting limits on this or else you're going to get burned out."

Ben nodded and JW said, "Well, I was hoping Ben would retire and take up some of the slack, but he seems to like getting paid to go to work."

Ben kicked at him from his chair, but purposely missed. "It's not that and you know it, JW," Ben said. "I just want to be sure this is going to fly before I make that kind of commitment. I don't have the financial reserves you do."

"You're right, my friend. It was a lot easier for me, but I've always known this would work, even before I knew I had any financial reserves."

JW and Ben jabbed at each other good-naturedly for a while before Allen interrupted and asked, "JW, the question remains, what do you do if the FBI never calls?"

As soon as Allen had asked his question, JW's phone began to ring. "Well, it's not the FBI, but it is the Communications Center."

JW answered his phone, "This is North."

"Hey, LT, this is Anne in the Comm Center. I have a 10-21 for you to call the chief ASAP."

"Chief Estrada?" asked JW, unsure if that was who she meant.

"Ten-four, sir. Do you need his number?"

"No, I have it here in my phone. Thanks, Anne."

"You're welcome, LT. Be safe."

JW turned to his friends and said, "Well, that's weird. I have to call Chief Estrada ASAP."

JW found the chief's number and dialed. The chief answered immediately and said, "Hey, JW. I hope you don't have plans. I have a request from Las Vegas for you to respond and assist with a trail. I'm calling you directly rather than going through the normal protocol on a call-out."

"Alright, sir. Did you say Las Vegas, as in Nevada?"

"Yes, I did, JW. I have no idea how they heard about you, but they did and they are asking for our assistance. I know the sheriff there—he's an old friend, we went to the National Academy together—so I decided to approve this. You are cleared to assist and, if he is available, you can take Kellum, too."

"Roger that, sir. Ben just happens to be with me right now. I'll check with him and get underway. Do you have a contact there for me?"

"As a matter of fact, I do." Chief Estrada relayed the name and phone number for a Las Vegas SWAT lieutenant.

JW started taking notes on a business card he had in his wallet.

After he got off the phone, he sat for a moment, thinking. "Ben, how would you like to go to Las Vegas?"

Ben looked at JW, did a double take, and asked, "Vegas?"

"That's what I said."

By now, other members of the party had gathered around. Their eyes were a mix of acute interest, with a tinge of fear thrown in. If the guys were going to Vegas, it was a big and potentially dangerous mission.

Ben said, "Well, I haven't been to Vegas in a while, probably since the last time I ran in the Baker to Vegas race." Ben was referring to the 120-mile, twenty-person relay race from just outside Baker, California, to the Las Vegas convention center. JW and Ben had both run in the race, but that had been years ago. They both loved to run, but the race was highly competitive and both men had lost their speed a long time ago. Since then, JW had worked in a support role on the team, helping coordinate runners on the course. It was usually a fun race to participate in, but one year JW ran a particularly challenging leg when it was 105 degrees. A couple of runners got heat stroke and had to be air-lifted via helicopter from the course to the hospital.

JW stood and made a brief announcement. "Everyone, I apologize, but duty calls. Ben and I have just received a call-out to assist the Las Vegas Metropolitan Police Department. That's all I know right now. Everyone not named JW or Ben is welcome to stay and enjoy what smells like a delicious meal."

With that, JW pulled Bonnie aside and said, "I'm sorry, Hon. I certainly didn't see this coming."

"I understand, babe. We just weren't meant for the quiet life."

JW smiled. He loved how she accepted his life, even though inside he suspected she was screaming at him, *What the hell is wrong with you, JW? Why can't you be normal?*

"OK, I need to change and make a phone call before we leave. Ben, can you start pulling items from the out-of-town call-out list?"

JW and Ben had planned for just such an instance. Lists were never more important than when you were under extreme pressure and needed to perform. The various contingency lists they had prepared in advance would now make an interstate drive much easier. One less thing to worry about: Did we bring everything we need?

After talking to Lucy, Ben went to his car and retrieved a call-out bag and his external ballistic vest from the trunk, along with his duty weapon. He came back and JW directed him to the spare bedroom to change. Most of what JW would need later was already in the Tahoe, but his uniform, duty belt, and Springfield Operator were in the house. He went into his bedroom and quickly changed. Both men made a well-coordinated entrance, leaving their changing rooms at the same time. Ben walked to JW and said, "I was thinking while I was changing."

"Always dangerous," JW said without missing a beat.

"You're right about that. Anyway, I was thinking about trailing in Vegas. I think we need to know more before we get on the road."

JW nodded, they were both thinking along the same lines. "We may need both dogs. It could be long, or it could be out in the desert or it could be on the strip. I know one thing—I need to call this lieutenant in Vegas before we leave."

JW pulled out his phone and dialed the number the chief had given him. He could hear the phone ringing and then a voice said, "Takeo Van Geffin."

JW wondered if he had written the number down correctly. "This is Lieutenant JW North from Long Beach PD. Do I have the correct number?"

"Yes, Lieutenant North. This is Lieutenant Takeo Van Geffin of Las Vegas Metro SWAT. Call me Tak, everyone else does. We are a bit crazy here right now. We appreciate your willingness to help."

JW took that all in for a moment and replied, "It's our honor to assist. We will be on the road," he paused to look at Ben and Bonnie who were busy collecting things and carrying them out to the Tahoe. He looked at Ben and mouthed, "How long?"

Ben said, "RTR in ten mikes."

"OK, Tak, we will be ready to roll from Long Beach in ten minutes."

"Ten minutes, wow, I'm impressed. I only got the call from my sheriff thirty minutes ago."

This caught JW a bit off guard and he said, "Wait a minute, you didn't initiate the call-out?"

"No. I'll give you the details once you are en route, but this isn't the first serial we have had in Vegas. We worked with a group from the FBI a year ago. They helped us catch a serial killer that was working the Strip. Anyway, when we had our second killing that looked very familiar, the sheriff called those guys and someone there suggested we call you. That's all I know about how you got involved."

"Well, that's interesting. OK, what can you tell me about the case? I'm trying to understand what you have so I can bring the right equipment."

Three hundred miles away, Tak nodded and said, "We have had two homicides. The detectives tell me the two crime scenes look very much alike, especially when you take into account what he did to the victims. There wasn't much press on the first one, so they do not believe this is a copycat."

A copycat would be a different suspect, who mimicked the M.O. or victimology of a previous suspect. There were several possible reasons for such behavior, including the desire to make the police believe the first suspect had committed the second crime, or because the second suspect had not yet developed his own style.

"Both victims were found behind large casinos on the Strip. It looks like they were killed there. Both victims had prior arrests for prostitution."

JW thought for a moment and said, "So, it looks like we are going to be working in an urban environment, possibly right on the Las Vegas Strip. Oh, hell, do you guys think he could be staying in one of the big hotels?"

Tak answered, "We don't know. We were hoping you could point us in the right direction."

"OK, I think that's enough to get us started and on the way. We'll call you when we are en route, and we can do most of the pre-planning over the phone. How long ago did the last attack occur?"

"We located the victim this morning. We believe the attack was sometime last night."

"Last question for now; is the victim still at the scene?"

"Yes, we weren't sure how your program works, so we have asked the coroner to leave it all in place."

"Great. We're going to want to collect scent from the victim. It would be great if anyone who has had physical contact with the victim could be there when we start. That allows us to eliminate them from the all the different scents we collect."

"I'll see what I can do."

As soon as JW hung up the phone, there was a knock at the front door. Bonnie went to answer it and then called out, "JW, there are two gentlemen from the California Highway Patrol here."

JW wondered what the heck was going on and went to see. He was met by a lieutenant and a sergeant from the CHP who quickly introduced themselves. Lieutenant Mario Carbajal said, "I got a call from CHP Sacramento telling me to provide an escort from Long Beach to the California border on the way to Las Vegas. Is there someplace my sergeant and I can sit to work this and get organized? It won't take but a few minutes."

Bonnie looked at JW quizzically. He anticipated her question with, "CHP doesn't like people speeding on their freeways, even if they are on duty. Someone must have called them and asked for the escort."

JW pointed to the dining room and said, "You can set up in there. I appreciate the assist guys. We need to roll out in ten minutes."

Carbajal laughed and said, "Ten minutes, no problem."

JW found Ben carrying water bottles to the Tahoe and briefed him on what he knew so far.

JW said, "I'm having nightmares thinking that the suspect is holed up in one of the big casino-hotel buildings."

"Yeah, I have some ideas about that. I think we are going to need both dogs."

"I agree, I'll go tell Bonnie." JW turned and almost tripped over Bonnie.

"Tell me what?"

As JW stumbled past her, he said, "I think we're gonna need to take Addy too." He quickly told her what he knew.

"Well, isn't that why you trained her? You need to stop treating Addy like she is made of glass. She earned her spot on this team and she works just as well as Ares. And you definitely need to stop treating me like I'm some fragile China doll. Yes, I worry, but we are all tough and we can take it. You can stay on the porch and be safe or you can be a big dog and kick some ass."

JW smiled at her and said, "Well, I guess we all need to be Big Dogs. Hmmm, I like the sound of that."

28

JW and Ben got into the Tahoe, which was sitting in the driveway, idling. Ares and Addy were in the back, both of their heads crowded in the door to the cage, looking out and watching all the activity around them. Lieutenant Carbajal came up to the driver's window and told them they were ready to roll. He had two CHP cruisers that would lead the procession; he and the sergeant would bring up the rear. All JW had to do was stay in the middle and keep up. He handed JW a handheld radio and said, "This is in case you need to contact us."

As he walked off, Bonnie came up to the window. JW could see Ben's wife chatting with him on the other side of the Tahoe. Bonnie said, "I know what I said about being tough and all a few minutes ago, and I meant it, but I mean this, too, JW North. You better bring my dogs home safe and sound. And you better come home safe, too." She gave him a quick kiss and said, "A kiss for luck. Drive safe, crazy people on the road."

JW backed out of the driveway and took his place in line. Several neighbors had come outside, curious about all the police activity. They all waved as they drove by. As they turned out of the residential street and onto a larger roadway, JW spotted several blue and red flashing lights at the next intersection. As his caravan drove closer, he could see there were two East Division black and whites with officers out of their cars, stopping traffic in all directions. Off to the side, standing next to his assigned command car, was Javon Hudson. Seeing JW's Tahoe approach, Javon faced them, snapped to attention, and rendered a hand salute, just as sharp as the day he graduated the police academy.

In the Tahoe, Ben asked, "Was that the chief of staff of the Long Beach Police Department saluting us?"

"Yes, sir, it was."

"Huh."

The caravan got on the 405 freeway and headed out of town. JW grabbed the microphone from the dash, keyed it and said, "King 99 to log on."

The call came back instantly. "King Nine Nine, go ahead."

He gave the dispatcher their information and said, "King 99, we will be on a 924 to Las Vegas Metro until further notice."

The dispatcher responded, "King 99, I will show you 924 to Las Vegas Metro until further."

In the Communications Center, the dispatcher crossed herself in the Catholic tradition and said quietly, "God be with you, sir. Be safe."

Traffic was relatively heavy leaving the huge Southern California metropolitan area, but they made good time. When they ran into traffic jams, JW followed the lead vehicles onto the shoulder. Near Riverside, there was an accident that blocked several lanes, including the shoulder. The CHP lieutenant must have radioed ahead because several CHP officers who were investigating the accident stopped to block a lane of traffic and let them by. As JW drove by, one of the CHP officers there was looking at them. He could tell by the look on his face, he was wondering, *Who are you guys?*

When they made it out of San Bernardino County, the officers assigned to the caravan dropped off and were replaced by two others. The changeover went smoothly, and Ben said, "I'm impressed. You must be important."

JW laughed and said, "Ben, haven't you figured it out yet? The only important things in this Tahoe are in the back seat. I'm just the driver and you, sir, are the ringmaster."

They both laughed and Ben said, "Your phone is paired with the Tahoe. Let me use it to start making calls."

Ben called Lieutenant Van Geffin in Las Vegas to update him on their progress. Ben was able to get some additional details from him and continued to take notes on a yellow legal pad. JW listened in to the call, ignoring the administrative details, but focusing in when there were details to the crime or things specific to the trail they would run.

At the end of the call, Ben said, "Well, I know more than I did an hour ago, but I really don't have a clear picture of what we're going to do. Their killer has killed twice, which is probably why the FBI isn't there. It doesn't meet Dr. Gaurdia's protocol yet. By their rules, it's not a serial killing yet."

JW knew the FBI required at least three killings before they would label a serial killer. He added, "Well, we know of only two. What do you think, is this another test from Dr. Gaurdia?"

Outside Barstow there was another exchange of escort vehicles and they were able to pick up speed. JW watched the speedometer as it climbed and settled in at ninety miles per hour. The Tahoe took the speed without hesitation. The ride was smooth and the dogs napped in the back. Ben suggested they stop in Baker to top off the gas tank. They still had over half a tank of gas, but if they needed to let the Tahoe idle for long periods of time, they wanted to make sure there was plenty of fuel.

JW stood at a gas station gazing at the world's largest thermometer. It was a local landmark he had seen many times while coming to the Baker to Vegas Relay Race. Baker was the last stop before you went out on the racecourse.

The thermometer was 134 feet tall and was set to measure a temperature equally high. It was built by a local businessman and the height was based on the record high temperature in Death Valley. It has been standing for a long time and JW always welcomed the sight of it. Ben walked up with a couple of Diet Cokes in his hand and said, "It's like visiting an old friend."

"Yeah. Do you remember the restaurant that was next door? I think it was called 'Bun Boy.' They used to make the best strawberry milkshakes there."

"I do. They closed a few years ago. That's the one constant in life—change."

JW agreed and, after giving the dogs a quick break, they continued on to Las Vegas.

At the Nevada border, the caravan stopped and pulled off the highway. JW got out and thanked Lieutenant Carbajal and his men. He handed out challenge coins to thank the departing CHP officers, and then turned to speak with the officers from the Nevada Highway Patrol and the Las Vegas Metro Police Department that were waiting to take over. They shook hands and the highway patrolman said, "We'll take you into Las Vegas from here. Once we get to the city limits, Metro will take over and drive you to their command post."

They all got into their vehicles and back on the highway. As they sped along the interstate toward Vegas, JW let his mind wander, back to a time when he was a K9 handler. He was searching a warehouse near the Port of Long Beach. It was a huge structure and JW was working close to his partner, Asko, because he was concerned about his safety. JW had spotted rodent bait stations and, although they looked secure, he didn't feel good working away from the dog as he usually would. The place was full of palletized cargo from overseas, and Asko had run up and down the rows of pallets. JW was not sure why someone had broken into this particular warehouse, but sometimes things just didn't make sense.

Asko seemed to be working a scent cone but was having trouble isolating on the suspect. As JW and his cover officer reached the end of an aisle, the suspect charged him and they both went to the ground. The suspect tried to grab JW's gun, but as he reached for it, Asko climbed over his back and bit into the suspect's arm. The suspect cried out in pain and JW holstered his pistol and grabbed the man's other arm, trying to gain control of him. His cover officer stepped back, hesitant to join in the fray. He was afraid Asko might let go of the bad guy and turn on him. JW looked at him and said, "He's not going to bite you. A little help here."

The officer hesitated a moment longer and then came forward. Together they were able to bring the man's free arm behind his back. Now JW gave the release command, "Aus," and Asko reluctantly dropped off the bite.

JW grabbed the suspect's now-bloody arm and closed the handcuff on his wrist. The backup officer took control of him and walked him outside to other officers, then returned to JW and together they finished the search of the warehouse. Outside, the officer approached JW and said, "Hey, sorry about that in there. I've never seen anything like that before. It was crazy how quick your dog was on that guy after he knocked you down. I know you guys train for that problem, but I guess I froze."

JW considered that for a moment and said, "No worries, stuff happens. You got back in the fight. No harm, no foul."

JW came out of his haze as Las Vegas became visible on the horizon. He wondered why that incident had come to mind and realized, *I'm out here, away from everything I know, chasing a murderer. Yeah, I guess that's a slight cause for concern.* It was good to have Ben with him. He knew Ben had his back and wouldn't hesitate if it became necessary. They entered the city and continued on the Las Vegas Freeway until exiting at the Strip. They turned off onto city streets and then turned in on a service road. The lead car pulled into a large lot that was filled with vehicles including a large command post vehicle. As JW and Ben got out of the Tahoe and stretched, a compact, fit-looking officer in a medium-green SWAT uniform approached. "Tak Van Geffin. Are you JW and Ben?"

"That we are. Hey, Lieutenant, I gotta ask you about your name," said Ben.

"Easy story. My mom is very traditional Japanese, and my dad is German. They met in Europe while my mom was deployed there in the army. My father was a liaison with NATO forces, and they met and fell in love. Five years later, little Tak shows up and from there it's all history. Listen, I want to be up front with you. My guys are a little uncertain about this trailing you guys do. They're not certain how it works, and you know how cops are…"

JW interrupted him and said, "Anything new is not to be trusted. Don't worry, Tak, we're used to it. I'm prepared to stand in front of your guys and take it on. Not my first time out."

29

JW stood in front of a group of twenty SWAT officers. As was typical of their breed, they were all very physically fit, many with hard faces. There wasn't a smile in the group, but JW didn't expect anyone to smile. This was a pack of alpha dogs, each one challenging the others for their place in the hierarchy. Many of them had seen war and all had been involved with numerous high-risk search warrants and hostage situations. This was the best Las Vegas Metro had to offer. They weren't here to smile; they were here to work. JW was familiar with the SWAT mentality, it was similar to that of all police officers. You had to have supreme confidence to do the job and their job was that much more difficult. He wasn't going to try and bullshit these guys; he was going to tell them how it was from his perspective and let them do their jobs.

"I'm JW North and this is Ben Kellum. I'm a retired officer from Long Beach, California, currently assigned as a reserve officer in the trailing unit. Ben is still active and is a K9 handler as well as assisting me with this program. Our K9s there are Ares and Addy. I spoke with your lieutenant and he tells me you guys have reservations about what we do. I completely understand that; I do." JW then told them about their training and what they had accomplished. He needed to sell them on the idea that he could help them get one more asshole off the streets of their city.

"Based on what I know of your case, I believe we can be of assistance. Make no mistake, this is your show. We are not here to take anything away from you guys. Personally, if we can take care of business and then sneak out of town without having to talk to anyone, I am perfectly good with that. I know you guys are going to feel exposed out there with us. I haven't figured out a way around that. The bad guy has the advantage. I'm going to suggest we hold off on running the trail until later, after things settle down a bit."

Tak spoke up and said, "That was our plan, too, if it doesn't affect the dogs' work. No need to run a parade down Las Vegas Boulevard during rush hour."

"Good, we are in agreement there," JW continued. "I'm not going to BS you guys. This is not a perfect program. There are no guarantees of results and no guarantees, even if the dog does his job, that we will recognize it. This is as much art as science and, as good as I believe it is, I am not going to lie to you and tell you we are going to get your bad guy for certain. All I can promise is my team will do its best for you."

Tak again stepped forward and said, "Thanks for your honesty, JW. OK, guys, get together with your sections. You all have assignments to put together an action plan for the various scenarios we may face. I'm going to take JW and Ben over to the crime scene. They need to collect scent evidence from the victim."

Ben went to the car to get the scent transfer unit.

JW said, "Well, Tak, what do you think? Do you think they bought any of it?"

"I'm not positive, JW, but I think so. I can tell you that they are as good a group of guys as I have worked with. They are all professionals and they will do their jobs. It would be best if they believed in it, but I bet you won't be able to tell the believers from the non-believers."

"I can live with that."

When Ben returned with the STU, Tak said, "OK, follow me. Time to meet our victim."

They walked across the lot to an area adjacent to employee parking and some utility buildings. If not for the outdoor flood lights Metro PD had set up, it would have been very dark and private, just like a killer would want. They approached an area that had been screened off to keep the media from prying. Several members of the Metro PD's crime scene unit were there, as well as the county coroner. As they walked up, Tak took the lead and introduced everyone. One of the Crime Scene Investigators (CSI) asked, "Lieutenant North, do you mind if we observe as you collect scent evidence? We've read about it, but this is a first for us. We've seen the newspaper articles on the work you're doing in Long Beach with the professor from USC. It's really an honor for us to meet you."

JW considered this for a moment. Obviously, they had read about his work because they knew he was a lieutenant. No one had mentioned rank since their arrival. In this instance, his rank meant nothing. He was here to work, not supervise. JW was a little embarrassed by the attention. Here, in front of him, were believers.

"Hey, I want to thank you for holding the scene for us. I know it was a lot to ask, especially for the coroner, and we appreciate it. My partner, Ben Kellum, and I would be more than happy for you to observe. He'll brief you on the scent transfer unit and explain our processes. We're going to need you to put a scent sample into evidence, so it's best for you to be there to help maintain the chain of custody."

The CSI's faces lit up as if someone had just given them an extra Christmas this year, while the coroner yawned. JW looked at him for a moment, thinking, *Another quiet professional. Guy's probably seen more cases than I can count. He's been here all day and just wants me to get on with it. Work has probably been backing up while he waited for us.*

JW looked at the coroner and asked, "May I take a look? How should I enter in order to avoid disturbing anything?"

"Help yourself. We have all our photos and evidence, so there's nothing much to disturb. Thanks for asking, though. Please don't touch the body."

As Ben opened his hard case and retrieved the STU, JW could hear Ben explaining what it was and how it worked. JW walked behind the screen and looked down at the victim. She was young, maybe not even twenty. Her clothing was in a pile off to the side, appearing to have been cut off by the suspect. Although she was young, she looked older, maybe forty. Street life was hard and her arm showed the signs of drug use, with track marks on the inside of her elbow. JW knelt down and said, "I apologize for the delay. We had a long way to come. I am sorry for what happened to you, and I promise I will do my best to find the person who did this to you. No one should die like this." JW noticed there was a lot of blood, with some castoff on the bushes nearby. *Most likely killed here.*

JW stood and looked down at the victim. Her face was contorted into what looked like a painful grimace. He looked around and thought, *No one nearby to hear her struggle or scream, if she had a chance.* The victim's eyes looked skyward, as if beseeching someone for help. Her throat was cut and her chest was a bloody mess of gore. The suspect had sliced her breasts off. Tak was standing behind him and JW asked, "Was the other victim like this?"

Tak answered in a flat tone, "Yes, almost exactly the same."

"Did you find her breasts?"

"No, we believe he took them with him."

"I hope so, easier for us to track, more scent."

"I like the sound of that."

JW slowly turned to him and gave him a feral smile. "Me, too."

As they walked back to the command post, Tak asked, "JW, why did you talk to her?"

"I'm not entirely sure. Part of it is to make her seem more like a victim to me. I dealt with street prostitutes off and on in my career, so it's sometimes hard to see them as victims. Part of it is my unease around the dead. My subconscious probably believes if I talk like I'm having a conversation, then maybe it's not so unusual. It puts me more at ease. I need to be comfortable. The dog will sense my discomfort and may be distracted, so I talk to them. I sort of died once, and I guess I would have liked it if someone had talked to me."

Tak looked at him with a bit of concern. "If you don't mind me saying so, that's a little weird."

"I know. Sometimes I feel like I'm living a dream, other times, a nightmare."

Tak nodded and made a mental note to assign someone good to take care of JW. He liked him and didn't want to have anything happen to him.

As they walked back to the command post, Tak excused himself; he needed to make a call. Ben went to put the STU in the Tahoe. JW stood there, thinking how to approach this trail, as four members of the SWAT team walked up. One of them said, "JW, we're confused. You were a cop for thirty years and now you are volunteering to chase criminals. How does that happen?"

"I think your LT may think I am crazy. How about this, we go out and catch us a murderer, and afterward I will answer all your questions over a beer. I'm buying." That answer seemed to agree with them and they went off to their equipment truck to get ready for the night's work.

After giving both Ares and Addy a break, Ben disappeared, only to return a few minutes later with two cups of coffee. "Hey, one of those CSIs told me they're having a big convention here in town next year. She was wondering if you would be willing to come and speak about scent evidence. You're kind of a celebrity, you know."

"I don't know. I'm not much on speaking. Do you think they'll have tequila there?"

"Oh yeah, they'll have plenty of tequila. This is Vegas, after all."

JW laughed and said, "Don't give me that 'What happens in Vegas, stays in Vegas' crap. You know if we come, our wives will insist on coming along and keeping an eye on us."

Ben gave him his most solemn look and said, "I don't know what you are talking about, sir. I happen to be a model of proper behavior."

"Please, Ben, do not make me sick to my stomach just before we go run a trail. You won't like it when I puke on your shoes."

"Yeah, you're right about that. Seriously, though, there is one thing that bothers me about this trail. Are we assuming that our suspect is still in the area? Because I think he is long gone. I would be, I know that."

"Yeah, but you don't like to kill girls and cut their breasts off. I've done some reading about these kinds of killers. They're not like the average criminal and we need to keep that in mind. They certainly don't think like we do, and we should only expect one thing—the unexpected."

One of the SWAT officers came out and motioned to them. "Hey, guys, we're gonna start the briefing."

The briefing started with Tak speaking. "Alright, listen up. This is going to be the weirdest pre-mission brief I have ever given. That's because we have so many unknowns. We are the best and we train to be flexible, to adapt to changes on the fly and to win the fight. That's who we are and what we do."

JW looked around and saw a lot of Metro PD brass on the outside of the briefing area. There were so many people present, they had to hold the briefing outside, using the side of the command post as a projector screen. JW figured there was a lot of interest in this case for a number of reasons. Having a serial killer in your jurisdiction was not good for public perception and not good for Las Vegas tourism. Even though, so far, it was only prostitutes who were being murdered, tourists might stop coming to Vegas if they thought they might end up mutilated in a dirt lot. He scanned the group and saw the sheriff looking at him. JW nodded when their eyes met.

Tak continued, "OK, first off, JW North and his partner, Ben Kellum, will be joining us on this op. They drove in from Long Beach at the request of the sheriff. This is our operation, but JW's dog, Ares, is going to determine where we go and at what pace. JW, any idea on how fast Ares will work?"

JW realized Tak was talking to him and said, "The speed of either Ares or Addy is going to be driven by the scent. This is what I believe will happen here: the scent is going to be fresh and strong. The killer had direct contact with the victim and may have picked up blood and other scent from that contact. Additionally, the suspect mutilated the victim and carried off body parts. Again, an opportunity for more of a scent trail. This trail is only twenty-four hours old, so it's fairly fresh by our standards."

At this point the sheriff interrupted him saying, "JW, Sheriff Carroll here. You say a twenty-four-hour trail is fairly recent by your standards. Care to expound on that?" JW smiled inside. *Thanks for the soft toss, Sheriff.*

"Certainly, sir. Ares' certification trail was in a mostly urban environment, almost four miles long and two weeks old." JW paused to see if there were any more questions before continuing. "The trail should go pretty fast. I can see Ares trying to sprint. I won't let him do that because working too fast could make him miss a turn, and I don't think you want to attract any more attention than we already will."

"How does the dog know who to follow? I mean you're gonna have scent from the suspect and the victim, won't you?" asked the sheriff as a follow-up question.

"Normally, you would have anyone who contacted the victim there at the start. The dog would, based on training, eliminate any scent that is there at the start. In the case of our victim, we will start near the crime scene and if Ares tries to go to her, I will correct him and redirect. Then, we have to hope he follows the most recent scent, which will be the suspect leaving the scene. Mother Nature helps with this when a dog is following the scent of an animal it is hunting. If the dog starts the trail at a midpoint, the dog may go the wrong way and follow the back trail. If he does, he goes hungry."

Tak nodded his agreement and continued with the briefing. "I had four groups work on specific problems or scenarios. First off, Team One will brief on basic formations. I say formations, but unless we are close to our bad guy, I want everyone to keep a loose, low profile."

The Team One leader, a sergeant, stepped up. "Alright. At the start of the trail, we will mostly be in vehicles. Team One will be escort. I figure JW and the dog, with Kellum in the middle. SWAT officers on each side, and one assigned to JW. I will be in the follow position. JW's escort will be the team medic, Perea, in case anyone needs medical assistance. We will have four Team Two members in plainclothes. They will be in a loose follow and looking for a possible suspect running away. I want this movement to look like a couple of guys out walking their dog, in SWAT gear. Since we are looking for a low-profile movement, the only weapons will be pistols for the escort team, no long guns." JW knew that would not be popular with the team members. They were hunting a murderer and they would want everything they could carry.

Team Two was assigned the plainclothes mission but provided a briefing on who would be where and what their responsibilities were. They provided an in-depth briefing on the scenario where the suspect was found outside, during the trail. The plan, if that occurred, was for a simple takedown with a heavy reminder of watching the background. The trail was going to be early in the morning, but if the suspect was armed, it could become a deadly force problem and the Team Two leader wanted everyone to be sure there was no one behind the suspect. *There would be no friendly-fire casualties.*

Team Three briefed on the vehicle formation, where the heavy equipment of Teams One and Two would be located, and noted that a paramedic unit would be along in case of injury. The Team Three sergeant discussed several important administrative considerations and finished with, "If we have a serious injury, UMC Trauma Center is designated as primary and we have alerted them," referring to University Medical Center.

Team Four was last and discussed the biggest fear that JW had. What if the trail took them to a casino or large hotel on the Strip? The team sergeant discussed certain primary tactical concerns, but looked to JW for some advice. "JW, I think a trail in a large hotel will be different than out on the street. How do you want to handle this if it happens?"

JW stood again and said, "Ben and I talked about this while driving here from Long Beach. We have never had this exact scenario, but we see this going one of two ways. One, the suspect is in the casino and, if so, that is on you guys for the take down. Or two, the suspect passes through the casino and back outside. If that happens, we pick up the trail as we did originally. If the trail leads us to a hotel, then we are in a whole other scenario.

"At that point, we will swap dogs and use Addy. This is like what we see when we find a suspect in his own neighborhood. The suspect's scent is all over the place and some dogs have a hard time isolating and locating a suspect in that environment. Addy excels at that type of work and we will use her if we have to search a hotel. How you guys deal with the hotel and containment is up to you. I will need a cover team similar to that on the street, possibly smaller, but if we isolate on a suspect in a room, I'll back out and turn it over to you."

The Team Four leader briefed on who would do what in the hotel scenario and then stepped down. Tak resumed the lead and gave a few more words of encouragement and then asked, "Questions? Anything we missed?"

A SWAT officer in the front row said, "I see what you mean, Lieutenant. There are a lot of unknowns in this thing."

"There are more unknowns than knowns at this point. We have a robust outline and we will flex to meet the needs of the situation. Any other questions?"

JW raised his hand and asked, "What if we get a dog injured, where do we go?"

Tak paled and said, "Crap, we didn't think of that. Good question." He turned to one of the assigned patrol K9s and asked, "Who do you guys use?"

The officer was not used to the limelight, but stepped forward and said, "We use Las Vegas Pet Emergency over on South Valley View." He turned and looked at JW. He understood the gravity of the question. "They have excellent vets there. If your dog takes a hit, I say we load him in the paramedic unit and I will lead you over there."

Tak nodded his assent to this and said, "OK, if there are no further questions, let's get ready to go. We move in ten minutes."

As the group broke apart, JW pulled Tak aside and said, "Hey, Tak, I didn't mean to put you on the spot in front of your boss."

He shrugged and then got serious. "No big deal. That's how we operate. If there is a hole in the plan, someone calls bullshit. We check our egos at the door during the brief. The sheriff knows that; he was SWAT a long time ago. Besides, I'm going to be sick if something happens to one of those dogs. If something bad happens and we haven't planned for it, I don't know what I would do. I want this to work, JW, and more importantly, I want to get this asshole without any good guys getting hurt."

30

After the meeting, the group reassembled near the crime scene. JW was thinking about what they were going to do, when Ben asked, "Where is the organ grinder?

JW absentmindedly said, "What?"

"The organ grinder, you know, for the circus. Hey, earth to JW, come in, JW." JW looked at Ben like he was out of his mind and Ben said, "Get your head in the game, man. Where are you? I need you at your best, not lost somewhere in your mind. I'm not worried about us getting hurt, I'm worried you're going to make us look like idiots and kill all the hard work we've done."

JW shook his head as if Ben had slapped him. He shook his head again to help clear his thoughts. "Damn. Thanks, Ben. Sometimes I feel like I went for a walk and got lost." The truth was, JW was under a huge amount of pressure, much more so than during certification. Although this is what he had been working toward, he worried if he was the man for the job. He knew Ares would do the job, but how would he react when faced with the suspect? People's lives were dependent on them today. What if he failed them and someone got hurt?

Ben replied, "I'm using some of my best jokes and you are not appreciating the work. Would you care to join me for a little trail?"

"Yeah. I'm here, Ben." As JW collected himself, Tak approached. They were ready when he was. JW reached down and whispered to his dog, "Hey, buddy, this is it. Show time. Let's go find the bad guy."

JW and Ben had been concerned about the safety of the dogs from gunfire. Because of that, they had researched a small company that made K9 tactical vests. Their vests were made to order and fit the dogs well. This allowed the dog to move freely, but still offered some protection. The factory representative had met with them and provided samples and a full sales pitch. They offered a lot of benefits beyond ballistic protection, including a carry handle that would allow them to pick up the dog or rappel them, if necessary. Ben and JW liked what they offered and had ordered two of them.

The new tactical vests had arrived the previous week. They fit the dogs perfectly, but they had not had time to train with them on. Ares wore his new vest uncomfortably. He would have preferred his leather harness, but this was a high-risk trail. Like it or not, the vest could save his life. JW clipped the trailing lead on Ares, gave him the scent, and commanded, "Geo-say." Ares started casting about, slowly working his way toward the crime scene. Suddenly, he turned away and started pulling hard. He was on-trail. JW leaned back and applied the brakes, but Ares only pulled harder. Ben turned to Tak and the others and said, "And away we go."

Ares worked the trail well; as JW suspected, the scent was fresh and strong. They worked east, toward Las Vegas Boulevard. Ares had his head down, following the scent trail. Occasionally, he would pause to scent the air. *Is the suspect close?* Ares restarted and continued. When they reached the Strip, he went to the intersection. For a moment, JW considered signaling for the follow caravan to stop traffic. *This doesn't make sense. This isn't a pedestrian crossing.* He looked up and saw an overhead walkway. They had been installed years ago to keep pedestrians off the street and facilitate vehicle traffic. He remembered trying to drive up Las Vegas Boulevard in the past. It had been almost impossible to get across, as vehicles had to yield to pedestrians.

The dog turned and started working toward the escalator. *Well, this is going to be fun. Ares has never seen one of these.* JW paused and asked, "Any way we can stop the escalator? I don't want the dog to get injured." Tak nodded and called on his radio. In moments, an officer appeared with a set of keys and turned the escalator off. JW restarted Ares and the dog moved upward, uneasy on the metal stairs, but still climbing. At the top, Ares worked across Las Vegas Boulevard and, after the other side escalator was turned off, he worked his way down to the street, in front of one of the many large casinos. It was late, but the bright lights made it seem like midday. Even though it was well past midnight, there were still a lot of people outside enjoying the sights.

Ares continued across to another set of escalators. This time the officer with the keys anticipated their needs and shut off the escalator before he asked. They crossed over another bridge and then down once more. The dog worked a few moments to relocate the trail, and then pulled back toward the Strip and turned right. The trail continued north, and they had to cross another bridge. The whole time, the officers with them were watching, looking for someone too interested or wanting to leave a little too fast. JW kept losing track of the plainclothes officers. They were good. Of course, most of JW's attention was directed at Ares. JW took a quick glance at Ben, who responded by giving him a thumbs-up. Sometimes things were going so well, you just needed a reality check. Ares was on-trail, hard.

They were probably a mile from the original crime scene when Ares turned toward the entrance to a casino-hotel complex. He worked his way to the door, which opened automatically for them. One of the hotel employees working in the lobby stepped in front of them and said, "Sorry, sir, no pets allowed in the casino."

JW stopped and looked at the man. *Really? You have got to be kidding me.* Clearly, this employee was not hired for his ability to stare the obvious in the face and recognize it. JW turned to Ben and said, "Get Tak. I need to go outside before I choke this idiot out. He gives a whole new meaning to the term 'spit-drooling moron.'" As JW turned and walked back out front, he saw Tak talking with Ben.

After a short discussion with Ben, Tak walked over to JW and said, "Ben thinks our suspect may have gone inside. What do you think?"

"I agree. I don't know if he was just passing through or this is where he stays. First off, we need to get in contact with someone higher than a bellboy and get some cooperation."

Tak acknowledged, "Yeah. Take a break out here and I'll get some brass over here to get this coordinated. I want to try to set a perimeter, but this place is the Ultimo. It might be the largest hotel-casino complex in the world, depending on who you talk to and what you use to measure it."

JW looked at the structure and said, "That's an understatement. We'll get out of your way for now. Let me know when you are ready to roll again."

A lengthy procession of police vehicles began pulling into the valet area of the massive hotel. The valets were all looking at one another trying to decide what to do with this invasion of their space.

While JW stood waiting for the order to resume the trail, Sheriff Carroll's vehicle was driven to the front of the hotel. JW could see the sheriff, seated in the back, talking on his phone. He got out of his car, walked over to JW, and asked, "What do you think?"

"Well, Ares is telling me he went this way. Unfortunately, we have no way to know if he stayed or moved on from here. Not yet, at least."

"Yeah, Tak briefed me on the high level of cooperation you received. I know the owner, Maddox Christenson. I just got off the phone with him. He's calling the on-duty manager and then he is coming down. Don't worry about the idiot in the lobby. Maddox will fire him just for being stupid."

JW felt bad about the guy losing his job and said so. Reading the look on his face, the sheriff added, "Oh, don't worry too much about him. Maddox isn't heartless. He'll put the guy somewhere where his limited skills will be a better fit. Maddox appreciates finding out. Think about it; is that the face you want representing you to the public? I don't think so."

JW thought about this as he excused himself to give Ares some water and a break. Within a few minutes, a SWAT officer approached him and said, "JW, the lieutenant is looking for you. We're about ready to go."

Ben and Tak walked back to JW and Tak said, "It's amazing what happens when the owner shows up. They have rolled out the red carpet for us. Believe me, the money people in this town are well aware of the negative impact a story like this could have on their bottom line. They all want to help and get this guy off the streets. I have a pair of officers in the main security office, the one with all the cameras. They can control everything from there. We're scanning the casino, the exits, and as much of this place as we can. Maybe we'll get lucky and this guy will panic and try to run." JW knew none of them were going to get lucky.

As JW prepared Ares to restart the trail, a man in a business suit approached. JW wondered why he was able to walk around so freely, and then he saw him hug the sheriff. Ah, that would likely be Mr. Maddox Christenson. Christenson approached JW and reached to shake his hand. JW gave him a firm grip and told him it was nice to meet him. Christenson looked JW over and said, "If this guy is in my hotel, I want you to get him out. Shoot him if you need to, or if you want to." JW felt like he was in the most sensitive X-ray machine in the world while under the careful gaze of Christenson. *This guy is intimidating without even trying. No wonder he's so successful.*

JW put the tracking lead back on Ares and restarted him. The dog put his head down and instantly resumed the trail. No casting, no hesitation. The trail was strong in here. Ares worked across the lobby and into an alcove, stopping in front of an elevator door and looking back at JW. Ben looked up and read the lettering on the wall. "North Tower Elevators." He turned to his escort and said, "Well, this just got a lot more interesting."

JW unhooked Ares' harness and attached a patrol leash to his collar. He asked Ben to take Ares back to the car and to get Addy. It was time for her to earn her keep.

JW turned to Tak and the Team One sergeant and said, "OK, Ben and I have talked about this, here is what I want to do. Tak, you said you have guys in the security office. Let's find out if the North Tower is freestanding or has access to any of the other towers."

Maddox Christenson, who had been talking with the sheriff, overheard JW and said, "No, each tower is isolated. These elevators and the emergency stairs are the only ways in or out."

As JW smiled, the blue drained from his eyes and was replaced with gunmetal gray. "Excellent. I recommend we shut down the elevators for now. We are going to clear each floor, working up from here. After we clear it, you can allow the elevator to work from that floor down. We need this elevator right here. Our suspect used it and that's how we find him. We take the elevator up and restart the trail. If the scent is there, Addy will lead us to him. If there is no scent, she'll tell us that as well. We work our way up until we find him or get to the top. How many floors does the North Tower have?"

Christenson smiled and said, "Only sixty-five."

"Well, OK. I guess this will take a while. Let's get to work."

Ben returned with Addy and JW greeted her. "Well hello, Princess Adeliene. I hope we didn't disturb your nap." She wagged her tail vigorously. She was happy to be out and going to work. As the hotel security staff worked to comply with the instructions they had been given, JW talked with Ben off to the side. "You know, if this works, you'll be famous, too." The elevator doors opened, and the team entered, ready to resume the night's work. At the second floor, the doors opened and Ben held down the "Door Open" button. JW started Addy on the suspect's scent. She walked out, sniffed the area and looked at JW. Her expression read, "That's a big no. Next."

They continued up one floor at a time. JW was thinking, *This could take all night.* After the twenty-fifth floor, JW called a break for Addy. He gave her some water and returned to the elevator, riding up to the 26th floor. That floor was a no, also. Addy was showing no signs of fatigue. She worked each floor, sniffing and searching before looking back at JW. Next. The team continued upward. At the forty-seventh floor, Addy restarted as usual, but this time she pulled hard to the left. JW had become used to the routine of no scent and was pulled hard from the elevator and almost knocked over a table that was outside the elevator doors. JW whispered to her, "OK, girl, let's slow it down." He paused while members of the team came out of the elevator and deployed. One of the officers was carrying a full-body ballistic shield. He carried the shield in front of him, looking out a clear ballistic window with his pistol in his right hand, extended out to the side to engage the suspect if he were a threat.

Other officers reached into carry bags and deployed short-barreled AR-15 rifles fitted with red-dot, reflex sights, perfect for the close quarters environment they were in. Tak radioed down to the lobby and instructed them to take the elevator and bring Team Four up for backup. Soon those officers were also in the forty-seventh-floor lobby and had their heavier weapons deployed, along with a pick and ram, in case they needed to make entry into a room. With a nod from Tak, JW restarted Addy. Two officers worked in front of them; one covered down the hallway while the other pointed his gun at the door Addy was checking. JW wondered how many rooms were on a floor. He forgot to ask, but he figured it was a lot, since everything in this place was huge.

The rest of the team worked behind them. Ben was at his side and Perea, the medic, was right behind him. If he got any closer, he was going to be in JW's back pocket. JW could feel his hand on his back, helping him to keep from bumping into him. It was slow, tedious work. Everyone was on edge, except Addy, who happily worked each door and moved on. The only thing that seemed to bother her was the slow pace of work. *Safety first, little girl.* They were halfway through the floor when Addy slowed and turned to look at him. She moved a little closer to a door and put her nose down to the crack at the bottom. JW knelt beside her and she took a deep breath. Everything slowed and JW saw her look at him, she was smiling. *Oh, good girl! Good job, my sweet little dog!* As Addy started to move back to give her alert, the door exploded in the middle. The concussive boom of a 12-gauge shotgun blast in close quarters was so powerful it knocked JW back. There was a collection of holes in the door, all within a few inches of one another. He felt pain in his arm and looked down at it; there was a piece of wood from the door sticking out of his left forearm. He heard Addy cry in pain and suddenly everything sped up.

JW was pulled backward off his feet by Perea, who said, "Hang on, sir, I got you." Perea was so pumped full of adrenaline from the shotgun blast that he hardly felt the weight of JW. He pulled hard and all JW could do was take the ride, pulling Addy by her lead along with him. The scene at the door played out in front of him. As JW tried to regain his feet, one of the Team Four officers came past him with a battering ram to knock the door down. With a nod from his team leader, he slammed the ram into the door, just above the locking mechanism, knocking the door open. Another officer then threw a concussive grenade through the door and turned away to protect his eyes and covered his ears. Just after he tossed the flash bang through the door, another shotgun blast went off, peppering the wall across from the door. The nearest officer was hit in his vest by several pellets, knocking him down. The double bang of the flash bang grenade shook the floor. The officer reached into another pouch and retrieved a second flash bang and tossed it through the door, again yelling, "Bang Out!"

The officer with the shield pushed into the room. Several officers followed closely behind. He could hear voices yelling, "Police! Hands up!" Then there was a series of loud gunshots.

JW recognized the sound of rifle and pistol fire, but he did not hear any more shotgun blasts. He thought the suspect was most likely on the express train to hell. He was OK with that.

The next thing he knew, they were back in the elevator lobby. JW looked at his arm again and felt nauseous upon seeing the wood sticking out. He reached down to remove it and almost passed out as he did so. *Damn it, that really hurt. Bad call, JW.*

Ben was crouched down, checking Addy. Her new ballistic vest was covered in splinters. It had done its job, but it was trashed. She was going to need a new one. Ben continued to check for any injuries, then held out his hand as he looked up at JW. It was covered in blood, a lot of blood. Perea had been busy looking at JW's arm but stopped when he saw the blood pooling below her neck. "OH SHIT!" Perea keyed his radio and said, "K9 down. We are coming down in the elevator. Prepare for medical extract."

Ben looked at JW and yelled, "Scoop and go, JW."

JW realized his dog's life was spilling out on the forty-seventh floor. He reached under Addy and carefully lifted her. The elevator doors opened and they all stepped inside. Ben pressed the button for the lobby and prayed no one would interrupt their descent. Addy was losing a lot of blood. Perea slid a pack off his back and opened a pouch containing gauze. He began feeling around her neck, looking for the injury. He said to JW, "I can feel the injury. It's a deep laceration, probably shrapnel from the door. I can't tell how bad it is because I can't see it through all of her fur." He pulled out a thick wad of gauze and began forcing it into the injury. Addy felt the pain of his efforts and let out a small cry. Perea started talking to her. "I know that hurts. I'm sorry, but I have to stop the bleeding. You just hang on now, I've got you. You're gonna be OK."

JW's eyes began welling with tears. He was watching his little girl die right in front of his eyes. He bit down hard on his tongue and shook his head. "Not today. Not today, Addy. You listen to me. You are going to be OK. We're going to go home and you can tell Mommy how I got you shot. But you are not going to die today. Do you hear me?" Addy looked at him with glazed eyes. She was rapidly going into shock. Finally, the elevator doors opened to the lobby. There were a dozen police officers standing in the lobby, blocking the guests from getting in JW's way. It was a good thing, as he would have just run them all over. JW ran out of the elevator, toward the entrance to the street, with Addy in his arms. A woman who was arguing with a police officer saw Addy and her jaw just dropped open. He heard a voice from the side of the lobby, saying, "Over here, JW." He turned toward the sound of the voice and saw the sheriff and Maddox Christenson holding the side doors open.

JW ran through the doors and saw why they were there. The front of the hotel was packed with cars. Somehow, his Tahoe had been moved to this side door and there were two K9 vehicles ready to escort. The back door was open and JW climbed inside his Tahoe with Addy while Perea continued to apply direct pressure on her wound. Ben took Ares and the two of them got in the front passenger seat and the driver said, "Hang on!" As the sirens were turned on, JW looked back through the open doors and across the lobby. There was a continuous trail of blood all the way across. *Oh, Addy!*

Perea must have read JW's mind, as he said, "It's OK, JW. I have most of the bleeding controlled. A lot of that blood was yours. I need to look at your arm and get that leak plugged."

JW shook his head and said, "Later, after I know she's OK." The three police cars raced across Las Vegas. Their driver was a younger officer and he was cussing a blue streak at every car that got in his way. "God damn it, you idiot, do you not see the pretty lights?" He looked over his shoulder and said, "Don't worry, guys. I'll have you there in a few minutes. Dispatch has called the vet and they know we are coming in."

JW looked down at Addy and said, "Hang on, girl, we'll be there in just a minute." They pulled off the road into a parking lot for the Vet Emergency Center. The staff rushed out carrying a K9 stretcher and took Addy from him. He followed them in and kept talking to her. *You can't let her see you upset, JW. Be strong for Addy.* "You're gonna be OK, Addy girl. These people are going to fix you right up. Be a good girl and just stay with us."

The door to the operating room closed in his face. There was nothing more for him to do except wait and pray.

The veterinary doctor gave her a quick once-over and came back out to where JW was waiting. "OK, this looks bad, and it is, but I won't know how bad until I get in there. It's a deep laceration and it cut a vein, that's why there's so much blood. So, here's what we're going to do. We are going to sedate her and start pumping her full of fluids. Most of the bleeding has stopped for now, so that gives us a little time. We'll take some X-rays and then we'll shave that area and then get in there and stitch her up. I am praying the damage is not too great, but I just don't know. I'll come back out later and let you know how it's going."

JW listened but didn't fully comprehend what was being said to him. "She's going to be OK? She's not going to die, is she?"

"I don't know. I need to get in there."

JW, Ben, and Perea all grabbed chairs in the lobby to wait. JW pulled his phone out, looking at it like it was a rattlesnake. He knew he needed to call Bonnie, to tell her what had happened, but he didn't know enough yet.

Ben went outside to call the Long Beach Communications Center and update them, knowing that they would update the chief too.

After an hour wait, the vet came back to the lobby. "OK, here's the deal. We needed to stabilize her because she had lost a lot of blood. At first, I thought we might lose her, but she's tough. She's a fighter. Once she was stable, we went in and looked around. We never did find what caused the laceration, but whatever it was, it did a lot of damage. However, the repair was fairly straightforward, and she is resting now. I would like to keep her here for at least twenty-four hours."

"She's gonna be OK? She's not going to die?" JW asked, his voice breaking.

The vet smiled and said, "No, she's going to be fine. You might want to thank Officer Perea—he saved her life by stopping the bleeding."

JW turned to Perea and threw his arms around him. He whispered in his ear, "I owe you. Everything."

Perea smiled at him and said, "You don't owe me anything, JW. I'm just glad I was able to help. I really don't know much about dogs."

JW shook his head and said, "If you hadn't done what you did, she wouldn't be here. It's as simple as that. You saved her." JW sat down and put his head in his hands. All the energy was draining from him. He was emotionally exhausted.

Ben came into the lobby and said, "OK, I've made some calls back to Long Beach. The watch commander is going to your house to tell Bonnie. I heard on the Las Vegas radio from dispatch that Mr. Christenson is sending his jet to Long Beach to pick her up and bring her here. How is Addy doing?"

JW was looking down at the floor. His arm was still bleeding, but Perea had applied a pressure bandage to it. Perea looked at Ben and said, "She's gonna make it. They performed surgery and repaired the damage, but she's going to be OK. I think JW is going into shock; we need to get him over to UMC and get some fluids into him."

Ben nodded and said, "Hey, JW, we need to get you taken care of. You're leaking all over the floor and making a mess. Come on, let's go to the hospital and get you stitched up."

They led JW out and drove to the emergency room at the University Medical Center. The staff was waiting outside with a gurney when they arrived. Perea briefed the doctor on what happened and what he had done so far. The doctors rushed him inside and began treatment. JW was put on intravenous fluids and given some drugs for the pain. They took some X-rays and finally cleaned and dressed the wound. An hour later, the doctor came out to the waiting room and could not find the officers. He went back to the employee break area and found them there, drinking coffee. The doctor told them that, although JW had lost a lot of blood, he would be fine. He wanted to get some more fluids into him before releasing him. Ben went outside to make another phone call and updated police communications on everyone's status.

31

Bonnie North was sitting in her home office, drinking a cup of coffee. She had already checked her email and text messages and found nothing from JW. This didn't completely surprise her. JW had expected it might be a long trail and she might not hear from him until later in the day. She heard a car door close and looked out the front window. *What the heck? The chief is here. What on earth does he want?* Then it occurred to her, he didn't want anything, except to tell her JW was dead, or Ares, or Addy, or all of them! She ran to the front door; she needed to know what he was here to say. She threw open the door and burst out as he stepped onto the front porch. "Just tell me, who's dead?"

Chief Estrada was surprised by her sudden presence and even more surprised by her agitation. "No one is dead, Bonnie. They found the suspect in a hotel. The program worked exactly like JW said it would. There was a shootout and JW was hit by a wood fragment in the arm. He's OK. Addy was hurt, too, more seriously, but she will be OK."

Bonnie looked at him as if she didn't know him. *Addy was hurt. How did that happen?* Then she remembered Addy excelled at searching neighborhoods—a hotel could be like a neighborhood.

Bonnie felt like she was in a fog. The chief looked at her and said, "Bonnie, did you hear me? Do you understand, everyone will be OK."

She looked at Chief Estrada and asked, "Do you want some coffee?"

"Sure, Bonnie, but you need to get packed. They're sending a plane to take you to Las Vegas. I'll drive you to the airport."

An hour later, Bonnie and Chief Estrada arrived at Long Beach Airport. There, next to the LBPD helicopter hangar, was a Gulfstream G650. One of the crew was outside, awaiting her arrival. Bonnie thanked the chief for everything and walked across the taxiway to the door.

"Welcome, Mrs. North. Go right on into the cabin and make yourself at home. We will be departing momentarily."

As Bonnie climbed inside, Maddox Christenson stood and offered his hand. "Please, Mrs. North, come in and have a seat." Bonnie shook his hand and sat. "I'm Maddox Christenson. I own the Ultimo resort in Las Vegas. Your husband found a killer inside my hotel and was injured, along with your dog, Addy. The Las Vegas SWAT team killed the man when he did not surrender.

"I have been doing some research on your enterprise while I was waiting for you to arrive. I find this kind of thing interesting and I'd like to know more about your program."

He handed Bonnie a card that said only "Maddox Christenson" and a phone number. "Your husband has done me a great personal service. I believe in law and order, but I am also a businessman. I would never want the world to know a serial murderer had used my hotel as a base for his crimes. The fact that your husband found him, and Metro SWAT killed him, relieves me of the need to sell that hotel.

"I met your husband and spoke with him for a few minutes before all that happened. I like him and I believe in what you both are doing. I would be honored to provide any amount of support you could use, be it financial or other resources to which I have access. Now, please tell me more about this enterprise of yours; I find it fascinating."

JW was in the back of the veterinary emergency hospital where the large kennels were kept. He had sat quietly for hours, talking to Addy, telling her what a good girl she was, how sorry he was she got hurt and how they would be going home soon. Addy had come out of the surgery sedated. The doctor had pulled JW into an exam room and shown him the X-rays and explained what he believed had happened. There was nothing in the wound to recover, so he could not be sure if it was a piece of buckshot or a fragment of the door. Either way, it had sliced the outside of her neck and traveled deep into her tissue, and then passed back out. He told JW that the tactical vest she had worn had saved her from more extensive damage from the door. He handed the almost brand-new vest to JW and said, "Here, you may want to keep this as an example of its effectiveness."

JW had asked if he could see her and sit with her and they told him they would not normally allow it, but since he was in law enforcement and they had seen on the news what had happened, it would be OK. JW talked to Addy for hours, sitting on the floor for so long that his butt had gone to sleep. He told her how he wanted her to meet a nice boy dog and have some puppies. Finally, exhaustion won out and JW fell asleep. His phone was in his lap; he had been trying to figure out how to explain it to Bonnie. It all went to hell so fast. During one of the hourly checks on Addy, one of the veterinary technicians saw JW asleep. She smiled at the man, sprawled out on the kennel floor near his dog. She went and got a blanket and quietly put it over him. She thought about what had happened to these two. She considered whether she could do what they did and shook her head. Nope, no way. Both of them had the courage to stare evil in the eye and fight. She had always had a special affinity for police dogs, but now it was even stronger.

Ben was also asleep. He was sitting in the passenger seat of the idling Tahoe in the parking lot, with Ares in the back. There were two Metro Police Department black-and-whites there with him. Both officers were leaning on their cars talking quietly. They were there to make sure no one bothered these officers from California. Each officer had a cup of coffee in hand. Their counterparts in patrol came by every hour and gave them breaks or brought them something to eat or drink. The sheriff had been specific: two uniformed officers were to be there to ensure their privacy until JW North and Ben Kellum left. If they left and the dog that was inside stayed, they were to stay. If the media showed up, they were to stop them and call the public information officer: it was private property, after all. There were to be no interviews until Lieutenant North had sufficiently recovered from his injuries.

Bonnie and Maddox landed at Las Vegas International Airport in the Gulfstream and taxied to a private hangar. The crew quickly readied the plane for arrival and soon Bonnie was standing on the tarmac. Maddox directed her to a black and white police vehicle waiting nearby and told her, "I believe JW will need to stay around for a few days. I have a room at the Ultimo waiting for you should that be the case." He handed her another business card and said, "This is my personal assistant. Please call her if you need anything. I don't know if JW brought any clothing with him, but if you give her his sizes she can pick some things out for him, and you as well. The officer in the car over there will take you to the veterinary hospital where JW, Addy, and Ben are. JW doesn't know you are coming, so you can surprise him."

Bonnie said, "Thank you for everything. You know you don't have to do this?"

"Mrs. North, the joy of giving comes from not having to do it. Besides, I owe your husband a great debt."

Bonnie smiled at the man; she liked him. For someone with so much power and money, he was so genuine. "I will think about what we talked about on the ride over. I can see where your assistance may be needed in our future, but please don't say anything to JW about it. He is a proud man who likes to do things on his own. I will discuss it with him when the time is right."

"And that is why I spoke with you about this. He is the hero, and you are the strength and wisdom behind him. You cannot have one without the other and, in these troubling times, we need men like JW."

Bonnie nodded and started to step away, but paused and said, "Mr. Christenson, I mean Maddox, I haven't heard from JW—not even a text message. Do you know why he hasn't reached out to me?"

Maddox thought for a moment and then replied, "I can't say for certain, but if I were in his situation, I think it would be difficult to find the right words to tell you."

Bonnie nodded in understanding, hugged him, and said, "Thank you, again," and walked to the waiting police car.

Bonnie arrived at the veterinary care center with a building fury. *Why the hell had no one except Chief Estrada and Maddox Christenson called to let her know what happened? Why the hell hadn't Ben or JW sent her an email or a text?* As she exited the police car, she was confronted by two officers. They saw she did not have a pet with her and needed to make sure it was OK to let her pass. The driver of her car rolled the window down and said, "It's OK, guys. She is the wife of one of the two Long Beach officers." Their concerns assuaged, they stepped aside. They could see she looked pissed. Hell hath no fury and all that.

Bonnie first set her sights on the Tahoe. She walked up and saw Ben sleeping in the passenger seat and Ares in the back. She knocked on the glass and said, "Ben, wake up!"

Ben snapped awake and looked around, at first uncertain where he was. As he became aware, he looked at Bonnie and said, "Hang on a sec." Ben got out of the Tahoe and stretched. He said, "Bonnie, what are you doing here?"

Bonnie, in a foul mood to start with, snapped, "What am I doing here? What the hell do you think, Ben? I'm here to see about my dogs and my husband. I see Ares. Where are JW and Addy?"

"They're inside, Bonnie, but listen to me for one second, OK?"

Bonnie nodded and Ben told her what had happened since they had arrived. Bonnie was quiet, giving him the time to put the story together in his head. He had been asleep after all. "Bonnie, we did great. It was unbelievable, and Addy really shined. We did everything right, took the necessary precautions, but you know how it is. You are in front of the spear. We were at a big disadvantage and the guy started shooting through the hotel room door." Bonnie had not known some of these details. Ben continued, "Addy and JW were both hurt, and we bailed out of the hotel and rushed over here. Once we knew Addy was OK, and only then would JW allow it, we took him to get his arm stitched up." Ben paused a moment and said, "We were both exhausted. It's been almost two days since we slept. JW lost a lot of blood and was spent and they gave him drugs for the pain. When we got back here, Addy was out of surgery and recovering. JW went in and talked to her for hours and finally fell asleep on the floor.

"Look, I can see you're pissed; I probably would be too. JW is not doing well mentally. I should have called you myself. This falls on me, and I'm sorry you had to sit and wait for word and then get it from a stranger. I've seen this before with guys who had dogs shot or killed on duty. It is emotionally traumatic to them and their family. Addy is going to be fine. JW is my concern right now. It's hard to explain, but it's something like this: you get a dog and you work with it and you love it like crazy. You know you are placing the dog in harm's way, but that's part of the job. So, to help you deal with it, you tell the dog, 'You work with me and I will take care of you.' In JW's mind, he failed last year when he was shot, now he thinks he has failed, again. That's crushing to a guy like him. He is feeling a lot of guilt right now and questioning whether this was a good idea in the first place. You have to decide that too. If we continue with this, it could happen again; it could be worse."

Bonnie nodded and said, "I'm sorry, Ben. I shouldn't have yelled at you like that."

"No worries, Bonnie, I knew you weren't mad at me, you're mad at the situation. It's something we can't control and people like us hate that."

Bonnie went inside and the staff directed her to JW and Addy. When she arrived at the kennels, she saw JW sitting on the floor, staring at the ground. Addy was in the kennel, asleep against the front of the cage. Bonnie thought, *She is getting as close to him as possible. She feels his pain and wants to help him, regardless of any pain she is in. Dogs are incredible.*

As Bonnie approached, trying to be as quiet as possible, Addy woke up and looked at her. She had that Addy "I love you" look in her eyes and she was smiling. *Hi, Mom.*

JW also stirred and looked at her. His eyes were dead, not the normal blue or the gray of anger, just dead. They looked like two deep pools of agony that went on to infinity.

Bonnie sat down next to him and asked, "Whatcha doin'?"

"Sitting here waiting for you to come and execute me."

She laughed and said, "Well, maybe later, but don't get your hopes up. JW, why didn't you call me?" She needed an answer to this, she needed him to understand he had failed her in this one thing.

"Well, it was pretty hectic at first, there was so much happening. Then they took me to the hospital and shot me full of doctor feel good. No, that's not an excuse. I should have called, but I needed to come here first and see Addy, and I fell asleep. Look, Bonnie, I'm sorry. I know I screwed up; I just couldn't find the words to tell you I got your dog shot."

Bonnie took a deep breath and decided she needed to channel her anger in another direction. Beating up on JW, although entertaining, would not serve any good purpose. "How can you sit on this concrete floor? My butt is killing me already."

JW just looked at her for a moment; that was not on the list of any of the questions he was expecting. "Well, after two or three hours, your butt goes to sleep. After that, you just don't care."

Bonnie laughed. "Well, can we please go sit in a chair before I have to spend the next week at the chiropractor's office?"

JW grabbed the kennel gate and slowly pulled himself to his feet. The pain of a thousand needles hit his butt and legs and served to snap him partially back to reality. "Wait a minute, how did you get here, Bonnie?"

"Oh, some guy named Christenson flew me into town on his private jet."

JW smiled and said, "Well, that must be nice. I had to drive." JW found a couple of chairs for them to sit and talk. He didn't want to leave Addy, not just yet. Bonnie and JW talked for close to an hour. He went over everything that had happened in detail. Bonnie had heard most of it from others, but she knew JW needed to talk this out. It was part of his healing process. Finally, he finished and looked at Bonnie. She thought about everything that had happened and asked JW a simple question: "What would you do differently?"

"I don't know. Honestly, I don't. This is my responsibility and I have gone over this in my head, over and over. I can think of a hundred things that need to be corrected or changed, but I cannot think of anything I could do that ends up with the suspect captured and Addy not hurt."

Bonnie considered this and asked, "Are you sure?"

"Well, I would find time to call you, but yeah."

Bonnie realized JW needed something along the lines of an intervention. He needed something to snap him back to reality. She decided to channel all her anger and frustration into a ball of fury directed at JW. She hoped she was able to break through to him and this would help. "OK, if there is nothing that could be done, then WHY THE HELL ARE YOU SITTING HERE FEELING SORRY FOR YOURSELF! I don't know who this guy in front of me is. JW, you haven't been the same since you were shot almost a year ago. You may have healed physically, but your head is a mess of scrambled eggs. You need to wake up and man up or whatever you want to call it. You are not doing that dog or me or anyone any good. You are sitting here wallowing in an ocean of pity. NO ONE FEELS SORRY FOR YOU, JW! No one. You knew going into this that a dog or a police officer could be hurt. I knew it and accepted it. Am I happy my dog was seriously injured? No, I am not. But you didn't hurt Addy, JW. The guy who hurt Addy is dead. The Las Vegas Metro Police SWAT team lit him up like a Christmas tree and blew his brains all over that room.

"NOW GET OVER YOURSELF and start doing what God put you on this earth for. You're a cop, JW, a damn good one, and you have been given the gift of two wonderful dogs and a wife who loves you. You have the gift of an insane talent to read and work with those dogs. They can do what I think is impossible and not even break a sweat. Now get up and get your ass back to work or we will just toss this whole thing in the trash and have the two best pets in the world. This is your call, JW. Make a decision and move on. There is too much work to do to just sit around and do nothing."

Bonnie took a deep breath. That was a lot of frustration tossed out, most of it aimed at JW. Bonnie got up and walked to the front lobby. As she passed the front desk, one of the techs looked at her and gave her a thumbs-up.

While Bonnie waited for JW to decide which direction they would go, a police officer came inside. As Officer Perea was introducing himself to her, JW came out of the back. His entire demeanor had changed. There was a light in his eyes that had not been there before. He saw Perea and his face lit up. "Honey, this is Officer Perea. He's a SWAT guy and a medic. He saved our Addy's life. She was literally bleeding to death in my arms and he saved her."

Bonnie looked at him and hugged him. Perea looked uncomfortable. He was obviously not used to this kind of attention. She whispered into his ear, "What's your first name, Officer Perea? We're on a first-name basis here at Big Dogs. I'm Bonnie."

Perea was embarrassed by the attention and said quietly, "Michael, ma'am. You can call me Mike."

JW started talking to Bonnie as if Mike were not there. "I thought about what you said. You're right; this is too big to let it go. There is so much we can do. Addy and I talked while we were waiting for you. She told me she wants puppies." JW turned to Perea and said, "I see a puppy in your future, young man."

Mike looked at him like he was crazy. "Uh, I've never had a dog, sir. Neither has my wife. I'm not sure our homeowner's association will allow them."

"No worries, Mike. Ben can teach you everything you need to know, and I'll talk to the sheriff. You're a hero, man! No one is going to say no to the man who saved Princess Addy's life. No one is going to say he can't have a puppy from the hero dog that found the murderer of two women. No way."

Perea looked to Bonnie for help, but all he got was a big smile. "Just go with it, Mike. I'll make sure he doesn't get you into too much trouble."

Bonnie was still a little concerned about JW. He was manic right now, but at least he was manic in the right direction. It was going to take a while, but he would be OK.

Mike said, "I just wanted to come by and say thanks for all you did and see how Addy is."

JW said, "She's looking good, Mike. She knows she must get better. There's a lot of work out there and we need to find her a boyfriend."

Mike offered, "What about the other dog, Ares?"

JW looked shocked. "Ares is her brother, Mike! What kind of person are you?" Mike again looked at Bonnie with a "Help!" look plastered on his face.

"JW, you have to slow down. Mike doesn't know those dogs are related. Puppies? Where the heck did you come up with that idea?"

JW said, "I'm sorry. You didn't know," to Mike, and then to Bonnie, "It wasn't my idea, it was Addy's."

Bonnie started thinking that perhaps her husband was in worse shape than she thought. "Addy spoke to you, JW?"

"Oh, don't be silly, Honey, she doesn't talk." With that JW went out the front door to find Ben and check on Ares.

"Well, Hurricane JW has made landfall. There is no telling how much damage he will do."

Mike laughed at Bonnie and said, "It's not the wind, it's the storm surge." They both laughed.

Bonnie went to the front desk and asked how long before she could take her girl home. The veterinary technician told her the doctor wanted to keep an eye on her for another day. Bonnie thanked her and went in search of her husband. JW was out in the parking lot, chatting with Ben. Ben gave Bonnie a wide-eyed look as she walked up. "What did you do to him?"

"Who me? Nothing."

JW and Bonnie drove to the Ultimo hotel in silence. Ares was in the back, watching the world go by. He seemed a little upset; he was wondering where Addy was. Ben caught a ride with one of the officers on guard duty. They all arrived at the Ultimo valet station—it looked so different than just a few hours earlier. They walked into the lobby with Ares. No one said anything this time, at least not until the concierge approached them. "Good morning and welcome to the Ultimo. We have been awaiting your arrival. If you will come with me to the front desk, we have two suites ready for you. If there is anything we can do to make your stay with us any better, you just ask. Mr. Christenson has made it clear that you are all VIPs, including this beautiful dog." He reached down and petted Ares on the head.

"If there is anything you want while you are here, just charge it to your rooms, everything will be taken care of. If we don't have it, which is unlikely, contact the concierge desk and we will get it for you." He turned to JW and said, "Sir, what you did yesterday was nothing less than heroic. I have never seen anything like that. It is my personal honor to take care of your every need." The group was dumbstruck.

Bonnie managed a "Thank you," but beyond that, they were completely speechless.

"If you choose to dine with us, and I can recommend several restaurants here on the property, we will make sure you get a table. Is there anything I missed?"

Bonnie gave him a smile and shook his hand. "Thank you so much for everything. We all really appreciate it. Right now, I think these two could use some sleep. It has been a long couple of days."

JW looked around the lobby while Bonnie and Ben checked in. It was remarkable, but all the blood from yesterday was gone. Everything was perfect, just like before the shootout. He wondered what the forty-seventh floor looked like. They went to their rooms, matching suites next door to one another. Ben and JW were each carrying a small gym bag that contained a change of underwear and a fresh uniform. Bonnie told them to shower and get some sleep, she would go downstairs and get them something casual to wear. JW and Ben retreated to their rooms to get some rest. JW was overwhelmed by the size and plushness of the room. He wandered through the rooms looking at everything in awe. He knocked on the connecting door and asked Ben, "Is your room as nice as mine?"

Ben laughed and said, "This place is bigger than my whole house. I guess this is how the rich and famous live."

They both went back to clean up and JW was sound asleep within moments of climbing in between the sheets. Bonnie returned two hours later. She had picked out dressy casual outfits for both JW and Ben. Someone had to take care of them. JW slept soundly, with Ares also asleep at the foot of the bed. Bonnie brought out her iPad and starting reading. She stopped after a few minutes; something was tugging at her subconscious. She closed the book app and opened the calendar. *Wow,* she thought. *Almost one year ago, I was sitting in the Intensive Care Unit of Long Beach Memorial Hospital, waiting for JW to wake up.* She closed her eyes, looked up and said, "Thank you, God, for keeping my husband and dogs safe. Please continue to do so."

EPILOGUE

John Joseph Flannery sat quietly in his favorite restaurant. Life was good for him right now. He was becoming established here in Bowling Green, Kentucky. People recognized him only enough to ignore him as harmless; he maintained a low enough profile to avoid attracting any real scrutiny. He had been busy here, preparing for his hunt. He was going to show these people who the Shadow was, but a few more things needed his attention first. He was a planner and he wanted this to be perfect.

He had a newspaper spread out in front of him. He didn't really read it, but instead used it as a prop to allow him to look around and outside without making it appear he was looking for potential victims. He loved the women here. So many were to his particular liking, he was having a hard time narrowing down his list. His waitress came by and smiled at him. She was friendly and seemed interested in him. He laughed to himself. I can't take her. It might point directly to him. He needed to be careful, he had almost been caught in Long Beach and he wanted to avoid that. Long Beach—the word triggered something in him, and he looked down at the paper. There, on page three of *USA Today*, was an article talking about a police shooting in Las Vegas and how a police officer from Long Beach, California, had used his dog to track down a serial murderer.

He looked at the picture that accompanied the article. He thought he recognized the face. He did. He read through the article completely and thought, *What a small world.* It made him angry that this officer had killed one of his brethren. Although to be truthful, he considered others who killed like him to be inferior…savages. He looked at the name and the face. Yes, that was the police officer he had shot in Long Beach. This outrage must not stand. The Shadow started making plans, plans for when he finished his hunt here. The man in the picture scared him. He had tried to kill him and he had failed. Somehow, he needed to find a way to finish the job, but he was afraid.

End…for now

ACKNOWLEDGMENTS

Greetings and welcome to the second edition of *Big Dogs: The Adventure Begins*. As my second effort at the first book, I needed to revisit this section and add some new friends. I was a police officer in Long Beach, California, for twenty-eight years. I worked as a patrol and narcotics dog handler and unit supervisor for nine years. It was one of the best jobs I had, and I had a lot of great jobs and worked with many incredible officers. I wanted to create a story that combined the life of a police family working in a dangerous and stressful job. This book is the result of that dream.

I read a lot and occasionally watch cop shows on TV. I hate it when they are inaccurate and create an incorrect impression in the minds of their viewers or readers. The writers do all law enforcement and their community members a disservice. For this reason, I tried to be accurate but, hopefully, not dull. This is not a training manual. It is a story, and I have chosen to leave much of the tedium and repetitiveness out of the book.

Accuracy and correctness were crucial to me with his project. I hate reading a book about a cop who does dumb stuff, saying, "That is not how I was trained." Please understand that police training across the country varies greatly, as does the language officers use. There is no national standard; however, being safe is universal.

This book has been a goal of mine for a long time. It was stewing in my mind, and finally, I had to get it out. The writing was, for me, the easy part: I have been thinking of this story for ten years. Everything that came after that has been so much work and is the reason for the acknowledgments section.

Before saying anything else, I need to thank you, the reader. I would have written this book, whether anyone read it or not because I needed to. This book was designed to be the first of a series; if no one reads it, it will be the last. If you enjoyed it, please leave a positive review. If you didn't like it, please forget you ever saw it. Also, if you have friends that enjoy this genre, please tell them. I realize there is a lot of competition for your time and money in the book world. Thank you for choosing us, and I hope you enjoyed *Big Dogs*.

When I first decided to write this, I knew I would want a team to work with me. I have always worked that way, so why should this be different? My team of beta readers is made up of friends. Some are experts in a variety of fields; others are people who know nothing about police work except what they see on TV. I needed this story to be entertaining, as well as accurate, for both law enforcement and those whom they serve. I hope we achieved that.

The first person to read this book was my wife, Barbi. She can be brutally honest, and I was worried. Please understand that I have never written fiction before. A lot of police reports and college papers, but there is no history of creative writing in my life. Hopefully, you can feel my trepidation when I handed her the first copy. She read it, and her first words were, "It's good." But if you heard her voice, you knew she thought it needed a lot of work.

She went through the first draft with a red pen. I have no idea how many she used, but when it came back, there was more red ink on the pages than black. Many long nights followed with us sitting in my office, going through the edits. There weren't many arguments over content, and I generally deferred to her on grammar. But, hey, you can't say we don't spend quality time together. Barbi, this book would not be the same without you! Thank you, and I love you.

The second draft was printed and went out to my beta readers. The reviews came back, and I received various comments from them. Most were positive, but there were a lot of constructive suggestions. In some cases, I listened; in others, I chose to stay with my original idea. After all, I know where the story is going after this book. One of my favorite authors is Stephen King. I love the way he tells a story and especially how he links books and stories together. So, if you are wondering why I put so much effort into a minor character, you might see them later.

I was amazed at the number of continuity errors I had. My style of writing is to just sit and write. No notes, charts, or three-by-five cards tell me where to go. As I said earlier, I have been storyboarding this in my head for ten years. I know it pretty well by now. My readers were great at finding these things. Their hard work has improved the quality of what you read. Thank you to Jennifer Murphy, the first to read the second draft, Laurie and Floyd Enault, Sue Westbury, and Paul and Sheryl Sanford. Each of you gave of your time to help me. Thank you. Special thanks to Steve Murphy, my golf buddy here in Arizona, who had to listen to me ramble on about all this each time we played a round together.

My brother, Kerry Ditmars, deserves special mention. I sent him a copy of *Big Dogs* to read, not thinking he would become a member of the beta reader team. Instead, he asked what I wanted him to do, and I told him to read it and let me know if he liked it. He not only read it but reread it— six times. His help with continuity and word usage was unexpected and extremely helpful. Thanks, big brother.

Kerry introduced me to a friend of his, Hildie Rush. She is an artist who helped design the Big Dogs challenge coin. Unfortunately, I neglected to thank her in the original edition of Big Dogs. My apologies Hildie; thank you for your help.

Billy Kift was the original Big Dog for Long Beach PD. No, he is not JW North, but he took a simple idea and turned it into a powerful law enforcement tool for us. Long Beach PD was not the first department to use bloodhounds to help solve crimes and catch criminals, but Billy's hard work showed in the respect others paid to our unit. Another Human Scent Detection expert who assisted was Curtis Fish. Between Curtis and Billy, you could not ask for two people who know more about this field. Billy and Curtis took the time to read this book and lend their thoughts. It was a challenge to give the reader a taste of what it takes to train a trailing dog without boring them to death. I hope we have created that for you, and if we did, Billy and Curtis have a lot to do with it. Also, thanks to another former K9 handler, David Cannan, for his efforts.

Although he was not asked to help with *Big Dogs*, I must thank Larry Harris. He knows more about bloodhound trailing than anyone else I know. When I first learned about the hounds and how all this worked, Larry always took the time to explain things to me. I appreciate all you did to help me, Larry. I hope some of your wisdom has made it onto these pages.

My friend, retired Sergeant Marc Cobb, who has been the National Police Shooting Champion twice and won more other awards than I can imagine, reviewed the book for any issues with guns and shooting. He is not only a great shot but a fine golfer too. We have spent many days on the links together. I appreciate his insight and assistance.

Being a new author can be challenging. It helps a lot if you have someone to assist in navigating the backroads of this business. Although he was not a reader on this project,

Danny R. Smith, a retired homicide detective from the Los Angeles Sheriff's Department, provided sound advice and insight. If you like well-written murder mysteries, check out dickiefloydnovels.com/.

Another friend and retired Los Angeles Sheriff homicide detective, Bobby Taylor, was also a big help to me. I have never worked as a detective, so his insights and encouragement were great. Thank you, Bobby.

A former colleague, Elana Quinones-Conant, provided helpful insight into the forensics portions of this book. Although I did not have much of this type of work in this book, her assistance was invaluable. In addition, it does give me the flexibility to include more cutting-edge information in the future.

Barbi and I have two German Shepherds, Gunnar and Missy. They are rescues we got from the German Shepherd Rescue of Orange County (GSROC) in Southern California. We sometimes wonder who rescued who, but life is certainly better with a dog. We entrust Dr. Kenneth Skinner of Prescott Animal Hospital with their care. When I asked him to read *Big Dogs*, he told me he didn't have much time for reading. However, he still took on reviewing the parts associated with veterinary medicine. Special thanks to you; you created time to help when I know you didn't really have it.

Dawn and Geoff LaGary are both retired medical professionals. They were one of the first couples we met when we moved to Prescott, Arizona. They agreed to look at the medical parts of the book and were a great help to me. I think Geoff took a particular dislike to the Shadow. I will have to devise a particular fate for the Shadow when he meets his ultimate doom...or will he?

I need to thank Robin Samuels, my first editor. If you read Stephen King's *On Writing*, he will tell you an essential rule: trust your editor. Unfortunately, trust is hard to come by in my world. Robin took a stern but gentle approach with me and was a great help in editing *Big Dogs* and navigating the maze of modern authordom. When I looked at what she did with a small sample of the text, I was amazed and sold at the same moment. All I can say is that if you ever write a book and need an editor, I can strongly recommend her.

Those who have been around *Big Dogs* for a while will notice that we are now published by WildBlue Press from Denver, Colorado. Another author friend, Mike Rothmiller, recommended them to us. We submitted the second book in the series to them, and they responded with their desire to publish both the first and second books with options on the third and fourth.

I want to thank Steven Jackson and Michael Cordova, partners in WildBlue Press, for giving us a chance. If you can imagine the volume of books published yearly, it makes it all the more gratifying for their faith in *Big Dogs*. In addition, it has been a joy working with WildBlue's Ashley Kaesemeyer, Stephanie Lawson Johnson, Devyn Radke, and our editor, Tanya Mravik.

All of the above and many others were fantastic in their assistance in making *Big Dogs*. If there are any errors in this book, they belong solely to me.

Again, thank you to all my readers and my reader team. Thanks for joining me on this journey. It has been long and hard work, but I hope the results are worth it.

I look forward to entertaining you all with *Gasping for Air* sometime soon.

Steve Ditmars

ABOUT THE AUTHOR

Steve Ditmars, born in Long Beach, California, is a proud graduate of the University of Southern California. He served as an officer in the United States Marine Corps and is a twenty-eight-year veteran of the Long Beach Police Department. He was a police service dog handler for six years and supervisor of the K9 Unit for three years. Steve retired from the LBPD as Commander of the Special Operations Division, which included Homeland Security, Counter Terrorism, Communications, and the security details for the Long Beach Airport, the Port of Long Beach, and Long Beach Transit.

He currently lives in Prescott, Arizona, with his wife, Barbi, and their two German Shepherd rescues, Gunnar and Missy. Steve enjoys hiking the many trails in the area and finds some of his inspiration in the beauty and history of the area. *Big Dogs* is his first book. When not writing, he enjoys woodworking, computers, and spending time with his adult children, Eric and Cynthia, and granddaughter, Charlotte.

Steve has enjoyed competitive marksmanship since he was in high school. He appreciates the challenge of shooting, bringing man and machine together in harmony to achieve that perfect shot.

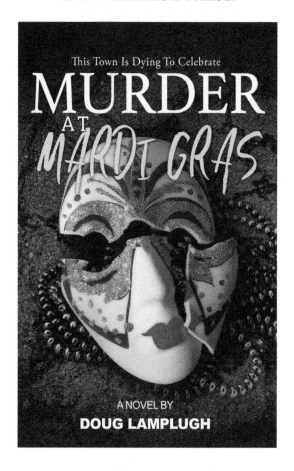

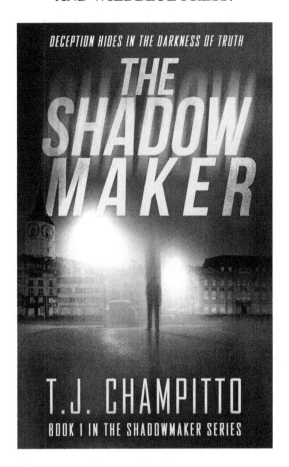

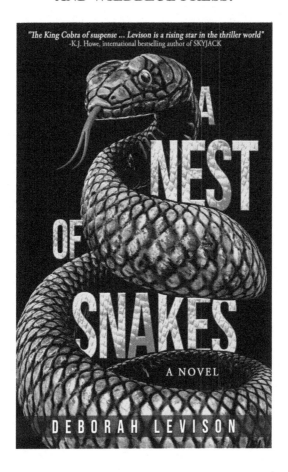

Made in the USA
Las Vegas, NV
15 December 2022

62860492R00174